Of Flesh and Steel

AN AKRANI GODS NOVEL

Cover Design | Editing | Book Design and Typesetting:
Enchanted Ink Publishing
Map: Alyssa Green, using Wonderdraft software.

ISBN: 978-1-7368365-2-1 (E-book)
ISBN: 978-1-7368365-3-8 (Paperback)

Printed in the United States of America

To Mom and Dad:

Thank you for always believing in me.

For seeing my potential even when I didn't see it in myself.

ALYSSA GREEN

AN AKRANI GODS NOVEL

N
W
E
S
BEHEMOTH T
MELIWE FOREST
CALUN
THESSALY
AZUREDEN MOUNTAINS
ATTLEMIS OCEAN
GRELAN FORES
HAVEN
LET
AADER FOOTHILLS

RRENMIS MOUNTAINS

BALAM

N FOREST

WYNDOVER WOODLANDS

KE

ONYX MOUNTAINS

BLACKROCK HARBOR

ATORA

LAOSIAN SEA

CRENTHA

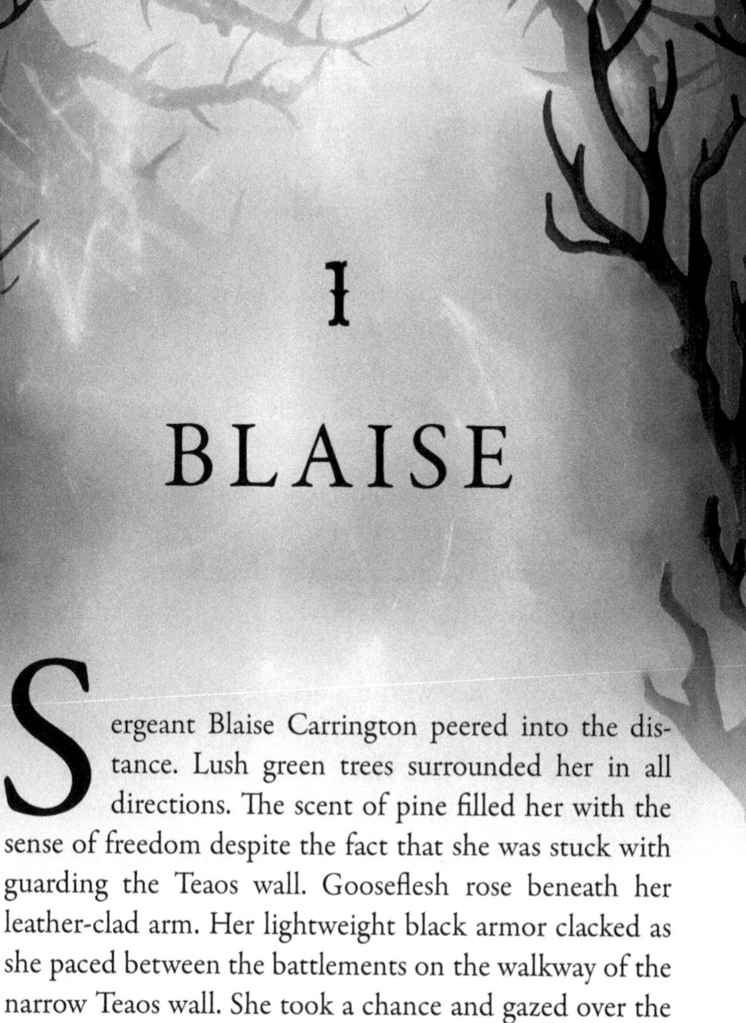

1

BLAISE

Sergeant Blaise Carrington peered into the distance. Lush green trees surrounded her in all directions. The scent of pine filled her with the sense of freedom despite the fact that she was stuck with guarding the Teaos wall. Gooseflesh rose beneath her leather-clad arm. Her lightweight black armor clacked as she paced between the battlements on the walkway of the narrow Teaos wall. She took a chance and gazed over the embrasure. A sinking sensation crept through her stomach, and a wave of light-headedness washed over her. In the twenty-four years of her life, she'd hoped her fear would've lessened. Her knees buckled. She regained her balance, leaning against the merlon. The wall enclosed the kingdom of Elatora and wasn't there to keep people in, but to keep them safe. *Gods, I hate heights.*

Her knees wobbled as she turned around and caught sight of the miles of farmland that served as another barrier. If the wall was breached, the sentinels would have ample time to warn the people. Though she couldn't see it through the overcast, Cloveshire Castle was about one hundred miles inward.

A lower-ranked sentinel walked up to her, clad in black armor, a sword on his hip and a crossbow in hand. "I'm here to relieve you from your post, Sergeant."

She nodded, thankful and ready to go home. "Nothing out of the ordinary."

"Are you okay?" the young sentinel asked, adjusting the strap on his ten-barrel crossbow.

"Yes, Corporal. I was just admiring the view." No one knew of or had noticed her fear, and she hoped to keep it that way.

He studied her with a sidelong look, then raised a shoulder. "Hey, the captain left to take care of a skirmish on the other side." His voice lowered in volume, his lips curving up. "Shoot the trunk of that tree over there."

With a sigh, she grinned and pointed her own crossbow at said tree, about one hundred yards away, and aligned her iron sights. Then, with a quick inhale and a slow exhale, she pulled the trigger. The arrow whizzed through the air and hit the trunk. It split her previous arrow from days ago in half.

His jaw dropped. He studied her for a moment. "*Why* are you assigned to this post again?"

Blaise shrugged. One reason was she had no desire for any other assignment. And no one seemed to bother her here. The walk down the tall, winding staircase was like muscle memory. How many times had she ascended and descended those steps in her sentinel career?

"I'll see you tomorrow, Corporal," she called from halfway down the staircase.

Blaise mounted her horse, Aero, and headed down the dirt path, passing crops of wheat and corn. Upon riding through the marketplace, she came across the bakery, which appeared to be closing down for the evening. They'd most likely sold out of everything. It wasn't uncommon. The boutique window on her left displayed a gaudy purple dress with puffy sleeves and a black corset, the current trending fashion amongst the women—and some men—of Elatora.

Aero let out a huff.

"Yeah, I don't like it either," Blaise said, leaning forward and petting her horse's neck.

Karasi save her, she was tired. She came across the noisy tavern, and the barkeep tossed a drunkard into the street. She veered Aero right, careful not to hit the man as he vomited into the gutter. The bustling street calmed as she turned the corner and entered the residential part of the kingdom miles away from the Teaos wall. She beheld Cloveshire Castle farther up the slight grade. Four gray towers with stained glass windows stood tall in the setting sun. An orangey gold tinted the barrier of the massive structure. The residential homes surrounded the monumental building in a circular formation, then the businesses, and finally, the farmlands.

Blaise's lips parted, and she let out a breath upon approaching her home, the third estate on the left. At least a few acres separated the houses on this street, leaving the residents—mostly sentinels—with plenty of privacy. Her home had been in the Carrington family for generations. She rode through the iron gates of the estate on Aero and gazed at the linear structure ahead. The double-doored entrance, built from oak, accented the gray stone of the building. Many shade trees were spread throughout the property. Lavender, roses, and chrysanthemums lined the walkway of the magnificent courtyard. The house had four bedchambers. Hers was connected to the stone terrace on the second floor, which had steps that led to the stable.

She'd just started the long process of removing Aero's saddle when a young man with brown hair and eyes to match walked in, guiding his horse by the reins. He started undoing the straps of the saddle a few feet from Blaise.

"You beat me home. That's a first," the seventeen-year-old said, taking the bridle off his horse.

She grinned at her brother, Daniel, as she removed the saddle from her horse. "How was training? Do you regret becoming a squire yet?" He had mud and grime from his boots to his black wool jacket. "I see they have you running the obstacle course."

"Yep, how'd you know?" he asked, but he didn't stop what he was doing.

When she'd been a squire, mud had covered her jacket, and it'd been more soaked than Daniel's was. She reached for a brush sitting on a bale of hay. "Lucky guess," she mused, running the brush over Aero's reddish-brown coat. "I wonder what Grams is doing."

Daniel finally undid the buckles of the saddle and heaved it off to the side. "Probably something she's not supposed to be doing." His dark features expressed amusement.

Blaise settled Aero into her stall after thoroughly brushing her down. She stood there praising the horse for being such a good girl that day.

"You do know she doesn't understand you, right?" Daniel had taken the pad off his horse's back and set it in the used pile in the corner of the stable.

Blaise shot him a narrow-eyed glare. "You don't know that."

He reached for a brush. "Whatever you say."

"Aero, I believe Daniel just called you dumb," Blaise said with a grin. The horse huffed, and Blaise's eyes widened along with her brother's. She chuckled. "See?"

He shook his head, lips curving. "You're hopeless."

She aided him in brushing his horse. Once he'd settled his horse into her stall, they passed through the open stone-pillared corridor to the front door.

"Hey, did you hear?" Daniel held the door open for his sister.

Blaise crossed the threshold, asking, "Hear what?"

A crash came from the kitchen, and she rushed into the spacious area. An old woman with white hair reached into a cupboard. There were tall windows on one side, allowing for ample amounts of sunlight. The beams shone through the glass panels onto the stone floor and the broken mug.

"Grams, what're you doing?" Blaise walked up to the woman.

Helena wore a long-sleeve ocean-colored dress that complemented her dull blue eyes. "Why do you put the mugs up so high?" She huffed, crossing her arms as the pot of water boiled on the cast-iron stove.

Blaise took it off the fire, then walked over to the cupboard by her grandmother and retrieved a mug effortlessly. "I'll make your tea, Grams. Go sit down."

"You're lucky. You and your brother were blessed with height," Helena muttered grumpily and sat at the four-person table just a few feet away.

Grams was right. At first, Blaise had hated how she towered above most of the women—and some of the men—in Elatora, but her height had proved useful once she began training with the sentinels. Throughout the years, she'd learned to appreciate her body and what it could do.

Blaise brought the cup of steaming tea to Grams, and by that time Daniel had gathered the broom and began sweeping up the shards.

"Anyway, as I was saying," he began, "King Vaughn is putting together a new task force, seeing as the one before got obliterated."

Grams's eyebrows came together. "Daniel Briar Carrington."

Blaise wanted to laugh at his demise but refrained.

"What?" He raised his shoulders high.

"Those are lives you're talking about, young man." Grams sipped her tea. "What is this task force for precisely? And how do you know such things?"

It was Blaise's turn to chastise him. "And what have I told you about eavesdropping?" She crossed her arms over her chest.

He straightened, putting the dustpan back in the pantry. "I didn't get caught. Besides, you're a sergeant. I thought you would've known this."

Despite her rank, there were many things she didn't know. Her head hurt. She undid the bun in her hair, releasing long onyx waves down the front of her shoulders, and started undoing the buckles of her chest plate.

Grams chimed in, her eyes full of hope. "Do you think you'll join, Pooka?"

"What? No." Blaise had said it as if it were a ridiculous thought. She slipped the connected chest and back plate over her head.

"Honestly," Grams muttered. "I don't know how you can walk that post every day. Aren't you afraid of heights?"

Daniel leaned against one of the marble counters closest to Blaise. "You're afraid of heights? Why didn't I know this?"

Blaise let out a sigh as she threw her free arm up, then walked a few feet only to stop again. "Did it ever occur to you that *maybe* they don't want this information to be disclosed?" She looked at her brother.

"I think you should look into it more," Grams said with both hands around the porcelain mug.

"Why? So I can die like the last task force did?" Blaise shook her head. Why would Grams say that? Didn't she know about all the failed units King Vaughn had sent out in the past?

"I just . . ." The old woman stared into her tea. "Believe you're capable of so much more, Pooka. And no one said anything about you dying."

"I don't want to hear or speak about this again," Blaise said.

Daniel stood there, appearing dumbfounded.

"Do me a favor and keep this to yourself," she ordered him, then turned on her heel and walked out of the kitchen. Why couldn't he be the quiet, reserved squire she used to be? She hadn't been nearly as nosy as he was. *His wandering ears are going to get me in trouble one of these days.*

BEFORE BED, BLAISE walked into the large basement training area. When she entered, she glanced at the weapon wall. Some were heirlooms passed down through the generations. Her eyes examined the sword hanging closest to the staircase. Edgar Carrington—her father—had wielded that sword when he was a captain in the Sentinel Order. She padded to the cabinet that sat in the corner of the large training room. Inside, her mother's tools were collecting dust.

Blaise missed Jocelyn's gentle voice and the warmth of her maternal embrace. Her mother had been an akrani gitros—a healer. The cabinet hadn't been touched in years, and Blaise had never had a reason to go into it. But Grams had sparked something in her. *I just believe you're capable of so much more, Pooka.*

She shook the thought from her head and slammed the doors shut. A clatter came from inside, and she opened it back up. In the corner, a small vial of dark liquid had toppled over. It hadn't broken or spilled, thank the gods. She retrieved it and examined it, then opened it and sniffed the substance within. No scent. What type of healing tool was this? She sealed the vial and put it back where the circular outline of dust blanketed the bottom of the wooden shelf.

Her mother had warned her never to use akrani in public, that it would be dangerous. Blaise had obeyed the command without fully understanding the reason behind it. Though few, there were people in Elatora who practiced their akrani without consequence. What would happen if the sentinels knew about it? Would she still be on that wall?

Daniel had yet to find out about her akrani katai—the ability to wield all the elements. Grams knew, though, and didn't exactly agree with Jocelyn about hiding Blaise's abilities.

She knew how to discharge the overflow of energy from her body. Akrani was a separate life source said to be a gift from the gods. To her knowledge, the number of akrani was equivalent to that of the gods: four. Jocelyn had died when Blaise was twelve, before she could teach Blaise anything else of her forbidden gift.

It had become routine—a weekly habit, like rinsing Aero's coat. With the snap of her fingers, a small spark of electricity formed in Blaise's hand. She always flinched when it happened. Her mother and father had reinforced the basement with brick and mortar, so if an accident happened while she was practicing her katai, it wouldn't affect the rest of the house. Blaise couldn't help but think it was more than that but had always been too timid to ask. Not using her akrani didn't frustrate her. The ability to only manifest lightning baffled her. But she knew the other elements took more akrani. If she ever wanted to use katai *fully*, she needed to build up her stamina.

Her senses would go haywire whenever her well overflowed. A wave of cold would consume her from the inside out, and she'd develop light-headedness. If she used akrani regularly, like a normal practitioner, she wouldn't have that problem.

The spark on her fingertips gradually transformed into a ball, and the more energy she put into it, the more it grew. Once enough energy had emptied from her well, she slowly let it fade.

2

KAIDEN

Responsibility weighed heavy in Kaiden Atherton's chest as he stood on the wooden stage in front of the rows of sentinels. The day of his promotion to captain had finally arrived. He ran a clammy hand through his short dark hair. Beyond the green training grounds stood Cloveshire Castle, a vast and resplendent structure with rooms and corridors and towers that reached toward the clouds.

The ceremony continued, and his mind wandered to Elatora's ongoing struggle with Balam and its ruler. Queen Rowena wanted nothing more than to become the queen empress of Crenitha. She desired to unite all three kingdoms as one. Her frequent attacks on Elatora and Haven were gradually manifesting that desire to reality.

His eyes drifted back to Commander Peter Rykeworth, a dark-haired man with rugged features.

"Today is a momentous event," the armor-clad man began.

Kaiden held back a yawn. He expected the same speech he gave at every promotion ceremony. He'd talk about honoring the gods, how the Order was family, and servitude to the king and the people. But his eyes widened as the speech took a different turn.

"Kaiden Atherton has been training for this his entire life," the commander said.

The man standing behind Commander Peter—Kaiden's father, the second-in-command, Stephen Atherton—gazed at his son with pride. "King Vaughn noticed my son's strength and sense of duty from a very young age," he said. "And the potential to one day lead a unit of his own."

What in gehheina were they talking about? Kaiden had received no special treatment or training that he knew of. His lips formed a straight line, and he clasped his hands behind his back, rolling the tension from his shoulders. He would definitely speak to them in private about it.

Commander Peter unsheathed his longsword. "Take a knee."

Kaiden obeyed.

"Do you promise to keep the oath of the sentinel? Loyalty to the king, commitment to the Order, and servitude to the people of Elatora?" he asked.

"Yes!" Kaiden lowered his gaze to the wooden platform

while the commander tapped each of his shoulders with his blade.

Commander Peter announced, "Arise, Captain, and face your fellow sentinels."

Kaiden turned toward the company of soldiers.

"I present to you Captain Kaiden Atherton!" Commander Peter proclaimed.

The sentinels' traditional barbaric chants boomed throughout the training ground like thunder as they celebrated their fellow brother-in-arms. Kaiden grinned and was sure their cries echoed beyond the castle walls.

After the ceremony, the commanders requested Kaiden's presence. He reported to the castle armory, a sizable room capable of holding about one hundred sentinels at a time. It had a fireplace with a brick mantel and shelves along the walls that stored the sentinels' armor when they weren't on duty. The weapon racks were in front of those shelves but were seldom full since the sentinels usually took their weapons home with them.

A large rectangular wooden table sat next to the grand fireplace with twenty chairs surrounding it. Both commanders awaited Kaiden's arrival.

"I want to congratulate you once again on your promotion, Captain. You deserve it," said Commander Peter. He sat at the end of the table.

"Yes, son, well done," Commander Stephen chimed in. He sat to the left of Peter.

Kaiden approached, nodded, and took a seat across from his father. "Thank you." Before the commanders could speak, he said, "With all due respect, I'd like to discuss that speech first."

Peter looked at Stephen as if letting him take the lead. "Of course. You must have many questions."

Kaiden organized his thoughts. "What did you mean by I trained for this my whole life?"

The commanders exchanged glances once more before Stephen finally said, "The king thought it would be best if we came up with a different training regimen for you."

"What in Teival's name are you talking about?" Kaiden hadn't meant for it to come out harsh, but he'd thought he was getting the same treatment as all the other men and women in the Order. "What about the others who were in that class?"

Commander Peter replied, overlapping his gloved hands on the table, "A facade to make you think there were others. But it was only *ever* you, Captain."

Kaiden wasn't anyone of great importance. Sure, he was descended from a long line of sentinels, but there were many who were like him. He shook his head. Why would they deceive him like that? What else weren't they telling him? There wasn't much to do but accept it. He stayed silent in his bewilderment.

"Right, let's get to it, shall we?" Peter began. "The king is putting together a task force. He wants to send another unit to Balam to eliminate Rowena."

"Eliminate her?" Kaiden cocked an eyebrow.

Peter nodded. "The last survivor from the previous task force claims she has an akrani alchime and that she's keeping him chained to the dungeon wall while he creates these revenants for her."

"I thought alchime was a lost akrani practice," Kaiden said.

"It was," Stephen remarked, stroking the salt-and-pepper stubble on his chin.

"Why are you telling me this?"

Stephen shot his son a half grin and stated, "This is what we trained you for, Captain. King Vaughn has arrangements with young King Theod of Haven. He has two others who will join you on this mission."

"I still don't understand. Why train me alone for this? Why not train an entire unit?" Kaiden leaned forward in his seat. He looked at the mantel, where a large painting of the goddess of chaos, Jynx, sat. Her fiery red hair fell in tight curls around her tan face, and her silver full-body armor glistened. He wasn't entirely sure if that was her true appearance or just the imagination of the artist. She was one of the lost gods no one bothered to worship anymore. The realm of Alymeth and the lands within hadn't seen or heard from the gods in decades.

Stephen glanced at Peter before saying, "A unit is as good as their leader."

What a vague answer. Kaiden expected it from his father though. He sat back in his seat, crossing his arms. Both commanders knew Rowena had been unstoppable for over twenty years. Her akrani, satori, allowed her to see and prepare for the attacks made on her. Did his father care he was essentially sending Kaiden to his death?

"Do you have a list of sentinels you'd like me to recruit?" he asked.

"It's your team, Captain. You may choose your men or women accordingly," Stephen replied with a blank expression. "However, the king has someone specific he wants on the team."

"Who?" Kaiden ruffled his eyebrows.

"Sergeant Blaise Carrington," Commander Peter said.

The name didn't ring a bell. "Why does the king request that specific sentinel?" Kaiden asked.

"He wouldn't say, but he was *adamant* about making sure she joins," Commander Stephen said, dropping his hands into his lap.

"What if she refuses to join?" Kaiden knew he was asking too many questions, but he had to be sure to cover all bases.

A grin crept onto Commander Peter's face. "Then make it so she *can't* refuse."

What could he say about the matter? It wasn't as if Kaiden had a choice. Following orders was what he did best. His chest rose and then fell as he exhaled. He hadn't asked for this promotion and didn't even think he deserved it. He always went above and beyond everyone's expectations, something his father had instilled in him. However, Kaiden was in no way perfect. He just knew how to follow directions accurately, and that was half the battle.

King Vaughn was known to be stern and blunt in his meetings. He'd taken the liberty of briefing all the past task force units instead of leaving it to his commanders, and it wasn't odd for him to take matters into his own hands. Oftentimes the commanders didn't know about his plans until it was too late, which was why Kaiden didn't look forward to taking his father's place as second-in-command. But since Commander Peter didn't have a son, there was a possibility that Kaiden could be promoted to first-in-command. The thought made his stomach clench.

"How long do I have to get this unit together?" he asked half-heartedly.

"Half a fortnight," Commander Peter replied.

Captain Kaiden stood and said, "Well then, I shouldn't waste time." With one final bow, he took his leave.

There was only one person Kaiden could trust to assist in leading the unit, someone who could take over if something ever happened to him: his loyal, sarcastic, and sometimes infuriating best friend.

IT WAS THE trading season, which resulted in many wagons roaming the streets, eager to sell the fruits of their labor. Countless Elatora citizens filled the marketplace. The sound of their bargaining was loud enough that Kaiden couldn't hear his own thoughts.

Kaiden kept a swift pace toward the tavern. It was only a mile away, and it was a beautiful day for a brisk walk. The bakery was on his right, and as he passed, the sweet aroma of pastries filled his nostrils. He'd make it a priority to stop for a custard tart later.

He approached the Bootless Sentinel on the corner of the street. There was a commotion inside and a loud banging noise. Before Kaiden realized it, a man crashed through the front door of the establishment, shattering it.

A tall young man with blond hair emerged, clad in sentinel armor, wiping the dust off in a nonchalant manner. His blue eyes met Kaiden's hazel ones, and then his lips curved up.

"Nice to see you staying out of trouble, Mathias." Kaiden shook his head, feigning disappointment.

The man Mathias had sent crashing through the door stood and ran away from the scene.

"It would do you well to respect the people who serve you!" Mathias bellowed after the drunkard before turning to Kaiden, shooting him a coy smirk. "Have you come for a pint?"

"Sure." After his meeting with the commander, he could use one.

Kaiden sat down at a table away from the other patrons. Mathias joined him with two pints of bubbling apple ale before taking a seat across from the captain.

"Congratulations on making rank, by the way." Mathias sat back in his chair. "Sorry I couldn't make it to the ceremony. I had to deal with a skirmish on the north side of the kingdom."

Kaiden waved his hand. "Don't worry about it. You know how I feel about these promotion ceremonies."

"So." Mathias swallowed a big gulp of the liquid. "What's this about?"

"What?"

"Well, you rarely go out of your way to come here." Mathias ran a hand through his short hair.

Kaiden heaved a sigh. "Can't get anything past you, can I?"

In the twenty-six years of Kaiden's life, he'd known Mathias for twenty. They'd served as squires at Cloveshire and had been horrible troublemakers. It had mostly been Mathias causing the mischief and Kaiden covering for him. Of course, Mathias returned the favor, but it was a rare thing for the second-in-command's son to get into trouble.

"I have a favor to ask," Kaiden said.

"And what is this favor?" Mathias crossed his arms over his chest.

Kaiden summarized what Commanders Peter and Stephen had told him, then continued to ask, "So, will you join the unit?"

Mathias narrowed his eyes and leaned forward, placing his forearms on the wooden table. "So, you're telling me the king is having you put together a task force to invade Balam, somehow break into Queen Rowena's fortress, off her, and save this akrani alchime prisoner, therefore ending Queen Rowena's reign?"

"Well, when you put it that—"

"Count me in." Mathias straightened and hammered his fist onto the table.

Kaiden raised an eyebrow, confused for a moment. "Well, that was easy," he muttered, then took a sip of ale from his pint glass.

"You know I would fight to the death for you, and besides, it beats patrolling Teaos every day." Mathias raised his pint and chugged the rest of the frothy liquid down, leaving a foam mustache on his thin upper lip.

"Well, if you would stay out of trouble and stop breaking shit." Kaiden gestured to the tavern entrance.

Mathias shrugged, and a cunning grin then formed on his lips. "So, how'd you get stuck with this assignment?"

"Both commanders pulled me into the armory right after my ceremony. I assume they've known the king wants me as his next task force lead for a while now." Kaiden took a swig and stole a glance at the curvy barmaid across the room.

"Gods, she's a wild one," Mathias remarked. "Likes the top."

Kaiden hadn't even realized he'd been checking her out, but she was a beautiful woman. There was no law saying he couldn't admire from afar. "Of course you've already been under her skirt."

Mathias was notorious for his philandering ways. Kaiden was no stranger to alleviating his . . . urges, but his duties always took precedence over the women in his life—except for his little sister, Elizabeth, of course. He assumed his father had a wife picked out for him for when the time came, most likely Commander Peter's daughter, Cecilia. With a task force to assemble and a queen to defeat, there would be no time to think about relationships and marriage.

"I have another request," Kaiden said hesitantly. He'd discerned the danger in asking his best friend to join the team in the first place, but Kaiden needed the best, and Mathias was just that. He had a knack for persuading people to do what he wanted, and Kaiden needed someone he could trust to carry out this mission in case he failed to do so.

"What now?" Sergeant Mathias deadpanned.

"Help me gather the rest of the team. Do you have anyone in mind?" Kaiden knew the answer to that question.

"I have a few in mind." Mathias leaned back in his seat once more and grinned.

"Do I know them?"

"One of them is Audrey Black," Mathias replied.

Kaiden let out a breath. "I've heard of her. She specializes in close combat."

"That's not the only thing she specializes in," Mathias muttered before taking a drink.

"I'm going to ignore that." Kaiden's lips formed a straight line. "Who else can you think of?"

"Well, we're probably going to need some brute strength on the team." Mathias placed his index finger to his chin. "George Mapilton. He's a family man. Loyal to the Order. I think he has eighteen years under his belt."

Kaiden's eyes widened. "Shouldn't he be getting ready for retirement?"

Mathias laughed. "He always says he's in the prime of his life. The man has six kids and no intention of stopping."

"It wouldn't be right to take him away from his family," Kaiden said. He called to the barmaid for another two pints.

"Shouldn't we let *him* make that decision?"

Mathias was right. Kaiden couldn't take that choice away from George, which was also why he didn't like the idea of coaxing Sergeant Blaise into joining. But orders were orders, and from the king, no less.

The barmaid brought them their pints.

"Drink up. We have transcripts to go through." Kaiden raised his mug and chugged.

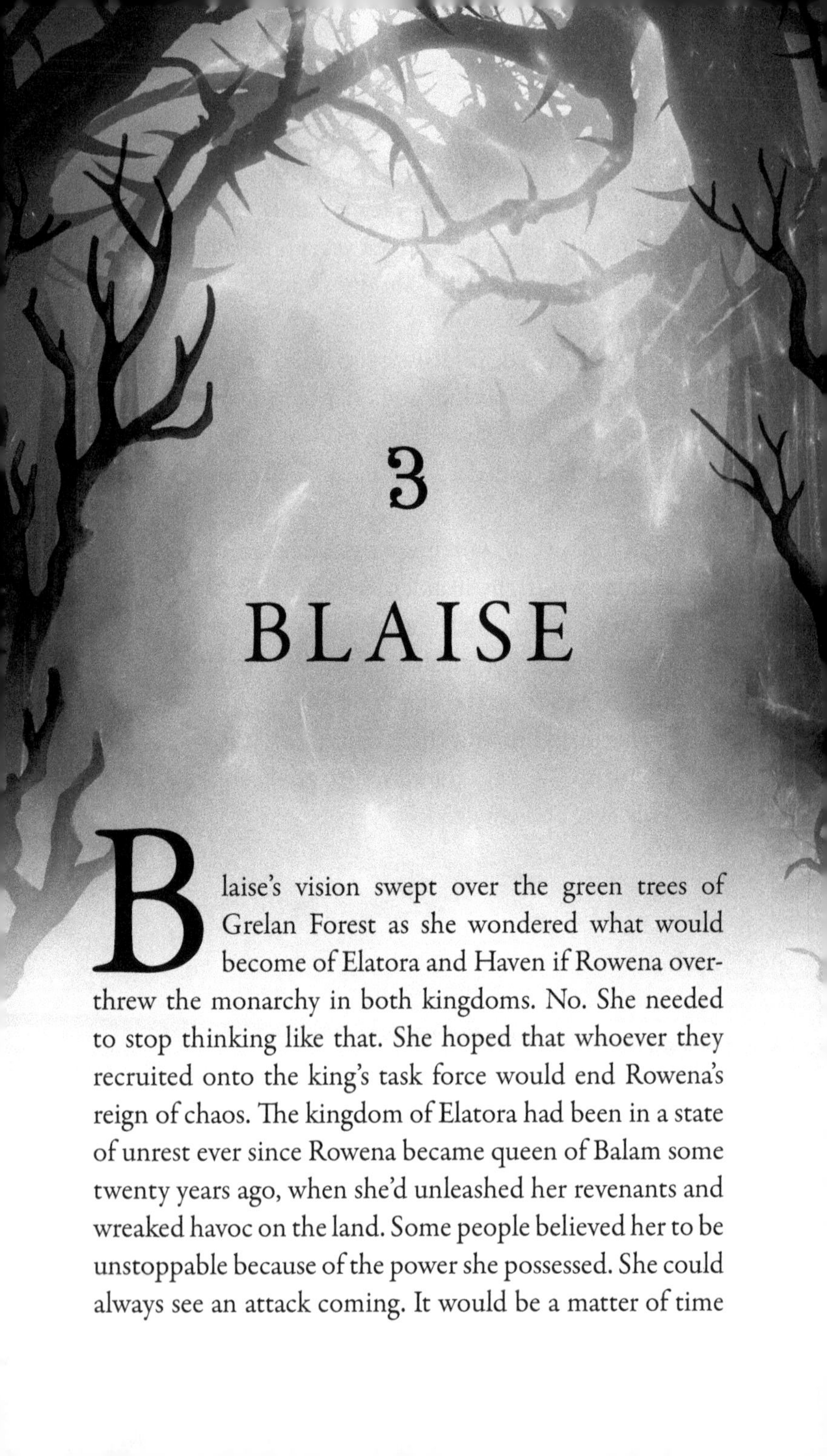

3

BLAISE

Blaise's vision swept over the green trees of Grelan Forest as she wondered what would become of Elatora and Haven if Rowena overthrew the monarchy in both kingdoms. No. She needed to stop thinking like that. She hoped that whoever they recruited onto the king's task force would end Rowena's reign of chaos. The kingdom of Elatora had been in a state of unrest ever since Rowena became queen of Balam some twenty years ago, when she'd unleashed her revenants and wreaked havoc on the land. Some people believed her to be unstoppable because of the power she possessed. She could always see an attack coming. It would be a matter of time before she overthrew King Vaughn and King Theod and reigned supreme as queen empress.

Blaise walked along the Teaos wall and gazed up at the sun as it beat down on her tanned face. Two sentinels walked their posts nearby. It was usually one per one hundred feet, sometimes double that distance if they were down a man. She slung her crossbow over her shoulder, ready to shoot at anything beyond or even inside the wall.

In the distance were the remains of an abandoned stone building. She'd been told that it used to be the temple of Karasi, the goddess of life. But the gods had long abandoned the people of Crenitha, and she wasn't sure why. Blaise's mother used to worship Karasi in thanks of her gitros. Blaise's katai came from Jynx, the goddess of chaos, and she wouldn't be worshiping her anytime soon.

She shook her head from the daydream and continued to gaze upon the vast greenery. A realization overcame her in that moment. *This is it*. The rest of her sentinel career would be spent guarding this wall. In her thoughts, she looked down the length of the barrier to the long drop below. A light-headedness hit her, and she leaned onto the merlon for support. Her chest tightened as she struggled to take deep breaths.

Blaise managed to regain control of her body in time to spot a crowd of people running in her direction from inside the kingdom. She counted the group. Twelve or thirteen of them approached at a quickening pace, setting Blaise's senses on high alert.

"Wayward incoming!" Just as she screamed it, some of the men and women pulled out crossbows and opened fire on the sentinels guarding the wall. Blaise immediately returned the gesture, picking them off one by one while dodging their horrible aim. Where in gehheina was her backup?

Iron sights lined up, she released a breath and pulled the trigger. The arrow whizzed through the air, puncturing an attacker through the chest. Another pull of her trigger, and an arrow plunged deep into the skull of another.

Her fellow sentinel archers finally arrived on scene, armed with their crossbows. They helped her finish off what was left of them. *What a waste.* The first time Rowena's followers—known as the Wayward—had attacked her post, it had disturbed Blaise. She'd killed her own people. But the more it occurred, the less she thought of them as such. They stood with Rowena's cause to rule all of Crenitha. There were many who were afraid of the queen, and some of the Wayward believed she would have mercy on those who followed her. Others worshiped her like a god because of her satori. Blaise thought they were all insane, including the ruler of Balam. She'd heard about the horrible things Rowena had done to sentinels and Haven soldiers alike. She'd tortured them, tore them limb from limb until the sweet release of death found them. Blaise cringed and pushed the thought away.

More sentinels arrived at the scene to help clean up the bodies as Blaise went back to patrolling her post.

A few hours later, two sentinels rode up to Teaos and made their way to her post. What had she done wrong? She glanced at the rank insignias on their shoulder guards. They appeared to be a captain and a sergeant.

She observed as they ambled up the open spiral staircase. Her eyes locked on the captain and the golden specks in his intense hazel eyes. The wave of his dark brown hair, which was cut close on the sides and a few inches longer on top, had one single strand out of place. Though not blatantly obvious, she still had the urge to reach up and run her fingers through it until it was uniform with the rest of his hair. The captain's good looks became more apparent with each stride toward her. She tried to steady her breaths. Gods, the women of the three kingdoms probably threw themselves at this man.

His tall form stopped in front of her. "Sergeant Blaise?"

"Yes?" she replied. Even at her height, he stood a few inches taller.

"I'm Captain Kaiden, and this is Sergeant Mathias." He gestured to the blond-haired man who stood next to him.

"Hello," Blaise said. She noticed the sergeant's defined jawline and the playful gaze of his almond-shaped blue eyes. He was very handsome as well, but there was something about the captain that made her heart flutter. Recognition of this man haunted her. Where had she seen him? Then it dawned on her. The captain was Commander Stephen's son. She swallowed.

"Don't be alarmed. We just want to ask you a few questions," the captain said, though his firm expression didn't put her at ease.

She nodded, simultaneously keeping watch over the horizon. "Am I in trouble, Captain?"

"Let's go into the guardhouse. I'll have someone cover your post," he said, already making his way to the circular structure about fifty feet from them.

A dozen guardhouses were built into Teaos, including the one at the main entrance of the kingdom, but they were mostly for show. The sentinels hardly ever used them because they remained vigilant during their watch. They were more for the higher ranked who occasionally visited the wall for the purpose of inquisition.

Blaise walked into the small space with the two men, trying to figure out the reason they were here. She fidgeted beneath their gaze as they studied her.

"Is it true you shot down most of the rebels with your crossbow today?" Sergeant Mathias asked as he crossed the room to the arched window overlooking the foliage of the forest.

"Yes," she replied slowly. "Is that a problem?"

"No. It's impressive," said the captain.

Her brow furrowed. "I don't understand. Aren't all guards required to have sufficient aim?"

The two men glanced at each other with amused expressions, then turned back to her.

"Not required, but it's preferred, and your aim isn't just *sufficient*," said the captain. "I don't have your eye, and the sergeant here sure as gehheina doesn't have it either."

Sergeant Mathias glared at the captain and muttered a curse under his breath.

Blaise sensed these two were likely good friends given the way they shared glances as if they could read each other's minds. "Oh no," she murmured. "Where there are compliments, there are requests." She shot them each a sidelong glance.

"Smart one, she is," Sergeant Mathias remarked. That amused grin stayed on his handsome features.

The captain appeared more annoyed than anything. "King Vaughn ordered me to put together a task force."

She shook her head and started for the door. "Oh, no . . . No way in gehheina am I going on one of the king's suicide missions."

The captain stepped in her way, and she couldn't help but notice how the gold in his eyes darkened. "Hear me out, Sergeant," he said.

What was this feeling? A calming sensation rippled through her, sending chills down her spine. *Weird.* If only he knew what he was doing to her. She tilted her head to the ceiling, let out a heavy sigh, and gestured for him to continue. He sure was persistent about recruiting her into his unit.

"We're going to Balam to free an akrani alchime prisoner and assassinate Queen Rowena," said the captain. "Most of the team has been gathered. We need one more who's strong in long-distance weaponry. That just happens to be you."

She raised an eyebrow. "You pulled my transcript." It was more of a statement than a question.

Captain Kaiden nodded, the guilt apparent on his face. "You have an impressive record." He paused. "Your brother, Squire Daniel, was more than willing to share your life story with us." Amusement crept onto his features.

I'm going to kill him! Blaise's cheeks warmed, and her nostrils flared. "I'm sorry, Captain, but you're going to have to find your team another archer. I'm not the one you're looking for."

He stood there, staring at her, unmoved. His lips formed a straight line across his beautiful face, and for a moment, it mesmerized her. *He* mesmerized her.

Sergeant Mathias cleared his throat loud enough to snap them both back to reality.

"Right," the captain began. "Well, is there anything I can do to change your mind?" His lips quirked into a half grin.

Her cheeks warmed again, but for a different reason. She didn't know what kind of game this captain was playing, and she wouldn't stand for it. "No," she replied firmly, then turned her back to him, hiding her blushing face.

"Fine. You're dismissed. For now." He moved to the side, opening the heavy oak door for her to return to her post.

The nerve of the man. No way in gehheina would she agree to free this akrani alchime prisoner from the Balam fortress and kill Rowena. She would see them coming from miles away because of her satori. The discussion with Captain Kaiden replayed in her mind for the rest of her watch.

WHEN BLAISE ARRIVED home after watch, she rushed upstairs and burst into Daniel's room. "You little snitch, you had no right to tell them about me!" She lunged at him on the bed.

He squealed and dropped the book he'd been reading and ran out to the landing of the staircase. She caught up and reached around him, tackling him to the cold stone floor.

Daniel grunted in obvious pain. "I thought you'd be happy. You've been stuck at the same post ever since you became a sentinel," he struggled to say.

"There you go thinking again." She had him in a choke hold for a moment until he slipped out and twisted her arms behind her back.

"Don't you want to do more, like Dad?" He squeezed her arms together.

She yelped. "What? No! Look where that got him." She huffed and shuffled backward, slamming his back into the wall and causing him to loosen his grasp on her. He gasped for breath from getting the wind knocked out of him. She stared at him. "Listen, the only reason I became a sentinel is because I was forced into it."

At first, she'd wanted to protect the people of Elatora. But when no one batted an eyelash after her father's death, she refused to go on any dangerous assignments. Her only concerns were taking care of Grams and her brother and the upkeep of the family home. At least that was what she told herself.

His face expressed disappointment as he rose to his feet. "When I become a sentinel, I'm going to be great. Just like him." After saying that, he walked back into his room and slammed the door.

Blaise stood there, staring at his door for a moment, incredulous about what he'd said to her. It hadn't been her intention to become a sentinel at first, but after being talked into it by her father, and once she'd discovered how much it paid, she couldn't turn down the opportunity.

"What is going on up there?" Helena bellowed from the foyer.

"Nothing, Grams." Blaise sighed.

"Oh. Well, if you're done doing 'nothing,' there's a young man in the courtyard waiting for you."

Blaise cocked an eyebrow and tilted her head sideways. "Do you know who it is?"

"I know he's quite the looker." There was a hint of amusement in Helena's raspy voice. "Go out there and see for yourself."

With an exasperated breath, she walked down the staircase and out the heavy front door toward the courtyard. She neared the large grassy area, which was accented with trees and had a small flower garden off to the side. There he stood, Captain Kaiden, in the center of the lavish foliage. He'd changed out of his armor and into casual clothing that accentuated the toned muscles in his back and arms. He stuffed his hands into the pockets of his black trousers. The movements caused the white sleeves of his button-down shirt to tighten more around his biceps. She really needed to stop staring.

Blaise approached him from behind, still clad in her uniform, long hair neatly wound into a bun. "If you've come to change my mind, you're wasting your time." She couldn't deny that he looked absolutely gorgeous, and she *hated* that the thought had even occurred to her. When was the last time she'd fooled around with anyone? Winter solstice, with some random guy from the tavern a few months back. The sex hadn't been bad, but it hadn't been good either. The captain definitely looked like he might be able to satisfy her. She bit her bottom lip.

He spun around, and the corner of his mouth turned up as he said, "Come to the tavern with me."

Her cheeks warmed. Gods, had he noticed the way she'd been looking at him? She hugged herself. "Excuse me?"

"Come to the tavern with me," he repeated, stalking closer to her. The leaves of the oak tree shaded them from the orange-gold glow of the setting sun.

Raising her chin, she replied, "I don't drink." That was the lie of the century.

"Okay, but I'm sure you eat. And I know for a fact you've just arrived home," he stated, gesturing to her uniform.

"I'm not hungry." She didn't move as he stepped even closer to her.

He studied her, his eyes intense with determination. "You're lying."

"I'm not." But she was. How could he tell?

A grin formed on his lips as he continued to stare at her. "*Yes*, you are."

I'm going to punch him. She didn't. A prison cell didn't sound appealing to her at the moment. Her eyebrows came together. "I'd appreciate it if you didn't pretend like you know me, Captain."

"I know your father was a sentinel and your mother was a homemaker. You live here, in your family home, with your grandmother, who's ill, and your brother, the young squire."

"And?" she grumbled and started toward the house.

He stepped in front of her, blocking her path. "And I know your grandmother requires a lot of care and elixirs."

"Get to the point, Captain," she exclaimed in frustration.

"Come to the tavern with me, and I will." That cursed grin she was becoming accustomed to crept onto his lips once more. He took a few steps backward and crossed his arms over his chest.

Her hands balled up into fists, and she replied through gritted teeth, "Fine." Then she continued toward the house.

"Where are you going?"

"To change. Unless you expect me to go in my uniform." She gestured to the armor she still wore.

"I'll be out here. Waiting." He then walked back into the shady courtyard and assumed the same position he'd been in when she'd first gone out to meet him.

Why was he being so resilient in pursuing her? It wasn't as if she had a plethora of experience on the battlefield, though she was pretty sure she could handle herself if thrown into that situation. "You do that," she muttered and couldn't help but roll her eyes as she walked into the house.

4

KAIDEN

He stood in the courtyard of the Carrington residence, waiting for the sergeant to come out. And when she emerged, all he could do was stare. In place of the armor, she wore fitted black trousers with matching shin-high boots. The long-sleeve shirt, dark green like the Grelan trees, highlighted the curves of her tall, athletic frame. Waves of her long ebony hair cascaded down her shoulders. Then his eyes wandered to the swooping cut of her shirt and the show of velvety skin it provided.

"My eyes are up here, Captain," she said with a hand gesture.

He turned, cheeks warm from embarrassment, and led the way through the black iron gates of the Carrington estate. It was a nice evening for a stroll. Besides, he didn't know how much ale he would have that night and didn't want to take a chance riding. Cedric—his horse—would not appreciate that at all.

If Sergeant Blaise had so much skill, why had she been assigned to Teaos? She had high marks with the barreled crossbow and throwing daggers. Her skills with the sword were adequate. An acceptable score in hand-to-hand combat. Something seemed off about this whole arrangement, and he intended to figure it out. He intended to figure *her* out.

The trek to the tavern would give him the perfect opportunity to further get to know the mysterious woman walking beside him. "So, can I ask you something?"

"You're giving me a choice?" She didn't look at him.

"Why don't you want to join my unit?"

She glanced at him. "I have my reasons."

"But didn't you join the Sentinel Order to be a part of something bigger?" The tavern was just another few yards up the hill. They would arrive there in no time, so long as they kept this pace. "Are you scared?"

"No, I'm not scared!" she retorted, shooting him a narrow-eyed glare. "Why do you care anyway?"

"I'm curious."

"Why?"

He grinned. "I have my reasons."

She rolled her eyes and huffed.

Kaiden hoped his unit had arrived already as he and Blaise ambled through the threshold of the doorless Bootless Sentinel. He scanned the tavern, and his eyes locked on the group of four people sitting at the table in the corner.

"I wonder what happened," Blaise muttered, looking at the broken hinges on the doorpost.

Kaiden didn't bother to tell her that his destructive best friend had done that. "Shall we?" His hand went to the small of her back as Mathias waved them over.

"What's going on here?" she asked as she stopped in her tracks.

"Come on, just meet them," he prodded.

She turned on her heel, and as quickly as she'd entered the tavern, she exited, shaking her head. Irritation was apparent on her face.

Kaiden cursed. She was not making it easy for him. He glanced at his unit and the bewildered expressions on their faces. He put an index finger up, signaling them to wait. And with a few quick strides, he caught up to Blaise on the street.

"Do you have something against meeting new people?" He skidded to a stop in front of her.

"Those aren't just 'new' people, Captain. That's your unit in there, isn't it?" She placed her hands on her hips, brow furrowed.

He nodded.

"Unbelievable," she scoffed and attempted to walk around him, but he blocked her once again.

"Wait." He put his hands up, and her chest almost collided with them. That would've been embarrassing.

"Why? So you can attempt to coerce me more?" she asked. "I've had enough of this."

"Are you forgetting who you're talking to?" He stepped

closer to her, leaving inches between them, but this woman wouldn't budge. She didn't even flinch, and although he never would've admitted it, her boldness impressed him. At the same time, it irritated him to the core. He needed her in the unit.

"My apologies, *Captain*," she hissed.

He grinned, both in annoyance and admiration of this stubborn woman. It couldn't be helped, but he really hadn't wanted it to come down to this. "A duel."

She frowned. "Excuse me?"

"Between you and me. If I win, you'll join my unit willingly."

"And if I win?"

"I'll pay for your grandmother's elixirs. Forever."

With brow furrowed in thought, she asked, "*And* you'll leave me alone?"

He sighed and nodded in agreement, sure that he wouldn't—couldn't—lose to her. He didn't want to think of the consequences if he *failed* to recruit her. Was that even an option? The king wasn't the type of man to falter in his decisions. If he wanted something, it got done in one way or another.

Her eyes seemed to study him as she bit her bottom lip. She took a few more seconds to think about it.

Kaiden stared at her lips, wondered what they tasted like. His gaze snapped back to her eyes, but that did no good either. She simply beguiled him. This had never happened with any other women in his past. How had they never met before? And what was it about her that left him feeling so . . . flustered?

"And if I don't accept this little deal of yours?" She leered at him.

"Well." The corner of his mouth rose. "I won't leave you alone until you do."

She tilted her head up, exasperated. "With all due respect, you are incredibly loathsome, Captain."

"I'll take that as a compliment." He held a hand out for her to shake. "Are we in agreement then?"

With a conceding sigh, she gripped his hand, sealing the deal. "Fine. When and where?"

"Tomorrow. Castle training grounds. Noon."

"I have watch tomorrow."

"I'll take care of it, Sergeant. Now, will you at least let me buy you dinner tonight?" He gestured toward the tavern.

Her arms fell to her sides as she rolled her eyes. "No." Then she walked around him and ambled toward her estate.

That woman made nothing easy. He watched her hips swaying gracefully with each step. Wait, why was he staring at her hips? He disregarded the fuzzy feeling in his stomach and started toward the tavern. She had to give in sooner or later. Right?

Inside the establishment, Kaiden made his way over to the unit, who still sat where he'd left them. An auburn-haired woman wearing all black smirked at him. Her pale features were soft and innocent, but he knew better than to underestimate her.

Audrey Black had incredible speed and an innate ability to find pressure points on her opponents, which would leave them temporarily immobilized. And for a woman who had a deadly touch, she was quite playful and cheery. "Well, it appears you've failed to secure the last member of our team. Again," she said, her voice like honey.

"We've worked out a deal," Kaiden stated, taking a seat next to Mathias, who was grinning with his arms crossed over his chest.

"She intrigues you," Mathias stated. That insufferable smug look crept onto his face.

"Had a few too many already?" Kaiden slapped him on his back.

On the other side of Mathias sat a young man with black hair and boyish features. Isaac Lytcott's maroon coat complemented his dark skin. Though he was adequate with a sword and crossbow, his knowledge about the realm of the gods, Alymeth, kingdoms, and politics surpassed that of everyone on the team. "What deal have you worked out with the sergeant? I hope you got it in writing," he said to the captain.

"A duel." Kaiden raised his hand to the barmaid and ordered drinks for everyone. "And no, I didn't get it in writing," he added.

George Mapilton sat across from Isaac. He was bigger than Kaiden and Mathias put together. His long brown beard covered his chest, a contrast to the neatly trimmed hair on his head. His dark tunic hugged the bulging muscles of his shoulders and biceps. Taking a blow from him would cause a trip to the infirmary or worse. "A duel? You're going to fight her to join our team?" George asked with a cocked eyebrow.

"We've smoothed all the details," Kaiden assured him.

The barmaid padded over and gave them all freshly filled pints of ale.

"I put my money on the sergeant," Audrey remarked after taking a small sip.

"You would," George spat, and she glared at him.

Audrey slammed her mug down on the table, and some of the liquid spilled over the edge. "Look, I've trained with her, and I think she has the captain outmatched." She leaned back. "I'm a bit disappointed she didn't recognize me."

"What do you have to say about that, Captain?" George asked, his voice deep and husky.

Kaiden glanced at everyone sitting at the table before replying, "I guess we'll just have to find out, won't we?"

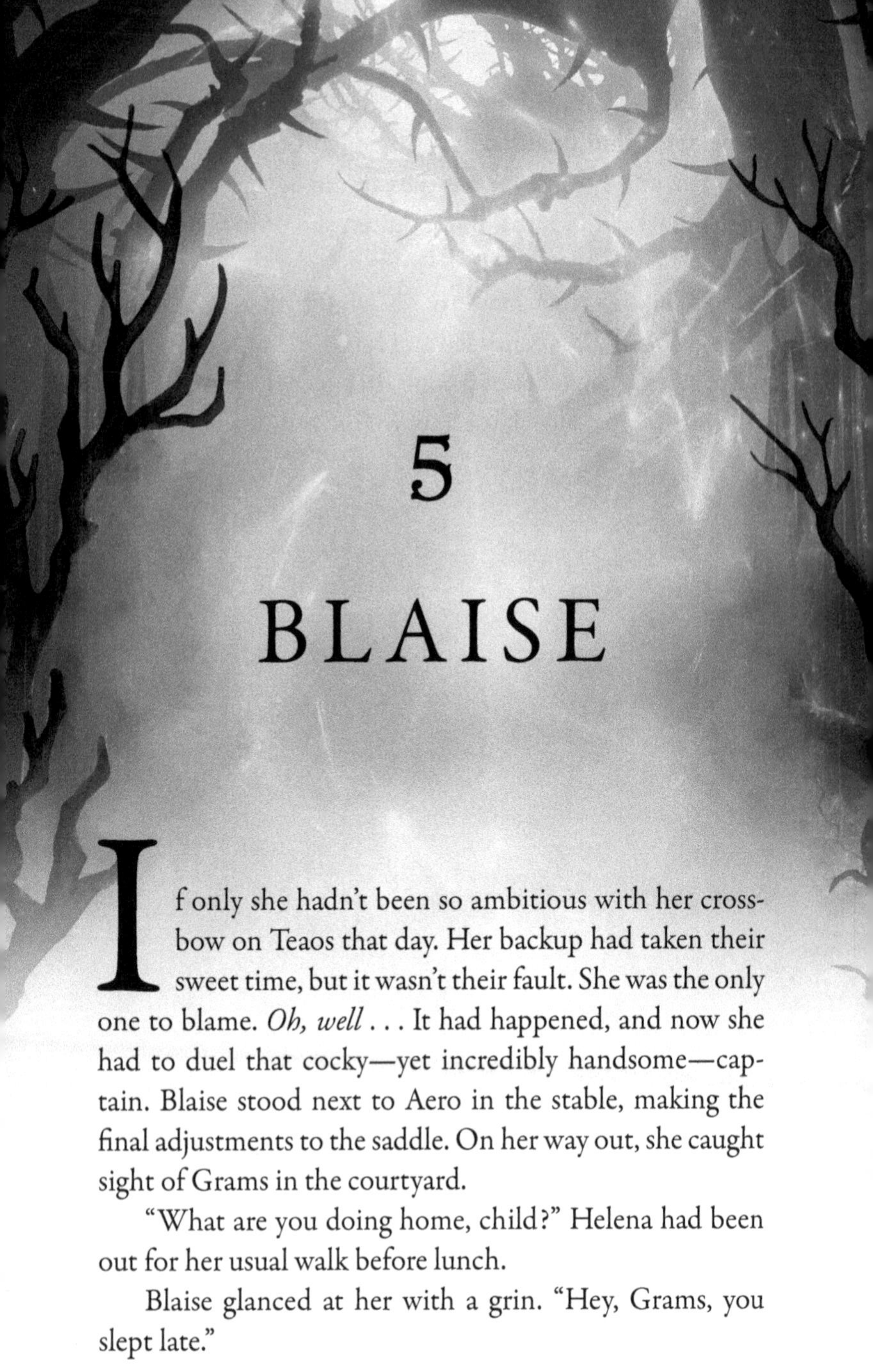

5

BLAISE

If only she hadn't been so ambitious with her crossbow on Teaos that day. Her backup had taken their sweet time, but it wasn't their fault. She was the only one to blame. *Oh, well . . .* It had happened, and now she had to duel that cocky—yet incredibly handsome—captain. Blaise stood next to Aero in the stable, making the final adjustments to the saddle. On her way out, she caught sight of Grams in the courtyard.

"What are you doing home, child?" Helena had been out for her usual walk before lunch.

Blaise glanced at her with a grin. "Hey, Grams, you slept late."

"No later than usual."

"True." Blaise raised a shoulder. Her nerves were getting the best of her. She couldn't lose this duel and leave the routine she'd become so accustomed to. Most of all, she couldn't leave Grams and Daniel. What would they do without her? What would she do without them?

Helena gimped up to her granddaughter in the stall and studied her for a moment. "Something the matter, Pooka?"

"I have a duel today," Blaise said, her voice void of any emotion. She didn't want Grams to worry, but she knew it would be inevitable.

Helena's eyebrows came together. "With whom?"

"The man you saw in the courtyard yesterday."

Still frowning, Helena murmured, "Gods, courting has become violent."

Blaise let out a brief laugh. "He's not courting me, Grams. He wants me to be on his task force."

Helena tilted her head, then nodded understandingly. "I thought you wanted nothing to do with that task force?"

"I don't. I'm dueling so I don't have to join his unit." Blaise placed the bridle on Aero. "I just want to be left alone. That's all I've ever wanted. Mom would *not* approve of this. I'm putting myself at risk." Her cheeks warmed at the thought of Kaiden's persistence. *Damn him.*

"Pooka, this is it. Why can't you see it?" Helena's voice filled with excitement, and it startled Blaise.

"See what?"

"Your opportunity to use your gifts. Your opportunity to make a difference in Crenitha. You don't really want to be stuck on Teaos for the rest of your sentinel career, do you? With all that potential bottled up inside you?" Helena stepped closer and gave her granddaughter's forearm a light squeeze. "Your mother wanted you to hide that akrani inside you, but I think it's high time you discover that power. It's high time you discover *yourself*." It appeared as though Helena wanted to say more.

"Is there something else?" Blaise asked.

"N-no." Hesitance dripped from Grams's voice.

Blaise didn't want to prod further and stress the old woman out. She only hoped that whatever secrets Grams kept from her weren't of great importance. And maybe she had a point. It might've done Blaise some good to be in a unit and put her skills to use.

The faces of those sentinels sitting in the tavern swarmed her mind. That young boy could have easily passed for a sentinel graduate. And the woman had looked vaguely familiar. She couldn't remember where she'd seen her before. Yet there they were, joining King Vaughn's task force, ready and willing to give their lives for his cause. The thought made her chest tighten.

Helena grasped Blaise's hand and caught her gaze. "It's time, Pooka."

Blaise slipped her hand out. "You're right, I should get going." She then mounted her horse and peered down at Grams. "Wait, time for what, exactly?"

"You'll find out soon enough," Helena said before Blaise rode out of the stables.

It had never been in Grams's nature to be so vague about things. Curiosity overcame Blaise at the old woman's words. What would she discover? And would going on this mission be the only way to discern whatever Grams had been talking about?

WHEN BLAISE ARRIVED at the castle training grounds, a crowd appeared to be gathered. Was he trying to put pressure on her? She let the stable boy take Aero from her, then stormed into the castle armory, straight up to Kaiden.

"Did you know all these people would be here?" she asked, her brow furrowed.

He turned, the golden specks in his eyes glistening in the dim lighting. "Good afternoon to you too, Sergeant. Do you mind?" He raised his arm and gestured to the buckles that secured his chest and back plates together.

She inhaled, fully aware that he was capable of doing this on his own, and then conceded, taking a step toward him. With a grin, she yanked the leather straps together to the last notch. He grimaced and shot her a glare. She disregarded the flutter in her stomach. Gods, why did he have that effect on her?

"How'd you know?" A corner of his mouth rose.

"Know what?"

He leaned in close. "That I like it rough."

Her nostrils flared, and her cheeks warmed. "Would you just answer the gods damned question?" She glanced around the room, thankful to the gods that they were the only two in there. He wouldn't act like this in front of other people, would he?

That devilish smirk stayed on his handsome features as one of his shoulders rose. "Word travels fast. What can I say?" He continued to adjust his chest plate. "Are you afraid to lose in front of all those people?"

Her eyes narrowed as she buckled the last straps together. "I'm not the one who's going to lose, Captain." After saying that, she walked out of the armory and onto the training ground to wait for him.

The rest of the unit had arrived to witness the duel. They all stared at Blaise as she stepped foot on the green grass. The familiar red-haired woman said, "Good luck, Sergeant."

"Thanks," Blaise muttered, and recognition of the woman flowed through her. Audrey Black had gone through sentinel training with her some five or six years ago. Blaise breathed, attempting to keep the nervousness in check and off her face.

In the middle of the training grounds lay a thick braided rope set up in a circle. The area had a limited amount of space to maneuver around in. This would be a quick duel. At least that was what she hoped.

She'd arrived on the training grounds ready to fight the captain, ready to take back her place on Teaos, ready to go back to her original plan of finishing out her twenty years as a sentinel on that wall, but she'd thought about the possibilities. What Grams had said about finding herself had resonated immensely, because she didn't know. Who was Blaise Carrington?

After a few more minutes, the captain finally walked out of the corridor and onto the grassy field toward her. His black armor glistened in the sun, and he had an intimidating look on his face, which she found attractive, oddly enough. *Focus.*

She took another deep, nervous breath and unsheathed her practice sword. Although the blade was blunt, it could still do considerable damage. "What're your rules?"

"First person to get knocked out of the circle loses," he replied, brandishing his own weapon.

Blaise staggered her stance and muttered, "Let's get this over with."

She made the first move, swinging in quick succession at him. Her strikes weren't perfect, but they were well-balanced. She flowed through the moves.

The captain blocked as she struck. He dodged and parried, which forced him to step closer to the edge of the circle. Taking the offensive, he swung down. Steel against steel, their blades crossed. The crowd cheered for their champion—mostly for Captain Kaiden, which didn't surprise Blaise.

Their eyes locked for a moment, both intense, both intent on winning. At least *she* was intent on winning. She predicted his movements and parried his attacks. With each swing, he badgered her closer to the edge of the circle. A frustrated grunt escaped her as his blade met hers for the hundredth time. She noticed he could read her movements before she even acted on them, but she could also predict his. It infuriated her. *Goddess of chaos, he's good. I'll give him that. And strong.*

Her heel grazed the rope. She rolled off sideways, simultaneously blocking one of his strikes. His breathing wasn't as labored as hers.

"Are you holding back?" she asked. Her sword met his with a clang.

"Are *you* holding back?" He shoved her and shot her a wink. The corner of his mouth rose.

Fumbling backward, she scowled. "You smug son of a—" With methodical movements, she swiped her sword upward, and her blade screeched against his chest plate. If she wasn't careful, exhaustion would set in earlier than she wanted. He was just so insufferable.

He returned with a blow to her leather-clad arm, which she blocked at the last second. The muffled cries of the crowd echoed in her ears.

Then each of his movements sped up and became more powerful, as if he was testing her strength. With every blow, with every block, the hilt of her sword rattled, causing pain in her hands. It was a familiar feeling and not one she missed. Her body ached. Her breathing was rapid. *I don't know how much longer I can do this.* She'd let her emotions get the best of her. She'd let the captain get to her. How could she be so stupid?

One combination after the other, the captain's fluid movements impressed her as she blocked all of them. But when she took the offensive, she hesitated. *Shit!*

With one final blow, Kaiden spun while swinging his blade. His shoulder met her chest, knocking her out of the circle. She landed on her back, and the breath was knocked from her lungs.

She lay there and gazed at the blue sky, resting her tired limbs. *Why did I think I could beat him? And why is he so gods damned strong?* She dismissed the rhetorical question as her eyes drifted shut, chest heaving.

Kaiden walked over, catching his breath. "You put up quite a fight, Sergeant." He helped her stand. "Unfortunately for you, this means you're officially on my task force. Congratulations."

She wanted to slap that smug smile off his face. Her eyes narrowed, but she kept her mouth shut and silently cursed the captain, hating the fact that she'd lost to him.

"Come on." He led her to the rest of the unit as the crowd dispersed.

Blaise introduced herself to the rest of the task force. They were all lower ranked, except for Mathias. She reacquainted herself with Audrey, a cheerful soul with a honey voice despite being proficient in close combat. Then she met George, the giant who stood at least a foot and a half taller than her. Isaac popped out from behind the giant, so innocent and young, completely naïve about what he was getting himself into. Then there was Mathias. Blaise didn't know what to think of him just yet.

"I saw what you did out there," Audrey said as she hooked her arm through Blaise's and pulled her aside. "Why'd you hesitate? You could've had that fight."

Blaise didn't have a simple answer for her. She shrugged. "Out of shape?"

Audrey scowled. "I don't believe that for one second."

Kaiden interrupted their brief reunion with an announcement. "I'll request an audience with the king. We'll regroup soon." He dismissed them.

"Either way, it was entertaining to watch," George said with a shrug as the rest of them dispersed.

Kaiden stopped her. "Tell me the truth, Sergeant. Were you holding back?"

She faced him. "Why does it matter? You got what you wanted." Her words dripped with irritation.

He stepped closer, not leaving much space between them. "It matters." His gaze bored into her. "You can't afford to hold back once we leave Elatora. Lives are at stake."

"If you're worried about me carrying my own weight,

don't be." She wielded a haughty glare and didn't falter. The midday sun beat down on them.

He let out a breath. "That's not what I said."

"No, but it's what you meant." She looked away as her mouth went dry, stomach tightening.

"Look, I know you're a capable woman, but it's a different world outside Teaos, and I want you to be fully aware of that," he said.

She heard the concern in his voice, and it annoyed her. "I *am* fully aware, Captain." She crossed her arms over her chest. The urge to punch him in the face slowly dissipated when her eyes met his. *Damn him.*

His lips turned up into a crooked grin.

"Why are you smiling?" she asked, gritting her teeth. "And are you usually like this with your other subordinates?"

His smile faded. He looked like he was thinking about what to say next. "Come to think of it, no. It's just you."

She didn't know how she should feel about his response. "You don't even know me."

"No." His expression became unreadable. "But I want to."

Her eyes widened, her cheeks warmed, and she tore away with a huff, not giving him a chance to see her in that state. "I'll see you tomorrow." Her sore legs moved beneath her. Why had she found dueling the captain easier than staring into his beautiful hazel eyes? She didn't know, and she didn't want to know.

"I'll see you tomorrow, Sergeant," he called after her.

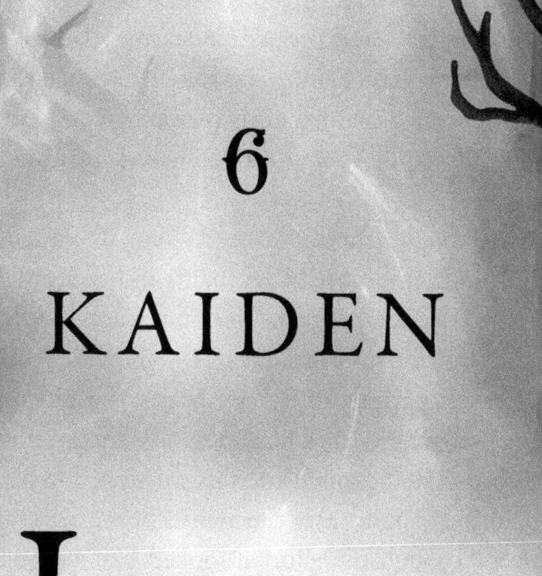

6

KAIDEN

He waited for King Vaughn in the war room of Cloveshire Castle. It was an impersonal space with no windows. Chandeliers hung from the high ceilings, providing enough light to illuminate the map of the realm, Alymeth. The map lay atop the marble table in the center of the space. It'd been a while since Kaiden had seen that map. He'd almost forgotten the size of it. He'd lived in Crenitha and had grown up in Elatora. The other two landmasses were Koshmena and Tarquinn, places he hoped to sail to one day.

King Vaughn Bere II entered in his usual dark royal garb with a gold crown upon his chestnut hair and an intense look in his brown eyes. This was the same man who had yelled at Mathias for crossing him without a formal greeting, the man who'd sent out five units of sentinels—over the span of twenty years—knowing full well that they had no chance of survival against Rowena and her revenants.

Kaiden bowed and greeted him.

The king's face expressed concern as he approached Kaiden. "Attacks on Elatora and Haven have been few. King Theod is worried that her army is nearing completion."

"Is there any proof?" Kaiden asked, turning back to the map.

King Vaughn shook his head. "No. We've sent scouts to confirm the number of revenants in her army. No success." He studied the map. "Tell me, Captain. How does one conceal an army of revenants?"

"I'm not entirely sure, Your Majesty," Kaiden replied, thinking about whether he should ask the king why he'd been chosen and trained for this mission. He glanced at the painting hanging over the mantel of the brick-and-iron fireplace. Though the ellorian looked like a regular man, he possessed great strength and speed. Known to serve the god of peace, Colvyr, the ellorians were also gifted with satori. Kaiden grinned, amused that the king would decorate the war room with that painting.

"Something funny, Captain?" the king asked, his lips forming a straight line.

"Not at all, Your Majesty. It's just . . ." He gestured to the hearth. "That painting of the servant of Colvyr."

The king's face softened. "Ah. I found it quite amusing myself." He glanced at the canvas. "The ellorians used to serve alongside the Sentinel Order."

"What happened?" Kaiden asked.

"They disappeared when the gods did," King Vaughn replied. His eyes went back to the map in front of him, and he changed the subject. "The first order of business is to travel to Haven. King Theod has two akrani soldiers who are brave enough to join our campaign."

Kaiden wanted to roll his eyes at the king when he said "our campaign," but he refrained. There were many things he wanted to ask King Vaughn. However, he would only ask one question. "Your Majesty, why did you request Sergeant Blaise specifically to be a part of this unit?"

"She's part of the mission," the king replied. "A woman named Philippa will approach you. That's all I'll say about it."

Kaiden wondered why it was so important to find that woman.

"Do not tell the rest of the unit about this. Not until *after* you've met with Philippa," the king concluded.

"Yes, Your Majesty."

The rest of the meeting was a discussion about the schematics of Balam and what routes the unit would take to get there. After discussing the general details of the mission, the king dismissed Kaiden.

"I have complete confidence in this unit, Captain. I hope you know that," said King Vaughn before Kaiden walked out of the room. "May the gods protect you."

The captain didn't believe in gods, not after his mother died when he was little. But he indulged the king, turned, and gave a bow. "And you as well, Your Majesty." Then he continued through the double doors.

KAIDEN GATHERED THE unit at the Bootless Sentinel later that afternoon. Thankfully, there weren't many patrons occupying the establishment that day. Mathias arrived early, and he finished a pint before George arrived. Then Audrey and Isaac strode in together. Where in gehheina was Blaise?

"Anyone see Sergeant Blaise?" Kaiden asked, standing from his seat at the table.

At that moment, *she* came traipsing through the doorway of the tavern.

Kaiden ground his teeth as he stared at her. "I said to be here at three." He kept the calm in his voice for as long as possible, but anything she did or said would probably set him off in an instant.

"I'm here now, so what's the problem?" she replied, slumping into her chair.

Everyone's eyes widened at her response to the captain, the leader of their unit.

Blaise didn't want to be there. Kaiden couldn't blame her for the attitude, but sentinels were supposed to be obedient and dutiful. He walked over to her, bent at the waist, and brought his face within inches of hers. "When I say to be somewhere at a certain time, you *will* be there from now on. Is that understood?"

Her chestnut eyes gleamed with antipathy for the captain.

He didn't care; he would *not* be humiliated in front of his unit. "Is that understood, Sergeant?" His voice, brimful of warning.

"Yes, *Captain*," she replied, gaze not faltering.

"Good." He walked back to his chair and sat, continuing with the information King Vaughn had disclosed. It took all but a few minutes to explain the route they were going to take and the stop they had to make in Haven. He left out that little part about ensuring a meeting between Blaise and the woman named Philippa. It appeared they needed time to process it all. They sat there in silence, sipping their pints.

What did Kaiden's father think of this whole situation? Was he even concerned for Kaiden's safety? That there was the possibility he wouldn't return? There had been no lines drawn between father and sentinel as Kaiden was growing up. Ever since the death of Kaiden's mother, the commander had drowned himself in work, which had been unfortunate for Kaiden's younger sister, Elizabeth.

The memory of cooking dinner for his little sister flooded Kaiden's mind. He'd taught her to do many things: how to ride a horse, how to properly tie her boots. He'd even helped her pick out her first expensive gown. She'd just turned nineteen and suitors had recently become interested in marrying her. It wasn't fair to leave her at this stage in her life. He could tell that the news had upset her, as she hadn't spoken to him since.

"Getting to Haven shouldn't be a problem if we stay in formation. We can rest the horses in Lerwick, which is on the way," Mathias said, breaking the silence. "All we'd have to do then is cross Thessalynne Lake from Haven and go through Daagan Forest."

"You're making this sound way too easy, Sergeant," Blaise deadpanned, her arms crossed over her chest.

"There're still those nasty revenants in Grelan Forest," Audrey remarked, scrunching her face.

George ran his fingers through his long beard. "I have experience in that forest. Mostly bone revenants. I've only seen one steel revenant, and that bastard was a bitch to kill." He took a gulp of ale and let out a satisfied sigh. "Almost better than sex."

Isaac cringed. "Inappropriate."

"The question is, what're we going to do once we sneak into Balam?" Mathias looked to Kaiden for an answer.

"I've heard her fortress is nearly impenetrable," Blaise said, sitting up straight.

"Not completely. The king claims these akrani soldiers from Haven know a way in," Kaiden replied. He knew half the battle would be breaching Balam.

"Wait, did you say we have to go through Daagan Forest?" Isaac blurted out, a worried expression on his face.

"Have you not been listenin' to anything, boy?" George asked, cocking an eyebrow.

"To get to that forest, we have to cross Thessalynne Lake." Isaac hyperventilated.

George shrugged as if to say, "And?"

"Have you never read a book?" Isaac glared at George from across the table.

"No." George gave another shrug.

"Calm down, Corporal Isaac," Blaise interjected. She turned to the large man sitting across from her. "Thessalynne Lake is said to be infested with sirens. Daagan is said to be haunted by trees that swallow you whole."

George laughed. "Those are just myths. You're overreacting." He placed a heavy hand on Isaac's shoulder, almost covering it.

"I suppose we'll find out, won't we?" Mathias teased, and a grin crept onto his face.

"That's enough," Kaiden said, running a hand through

his dark hair. "Get some good rest tonight. We leave in the morning." He dismissed them, and they left one at a time.

Blaise said nothing to the captain before she left, but their eyes met. She appeared as though she wanted to do violent things to Kaiden. He wanted to—no. He didn't want to do anything to that *member* of his unit.

Mathias and Kaiden sat across from each other in silence once their unit had left. The barmaid and barkeep gazed at the two men from behind the bar with stern expressions. Namely, they stared at Mathias for what he'd done to the door, which still hadn't been fixed.

"It appears we have an audience." Kaiden snorted.

"They always watch me," Mathias stated, brushing off their glares.

"I wonder why," Kaiden muttered before taking a gulp from his pint. He gazed into his mug and questioned whether his unit could make it through this mission. He'd gathered the best he could find, but would it be good enough to accomplish what King Vaughn wanted?

"So." Mathias interrupted his thoughts. "What's on your mind?"

"I don't know, Mat," Kaiden said. "I'm just ready for this entire ordeal to be over with." He studied his best friend. "And I'm worried about my sister. Leaving her alone with my father."

Mathias nodded. "I understand that, but Lizzie is a smart, strong girl. She's learned from the best." He punched Kaiden in the shoulder.

With an amused smirk, Kaiden said, "Thanks." He glanced up at a painting on the wall of the god of death—Teival—depicted in his mortal form, standing over a dead body, and siphoning the soul out to take it to gehheina. A dark picture for such a light and cheerful space. "Do you think our unit has a chance of surviving this?" He looked at his best friend.

Mathias shot him a crooked grin and replied, "I think we're the best gods damn team King Vaughn has assembled yet. We're going to send Queen Rowena and those revenants back to gehheina, where they belong."

Mathias was right. This time would be different. This unit would be different because Kaiden would be leading it. He was going to do whatever it took to keep everyone alive through the mission. He stared into the bottom of his pint glass once again.

"Something else bothering you?" A grin formed on Mathias's face. "And does it have to do with a certain *female* sergeant?"

Kaiden scowled. "She hadn't even entered my mind until you mentioned her. Thanks," he lied, then downed the rest of his ale, hoping the alcohol would cause him to forget about her, at least for that moment. He couldn't think of one female in his life who'd given him as hard a time as Blaise did. That mouth of hers infuriated him. That mouth flustered him. That mouth took him to that forbidden place in the darkest depths of his mind. He'd had the urge to shut her up earlier by tasting those lips of hers, savoring them. He'd wanted to fondle and caress that strong, curvy body of hers and do things that would make him forget his own name. *Gods, I need to stop.*

"What's going on in that head of yours?" Mathias squinted his sky-blue eyes.

Kaiden cleared his throat. "Nothing."

"Anyway, she's extremely skilled, I'll give her that. But she's also stubborn and a bit rebellious," Mathias said as he signaled for the barmaid to bring them two more pints. "We need to keep an eye on her."

"Don't worry. I recruited her, I'll watch her," Kaiden said, sounding more eager than he'd wanted to.

"I'm sure you will." Mathias's lips quirked.

Kaiden shook his head, disregarding that comment as the barmaid brought over two foaming pints. The meeting with the king and the information he had received weighed heavy on him. He finished half his pint in one gulp and let out a belch. "A few more of these and I'll be good for the night."

"That's the spirit!" Mathias chugged his own pint.

For the rest of the evening, Kaiden drank, determined to force the thoughts of Blaise out of his mind.

7

BLAISE

Stars shone brightly in the darkened sky, and the pale light of the waning moon gleamed as Blaise thought about the possibilities of what the next day might bring. She stood on the terrace in loose trousers and a fitted tunic. The cool night air caressed her cheeks, causing gooseflesh to rise on her tanned arms. She hugged herself, embracing the warmth within her body, and leaned against the stone railing. A muffled grunt echoed from the courtyard below.

Blaise frowned and grabbed a small dagger from her bedchamber, then walked down the stairs of the terrace and passed through the open corridor to check on the noise. She padded into the courtyard, barefoot, dagger in hand. Her hair flitted about in the crisp breeze. Another long groan came from the green bushes against the wall. Her grass-dampened feet led her closer, and then she peered over the side of it with a cocked eyebrow. She didn't recognize the person in the shadows. She pointed the dagger at the figure and crept in for a closer look. "Captain Kaiden?" She lowered her weapon and rolled her eyes at the sight of him.

"Sergeant. What're you doing here?" he slurred as she helped him stand.

Her brow furrowed. "I live here." She tucked the dagger into the waistband of her trousers.

He threw his arm around her, barely able to keep his balance. "You live here?" He looked up at the house, and confusion washed over his drunken face. "This isn't my house."

Blaise stared at him for a moment. His lips were curled into a clueless grin that she found endearing, though she would never have admitted it. "No, this is my house, Captain." She walked him over to the steps of her terrace, then peered through the window of her grandmother's room. *Sound asleep.* "Just keep it down." The volume of her voice lowered as Kaiden sat on the steps with his head in his hands.

Voice muffled, he said, "Goddess of chaos, everything is spinning."

"How'd you get here anyway?" She placed her hands on her hips.

He shrugged. "I walked?"

Blaise heaved a sigh. "Why would you pick tonight of all nights to get toasted?"

He didn't answer her question, face still buried in his hands. "Can I stay . . ."

"What?"

"Can I stay here?" he blurted.

The audacity of this man. She walked past him up the stairs. "No, you can't stay here."

"Why not?" He didn't raise his head.

"Why not?" she echoed and searched her mind for a reason. "Because you're a captain, and I'm a sergeant. It doesn't look good for us to be—"

"Blaise." He grabbed the railing and pulled himself up. She whirled around, and his eyes were glazed over as if he was hanging onto consciousness by a thread. His lips were parted like he wanted to beg.

How could she say no to him? He looked so vulnerable, so unaware of what was going on. It was a complete contrast to the sober captain she knew. Granted, she hardly knew him at all. She walked back down to him and threw one of his arms over her shoulder. Then she led him up the stairs, onto the terrace, and into her bedchamber. The bed would be big enough for both of them. He appeared too drunk to try anything anyway.

She helped him slip out of his armor and boots, and he made it a point to take his tunic off as well, revealing the cuts of his toned arms and chest. Like a fool, she stood there and stared at the defined muscles of his stomach. *Stop gawking at him.* With all her willpower, she tore her gaze away before he could notice.

He laid his head on the soft pillow, staying atop the covers. "Thank you for doing this." The gold in his eyes glimmered in the moonlight as he grabbed her hand.

"Please. Don't mention this. Ever." She bit her bottom lip at the half-naked captain in her bed. *What in gehheina am I doing?* She slid her hand out of his, walked over to her side of the bed, and slipped beneath the covers after she glanced at him. An arm's length away, he'd already fallen asleep, his back turned to her. His shoulders were broad, and the lines of his back muscles were prominent. Her fists clenched as she resisted the urge to run her fingers over his soft skin. The bed wasn't big enough. Maybe facing away from him would help. She turned on her side.

Within the span of a few days, she'd been forced into the king's unit. How in Alymeth had she let that happen? She'd been perfectly content on Teaos at that same post she'd been walking for over five years. Her chest constricted as she thought about how her father had died. They had assigned Captain Edgar Carrington as the king's personal guard. One fateful night, a single steel revenant broke into King Elias's chambers and murdered the king and the captain. Soon after, Prince Vaughn was crowned king, and he started developing a plan to stop Rowena's rampage.

She had hardly known her father. The sentinels had taken so much of his time from her that she'd come to resent the Order. He had lived for *them* more than he'd lived for his own family, and there was no way she'd turn out the same.

BLAISE AWOKE TO a muscular arm wrapped around her waist and warmth against her back. Who was it that held her so tight, leaving soft breaths on her nape? The sensation caused her skin to prickle. It was the captain. She didn't know what to do. She'd never been in this type of situation, and especially not with someone of higher rank. Her cheeks warmed as she felt the muscles of his chest against her back. *Gods, how did this happen?* Her eyes widened. She lost the ability to move.

"Are you awake?" he whispered.

Unable to speak, she let out a brief grunt.

"Sorry about this, by the way," he rasped, unmoving.

She flipped onto her back, inches away from his face. "If you're sorry, then why do you continue to do it?"

The captain's brownish-gold eyes locked onto her, and his lips curled into a grin. It was different this time; he beheld her more carefully, as if trying to piece together the enigma that was her. The hand gripping her waist gave her a sense of security and safety that she hadn't felt in a long while.

He leaned in closer, and his hand slipped beneath the hem of her shirt, roaming the soft skin of her stomach. "I . . . don't actually know."

Breathless, they gazed into each other's eyes. She seldom gave in to her desires, so maybe this time, just once, it would be okay. He inched closer to her lips, and just as they touched, Daniel burst into her room. "Blaise, don't you—oh, my—*Captain?*"

Kaiden moved so quickly he fell off the bed. Blaise followed suit, except she didn't fall. Her cheeks had become hot with embarrassment.

"Daniel, I can explain." She struggled to keep any remnant of calm in her voice. Her little brother had caught her in bed with a high-ranked sentinel. His reaction was warranted.

Kaiden stood on the other side of the bed, getting dressed. "It's not what you think it is," he said, clumsily slipping on his boots. "I came here drunk last night—"

Blaise glared at Kaiden and said, "Would you let *me* explain please?"

The captain gestured for her to continue.

"We were just sleeping together." That didn't sound good either. This was one of those moments where she wanted to stab herself with her own sword. "No, we were—"

Daniel waved his hand. "It doesn't even matter. I was just making sure you were up." He then gave the captain a warning look before walking out of the room and closing the door.

"I knew I shouldn't have let you stay here. What was I thinking?" She dragged her hands down her face.

"You weren't complaining a moment ago." Kaiden grinned.

She shot him a narrow-eyed glare and said through gritted teeth, "This stays between us."

"I don't think I'm the one you need to worry about," he muttered as he finished dressing.

"Are you saying my brother will tell?"

"Hate to break it to you, but he's the biggest gossip in the castle."

He had a point. Blaise couldn't argue with him there. "When you leave, please do so discreetly," she said, her arms crossed over her chest.

"For what it's worth"—he glanced at her—"I am grateful you didn't leave me out in the cold."

"Like I said last night, don't mention it." She placed a hand on her hip.

"I'll see you at Cloveshire." He turned to her and said, "Don't be late." Then he walked out of her room and exited through the terrace.

Blaise watched him as he crossed the courtyard and passed through the estate's black iron gates. She wondered what would've happened if Daniel hadn't barged in. It made her insides hot thinking about it. Yes, the captain possessed incredible looks and a muscular physique, but that was it. They were about to embark on an impossible endeavor. She didn't need to add more complication to it.

THE SCENT OF the morning dew lingered. Grams would still be in bed, but she couldn't leave without saying goodbye. The thought of leaving her caused Blaise's heart to sink into her stomach. She opened the door to Grams's room, being as quiet as possible. The old woman lay sound asleep in the enormous bed in her chambers, wrapped in a dark blue comforter.

Blaise sat on her bedside and hesitantly woke Helena. "Grams, I'm leaving now."

"Leaving? You're going on your mission?" Helena still had her eyes closed. She reached for Blaise's hand and missed.

"Yes, and I don't know when I'll be back." *Or if I'll be back at all.* Blaise left that part out. She grabbed Helena's cold, skinny hand.

Grams's eyes fluttered open and met her granddaughter's. "I know you'll do great."

Blaise smiled, holding Grams's hand a little tighter. "I'll miss you." A tear escaped from the corner of her eye.

She tried to keep her voice from trembling but couldn't manage it. "I'm scared."

"I know you are, Pooka. Change is scary. Terrifying. But I know you have what it takes." Helena paused as if searching for her next words. "Just remember, things are not what they seem."

Unsure of what Grams meant, Blaise let go of her hand.

"Wait." The old woman grabbed it once more. "As the sun rises in the east, she will rise."

"I think you need to take your elixirs now, Grams," Blaise said, eyebrows coming together. "I have to go now."

After Helena gave her an affectionate kiss on the forehead, Blaise took her leave and made her way to the stable. This was crazy. She barely knew anyone on this team. Not personally, anyway. How was she to know whether they could be trusted? Only time would tell. Until then, she would be on guard around them—the captain especially.

Grams's words echoed in her mind. *As the sun rises in the east, she will rise.* What had she meant by that? Blaise wished she'd had more time to confront her about it. Perhaps it was just the ranting of an elderly woman.

Blaise took her time getting Aero situated, attaching a bedroll and saddlebags for supplies. Once she'd done that, she climbed onto her horse. "Take it all in, girl."

The horse let out a breath.

"I know, don't be so negative." They made their way through the gates of the estate and down the dirt road toward Cloveshire Castle.

BLAISE WALKED DOWN the gravel path through the lush courtyard of the castle after putting Aero in the stables. The morning sun shone a yellow gold onto the approaching training grounds. Her thoughts were on the morning's events with the captain and the conversation she'd had with Grams.

Daniel caught up to her in the corridor that led to the armory. "Are you nervous?"

She glanced at him, taking in the sight of her brave younger brother, and came to terms with the fact that this might be the last time they saw each other. "Should I be?"

He shrugged and gazed down at his leather-gloved hands. "I'm gonna miss you." Sorrow overcame his boyish features, and he bit down on his bottom lip as if to keep it from quivering. "I just want you to know that I told them about you because . . ." He sniffled, avoiding eye contact. "I believe in you."

Her heart melted. She came to a halt and smiled at him as she pulled him in for a hug, which he returned. "Take care of Grams," she whispered. Tears welled up in her eyes, but she wouldn't let them fall. She had to be strong. If not for herself, for them.

His voice cracked as he replied, "I will." He hugged her tighter before letting go. "About the captain . . ."

She raised an eyebrow and placed a hand on her hip. "What about him?"

"Just be careful. He's a ladies' man."

Another grin graced her features. "How do you know I'm not a harlot?"

He cocked an eyebrow. "Is that a trick question?"

She raised her shoulder. "Maybe."

"Because I live with you," he replied, his lips turned up.

"I mean, you did catch us in my bed. How do you know I haven't been doing that all along?" She hadn't been, but she enjoyed ruffling Daniel's feathers.

He rolled his eyes. "I like to think I know you better than that, sister."

And he did. She swallowed, knowing she needed to get to the armory before she was late again, or she'd never hear the end of it. "I should go."

Daniel stopped her before she could walk off, wrapping his arms around her once more.

A lump formed in her throat. "I don't want to say goodbye, Daniel."

"Then don't," he replied. "I'll see you when you get back. The gods will protect you."

"You know, you're causing a scene," she teased, noticing a few passing sentinels and squires looking their way.

Voice muffled against her shoulder, he said, "I don't care."

"Okay, but I really have to go now, love," she said, pulling away from him, keeping the tears in her eyes from spilling over.

He nodded, swiping away the wetness on his cheeks. "Be safe."

"I will." She finally continued to the armory. *Dammit. Why'd he have to make that so difficult?* She and Daniel had spent most of their childhood fighting, but not because they hated each other. It had been more for entertainment and to push each other's buttons, as siblings do. That goodbye had caused an ache in her chest, mostly because she'd promised him and Grams that she would return when she knew it wasn't guaranteed.

8

KAIDEN

There wasn't anything strange about Kaiden's early arrival to the castle armory, yet Mathias stood next to the fireplace, a knowing grin plastered on his face. *For the gods' sake.* He gave the rest of the unit a look over, noting that same expression on their features. He swore he could read their minds.

"Daniel." It came out as a curse upon his breath. Perhaps if he ignored them, they wouldn't say anything. Kaiden adjusted his chest armor.

"So . . . how was your little sleepover, Captain?" Mathias sauntered over.

Kaiden sighed. "Nothing happened, Sergeant." And that was partly Daniel's fault.

"As much as I want to believe that, I know you better," Mathias teased.

"She's not like that." Kaiden and Mathias walked out of earshot from the rest of the unit.

Mathias feigned thoughtfulness. "Oh, really? Enlighten me. What *is* she like?"

"She cared enough to take me in last night so I could sleep off the ale you encouraged upon me," Kaiden said firmly.

"Hey, don't blame this on me. You're the one who *insisted* on going to her house at such a late hour."

"I did?" That part had slipped Kaiden's mind. He hardly ever drank over two pints of ale and couldn't blame it all on his best friend. The fact that Blaise had witnessed every drunken moment last night caused his chest to tighten. She'd probably see him in a different light, which wasn't a good thing. She already had an issue with authority.

Mathias nodded.

"Like I said, nothing happened between us," said Kaiden, remembering the almost kiss and the warm desire that had coursed through him as he'd stared into her chestnut eyes.

"What you do in your free time isn't anyone's business." Mathias shot him a teasing smile.

At that moment, Blaise walked into the armory, adjusting her wrist guard, and blended in with the rest of the crew. She and Audrey began talking to each other.

Kaiden stared at her from across the room. He didn't realize it until Mathias obnoxiously cleared his throat.

"Tell me again how nothing happened?" That damn grin never left Mathias's dumb face.

"Shut up," Kaiden said with an eye roll. Colvyr save him. He couldn't help but admire the way she carried herself with an air of confidence that demanded respect from others around her. He wanted to be honest with her and tell her about meeting Philippa, but that would go against the king's orders.

THE THOUGHT OF riding through the revenant-infested Grelan Forest left him with a sour taste in his mouth. On the way to Haven, the unit would stop in the small walled-in town of Lerwick. Kaiden considered their journey as his unit followed on horseback through the streets of Elatora.

Isaac rode up beside Kaiden and asked, "Were you able to say goodbye to your family, Captain?"

"My father and sister don't like goodbyes." Kaiden looked ahead at the drawbridge about a mile away.

"Still would've been nice to see them though. Right?" Isaac asked.

Kaiden shrugged. "I suppose."

His mother had been the last person he'd said goodbye to before she'd left on a mission to Balam. She'd never come back.

A few minutes passed, and they were all in front of the drawbridge.

Commander Stephen and Kaiden's teenage sister were standing on the side of the road, waiting. Kaiden stopped in front of the two and climbed off Cedric. He signaled his unit to stand by. They stayed at a distance, respecting his privacy.

"I thought you two weren't going to do this." He walked up to the pair.

The significantly shorter Elizabeth fiddled with her thumbs, her head downcast. "We couldn't let you leave without saying goodbye, Kai."

"I'll be back, Liz—"

"How do you know that?" She looked up at him with melancholy in her amber-colored eyes.

Kaiden gazed at her, moving a strand of her long dark blond hair from her face. She looked so much like their mother—or what he remembered of her—with her big round eyes, proportionate pointed nose, and high cheekbones. "Hey, I will fight tooth and nail to come home to you."

Elizabeth gave a conceding nod, accepting his answer. "Here." She pulled out a necklace constructed from rope with a circular purple crystal hanging off it. "I found this amongst Mother's things. Maybe it'll protect you on this mission."

Kaiden bent a few inches to her eye level and allowed her to place it around his neck. He gazed at it before tucking it away into the collar of his tunic beneath his armor. "Thank you, Liz."

She propelled toward him, throwing her arms around his torso, burying her face in his chest. "Don't go, Kai. They can pick someone else to lead the unit, can't they?"

A heaviness overwhelmed his heart. "I've already committed to the mission. To them." He gestured to the group. "What kind of person would I be if I went back on my commitments?"

With a nod and tears in her eyes, she straightened, letting her arms fall to her sides. She stepped away from him. "Words are binding."

He smiled, glad that she'd remembered that. "Yes."

She sniffled, wiping the tears from her cheeks with the sleeve of her blue dress. "I'll wait for your return then." She'd said that like a calm, mature young woman.

He raised his chin and shot her a toothy smile, thinking about what Mathias had said about her being strong. "That's my girl." He reached for her hand and kissed it.

Kaiden then took a few steps away from her with his father. His demeanor became firm and commanding as he said, "You're the only one here for her now."

Commander Stephen nodded. "I tried to recommend another captain for this unit—"

"Never mind that." Kaiden had raised his voice, though it had been unintentional. "Look at Elizabeth."

Stephen did. She didn't appear to know what they were talking about.

"That's your daughter. She's the only person in this kingdom—in this realm—who matters now. Do you understand me?" Kaiden met his father's saddened gaze.

Throughout the years, something had changed in Kaiden's father. Perhaps a brokenness from losing his wife? Years of servitude to the king? Kaiden glanced down at his clasped hands, and a sense of pity swept over him. He didn't know when things had changed in the man standing in front of him.

"I'm sorry I wasn't a better father to you," Stephen said, staring at the ground.

"It's okay." Kaiden honestly didn't blame him for having been so strict and distant. It had been difficult for his father to draw a line between serving the Sentinel Order and serving his family. Those two blended together most of the time, and Kaiden had learned from his father's mistakes. "Just be a better one to her."

Before Kaiden could walk away, the commander pulled him into a rough embrace. "I love you, son."

Kaiden hadn't expected the commander to express his emotions so readily. His throat tightened, and he pulled away from his father. He looked to the ground as he mounted Cedric. With an inhale, he gave his family one last glance. He signaled to lower the bridge. His ears rattled with the clunking and clinking noises coming from the bridge. When it reached the other side of the moat, he motioned for his crew to follow, and they rode over the wooden structure into Grelan Forest.

As predicted, they came across many revenants in the thicket. The ones they couldn't avoid and dodge had their heads sliced off. George and Audrey made it into a competition. Blaise picked them off with her crossbow as she guarded the rear of the formation, shooting them in the eye or right through their skull. Any other shot wouldn't have been effective. Isaac and Mathias stayed in the front with the captain.

Did Rowena know about the king's plan? About the unit? Kaiden constantly glanced around, ensuring the team stayed relatively close. He used his crossbow and shot at any hideous creatures who dared attack him. The rest of his unit were all occupied, fighting off the undead corpses rushing their way. The creatures moved quicker on all fours in an eerie crawling motion, their eyes void of any emotion except the hunger for flesh. Their skin rotted from the lack of circulating blood in their bodies. The akrani that had been forged into them by the akrani alchime made them strong but not invincible. These were bone revenants.

A few hours had passed, and the attacks continued to come in small spurts. "We don't have much farther to go!" Kaiden shouted, keeping Cedric at a brisk pace. His body had tired from riding and killing Rowena's monsters. He knew his horse had to be getting tired as well.

A revenant crawled on all fours at an inhuman pace. It leaped for Kaiden. He leaned back, then sliced horizontally, cutting the creature in half. Its thick dark red blood spewed everywhere. He glanced back and saw each half still squirming about on the forest floor.

Kaiden heard a shriek from behind. He twisted in the saddle to see that Isaac had fallen off his horse. Blaise quickened her horse's pace and rode up to him, shooting enemies on her left and one on her right. In one swooping motion, she grabbed Isaac's outstretched arm and pulled him up onto her saddle behind her. *Damn, she's good.*

A whoosh of air passed Kaiden's ear. Had someone in his unit shot at him? He glanced back at George, who had his crossbow aimed at him. The large man gestured at something in front of the captain. Kaiden turned back around to see that one of George's arrows had gone straight through a revenant's head.

"Nice shot," Kaiden bellowed.

George grinned, then pulled a small white ram's horn from his saddlebag and sounded it, alerting the guards on the Lerwick wall of their arrival. They opened the large iron-plated gate as the team crossed Cleree River's long wooden bridge.

Once Kaiden had safely made it inside the town's wall, he spun around. Mathias rode in next, followed by George and Audrey. Blaise and Isaac had fallen further back from them than Kaiden had thought. They were both shooting at incoming bone revenants while crossing the river's bridge. *For the love of Colvyr.* Kaiden had half a mind to go back out there.

Mathias seemed to read his mind. "Wait, don't go yet," he said.

Blaise and Isaac finally made it across. Her mare sprinted through Lerwick's barrier and skidded to a stop just a few feet from the entrance. The guards slammed the gate shut, smashing one revenant to bloody pieces.

"Cutting it a bit close, aren't we?" Mathias remarked with a smirk.

Blaise scowled at him, her breathing uneven. She said nothing and continued down the dirt road into the heart of the town. It had been built specifically for travelers because of the dangerous conditions in Grelan Forest. The kings of Haven and Elatora had agreed to share the economic responsibilities. They'd built the wall around Lerwick with the same materials as Teaos, but not nearly as high. It was about half the height and a quarter of the size in diameter. A small town indeed. Most of the people who lived there helped to upkeep and guard Lerwick.

Kaiden followed Blaise and Isaac through the marketplace, where vendors in small wooden stalls sold fresh produce. On his left, behind the wooden businesses, a long gable-roofed structure housed the butcher's shop, the tailor's shop, and the bakery. Barracks for the soldiers were on the other side of the street, and further down were small residential homes built in close proximity to one another.

"What a quaint little town," Kaiden heard Audrey comment.

"I hope they have good ale," Mathias added.

Kaiden just shook his head in amusement.

It took them thirty minutes to finally arrive at the square structure of the Lerwick Inn. The sun had begun its descent over the horizon. Unfortunately, the unit had to pair up because of the limited number of rooms. Kaiden assigned George and Isaac together and Audrey and Blaise in another room. He and Mathias would share a space like old times.

Once in his room, he couldn't sit still and began to pace. Mathias had gone somewhere with Audrey, and he wasn't sure what George and Isaac were up to. After changing out of his armor, he made his way down the stairs and into the tavern. He spotted Mathias and Audrey at the table in the corner. They appeared to be playing a drinking game with each other. With a grin and an eye roll, Kaiden continued out onto the dirt road.

"Captain!" Blaise caught up to him with quick steps.

He glanced at her. "Did you need something?"

"No, I just figured I'd join you if that's okay." She glanced down at her clasped hands. "Isaac and George are already asleep, and, well . . . I assume you saw Mathias and Audrey."

Kaiden nodded, and then a glint of light hit his eyes. It had come from a gold necklace Blaise was wearing. The neckline of her tunic barely covered it. He hadn't noticed it before and, out of curiosity, pointed at it. "That's a pretty piece of jewelry. Mind if I take a look at it?"

She pulled the rest of the necklace out from beneath her black tunic and held it up for him to view. What was that scent? He caught a whiff of lavender as he stepped toward her. It was the same scent that had nearly distracted him when they'd dueled in Elatora.

The necklace's thumb-size charm had a series of gold triangles woven together intricately and enclosed in a circle. He was no expert on the charms of Elatora, but he'd seen nothing like it. "It's beautiful."

With much care, she hid it away beneath her tunic and replied, "Thank you. It was my mother's."

He'd already known certain personal things about her life, the general details. He walked along the side of the road, fighting the urge to ask her more questions.

She followed and asked, "Where are we going?"

"The bakery." A wooden wagon passed them, carrying various produce. The man driving appeared tired.

The aroma of evening meals being cooked was potent as they passed through the small residential area of the street.

"Really?" She sounded surprised by his answer.

"Yes, I happen to love custard tarts," he replied.

Her mouth curved, amusement apparent on her face. "I never took you for someone with a sweet tooth."

He stopped in front of the bakery. "I love anything sweet." He leaned close and winked, causing her cheeks to redden.

She rolled her eyes. "Let's go get your tarts." She continued into the building.

At that moment, Kaiden knew making her flustered would be his new favorite pastime. He followed her into the bakery, although he could think of other ways to satiate his sweet tooth.

A woman with soft facial features greeted them.

There were a few tables on one side of the bakery where patrons could sit. On the other side of the small area was a display case filled with various mouthwatering pies, pastries, and breads.

"Hello there, what can I get you?" the woman asked as she wiped her pale hands off on her apron.

"Hello," Blaise greeted her with that smile, which made Kaiden jealous of the baker. "He wants some custard tarts."

The woman shot them each a smile. "Well, you're in luck. I have a fresh batch in the back." She then walked through a wooden door, leaving Blaise and Kaiden alone.

"You haven't told me what you like," he said, looking at all the baked goods in the display case.

She placed one hand on her hip and replied, "I don't like any of it."

He cocked an eyebrow and straightened. "Have you tried any of it?"

"You don't have to try something to not like it." The corner of her mouth rose slightly.

"No." He shook his head. "That's unacceptable. You're going to try a custard tart today."

"What?" She smiled. "Don't be absurd."

The baker walked out with a wooden tray. "Will you be eating it here?"

"No—"

"Yes," Kaiden interrupted.

Blaise squinted at him.

The baker smiled and continued to plate the pastry. "These sell rather quickly in the evenings. Enjoy." She handed it over to Kaiden with a utensil.

He scooped a small serving onto the fork and held it up to Blaise's mouth. "Open."

She bit her bottom lip and appeared as though she was going to put up a fight. He stared at the hint of green around the irises of her chestnut eyes and couldn't look away. Her lips parted for him. *For the love of Colvyr.* His heart thrummed as he eased the fork into her mouth, then dragged it out. She started chewing. He bit down on the inside of his cheek, resisting the urge to put his mouth on hers, tasting her and the piece of pastry he'd just fed her.

"Well?" the baker asked. "How is it?"

Blaise kept her gaze on him, and her response came out in a whisper. "Delicious."

Kaiden took a bite of the tart as well. He turned his attention back to the baker, who still had a smile on her face. "It's very good, thank you," he said, grateful for the interruption. Walking out of there hard would've been embarrassing.

He gave the baker a gald piece after eating the rest of the tart. Before he and Blaise walked out, the baker said, "Can I just say that you two are the cutest couple I've ever seen?"

Kaiden cocked an eyebrow, and all he could get out was, "Thank you." Then they headed out the door. Once outside, he noticed the flush in Blaise's cheeks. He smiled and asked, "Well, what did you think of it?"

She appeared distracted. "Huh? Oh, the tart?"

He nodded as they started the short trek back to the inn. The sun sat above the horizon. Hues of orange, gold, and pink filled the darkening sky. An enigmatic silence filled the streets of Lerwick as they strolled.

"It was good." She didn't look at him.

"New favorite?" His posture stiffened.

She smiled and rolled her eyes. "Yes, Captain."

He didn't know if she was telling the truth. It didn't really matter though. He'd actually persuaded her to try something new, and he couldn't wait for another opportunity like that to occur. The thought caused him to grin and made his stomach flutter. His eyes fixated on her as they walked side by side.

He'd seen the ocean as a young boy of five, before Rowena had begun wreaking havoc in Crenitha. Blaise reminded him of the waves that crashed onto the shores of Blackrock Harbor. Unpredictable. Unyielding. Formidable. But no less beautiful. *Gods, what is she doing to me?*

MATHIAS AND AUDREY'S drinking game had left them toasted. They'd kicked Kaiden out of his own room to . . . frolic. He didn't want to sleep in the tavern, nor did he want to be in a room with George and Isaac. All he wanted was a warm bed to rest in for the night. Maybe Blaise would pity him again and let him sleep in her room.

He walked down the hall, past George and Isaac's door, to the very end, and knocked. The light of the moon shone in through the rectangular windows lined up on the opposite wall. A short moment later, Blaise answered the door in her sleep attire, already appearing annoyed.

She leaned against the doorpost with her arms crossed. "What're you doing here? Are you drunk again?"

"No. Audrey and Mathias are . . ." He cleared his throat. "Bunking up for the night."

"Oh . . ." A thoughtful expression—followed by realization—washed over her face as her eyes widened. "Oh."

He nodded. "I hate to ask, but could I sleep here in her bed for tonight?"

She closed her eyes and sighed before gesturing for him to enter the small room.

Kaiden scanned the area. There was only one bed, a window, and a bedside table with a basin full of fresh water. The floorboards creaked beneath his feet as he stepped toward the full-size bed. It was much smaller than the one they'd shared at her house.

"Why is there only one bed?" He groaned inwardly. *Does this inn not believe in single beds?*

Blaise shrugged as she stood a few feet away from him.

"Would it make you feel more comfortable if I slept on the floor?"

Another contemplative expression overcame those beautiful chestnut eyes. "No. Just please try to stay on your side of the bed this time."

He agreed with a nod and slipped out of his tunic.

She stared at him as though she hadn't expected him to do that.

"Something wrong?" He froze at seeing her eyes roam the top half of his body.

"No." She gulped and quickly slipped beneath the covers of the bed.

He grinned and lay on the bed. The springs made a horrible creaking noise. He rested his head on the soft pillow with a sigh of relief.

"Is this going to be a regular occurrence?" She lay on her back, hands clasped on her stomach on top of the blankets.

"I don't know," he replied midyawn. "Seems to be my luck though." He paused, thinking about the day's events and fighting their way tirelessly through Grelan Forest. "What you did today for Isaac was brave."

"He would've done the same for me, I'm sure."

Kaiden remained quiet for a few seconds before changing the subject again. "You are quite difficult to figure out, Sergeant." He couldn't keep the tiredness from his voice.

She snorted. "Hardly."

"I just want to know one thing. Why did you hesitate?" He stole a glance at her. The moonlight shone through the single small window of the room. She lay there beside him, staring up at the wooden planks of the ceiling. *She's beautiful.*

She met his gaze, cocking an eyebrow. "What makes you think I hesitated on purpose?"

"Did you?" he prodded.

"You're going to be relentless about this, aren't you?"

"Probably." The corner of his mouth rose.

Shaking her head defeatedly, she replied, "I was thinking about my grandmother." She let out a slow breath. "Grams seems to think I have much more to offer, that I'm wasting away on Teaos."

"Sounds like a smart woman to me," he remarked. "And for the record, I knew you were holding back."

She rolled her eyes, holding back a smile. "You did not."

"Why do you argue with everything I say?" An exasperated sigh escaped his lips.

"I don't know." She shrugged. "To keep you on your toes." She poked his forehead playfully with her index finger.

He feigned a pained expression and rubbed it with his palm.

"This isn't very fair."

"What isn't very fair?" he asked.

"You know a lot about me, and I know almost nothing about you, yet here we are, sharing a bed for the second time." She chuckled lightly.

He let out a soft laugh as well. "Well, what do you want to know?"

She stayed quiet for a moment. "I know your father is second-in-command of the sentinels and you have a younger sister, Elizabeth. But what of your mother?"

He didn't enjoy talking about his mother. It wasn't an easy issue, but he knew about Blaise's family background, so it was only fair that he tell her, right? He breathed deeply before saying, "My mother was a sentinel."

"What happened to her?" Blaise asked.

"She died fulfilling her duty to them—to the king," he replied simply. There was a sadness he couldn't keep out of his voice. "I was about six when she died. She was on the king's task force. She died trying to stop Rowena from releasing her revenants upon the land." He stopped to take another breath. "It was a failed mission. Obviously."

He expected the silence that occurred between them. His mother's story wasn't one he told to everyone for that reason. Mathias even knew never to bring it up.

She broke the stillness in the air with a whisper. "I'm sorry."

"It was a long time ago." His gaze met the wooden ceiling of the room. "You want to know the sad part?"

"You mean apart from her death?"

"Yeah. I'm beginning to forget the way she used to yell at me when I got into trouble. Her comforting smile when I got hurt. The feeling of her arms around me when she hugged me just because." He'd blocked most of his childhood memories, except for those of his mother. His father had run their home like it was a sentinels' barracks after she died. All the warmth in his home had died along with her. He supposed his father loved him and Elizabeth in his own way, but he never showed it. Never *tried* to show it.

"There is something worse," she remarked with a yawn. "Not having those memories at all."

"I suppose you're right." He fiddled with his thumbs on top of the covers. "Blaise?"

"Yes?" she murmured, her voice dripping with exhaustion.

"Do you think the gods allowed Rowena to terrorize Crenitha?" It probably seemed random for him to ask that question, but his mother used to worship Colvyr. She'd blindly believed in him, in his peace.

Blaise's eyes were closed. "Nobody has seen or heard from the gods in decades. But who knows? Maybe they're in nehveina and gehheina laughing at our demise. Or . . ."

"Or?" He wanted to hear her thoughts on the matter.

"Perhaps they're just tired of our foolishness and have abandoned us altogether." She opened one eye to look at him. "Why are you asking me this?"

"I'm gathering opinions," he replied.

Her lips quirked, and she closed her eye.

"Blaise?"

She loosed a breath. "What is it, Captain?"

You're part of the reason we're going to Haven, he wanted to say, but instead he whispered, "Never mind." It had almost come out, the secret he so desperately wanted to share with her.

Some time passed before Kaiden heard the soft snoring of Blaise beside him. His lips turned up into an amused grin as he gazed at her sleeping countenance. He observed the rise and fall of her chest, the way her long onyx hair looked a shade of blue in the pale moonlight, how it draped around the pillow beneath her. He stared at the way her lips slightly parted on her exhale and couldn't bring himself to look away. He'd been dangerously close to tasting those potentially sweet lips the other morning. *Stop!* He needed to stop thinking about such things. Turning onto his side away from her, he pushed those thoughts from his mind, and soon after, sleep enveloped him.

9

BLAISE

Her eyes flickered open, and she glanced at the empty space beside her. Why had she expected him to still be there? He'd just needed somewhere to sleep. Blaise's stomach clenched at the thought. Sitting up, she swung her legs over the side of the creaky bed and stretched out her sore limbs. *Must be from traveling yesterday.*

She straightened and peered out the small square window. It was an overcast day, and the streets below bustled with people. A wagon full of various fruits and vegetables passed by the inn, heading toward the market-place. In the silence, she looked away, steadily scanning the small quarters. Audrey's things still sat in a corner of the room. Blaise couldn't help but wonder how her night with Sergeant Mathias had gone. Then she looked to the oak chest where her armor, weapons, and satchel lay in an organized mess.

The door opened, startling Blaise, and Kaiden padded in with a tray of various breakfast foods. The aroma made her stomach rumble. She raised a curious eyebrow at him and crossed her arms. "What's this?"

He appeared caught off guard by her question as he carefully placed the tray in the middle of the bed and sat down. "Breakfast?" One of his dark eyebrows rose.

She stared at him before joining him and buttering a slice of toasted bread, letting her long legs hang off the side of the mattress. "Thank you, Captain." Her stomach fluttered at his thoughtfulness.

"I don't know if you like grape or strawberry jam, so I just brought a bit of both," he said before grabbing his own slice and taking a bite.

Blaise wondered why he was being so . . . nice. It was a contrast from the bossy, arrogant, insolent captain she'd become accustomed to. She caught herself staring again and tore away before he noticed. "I actually just like butter on my toast." She held up her piece of bread, showing him.

"Never would've guessed," he said, finishing one slice and then moving to grab another. "I like mine plain."

With a grin, she teased, "Says the man who likes custard tarts."

He narrowed his eyes at her. "Don't deny it. That's your new favorite pastry now."

She didn't know what had gotten into her that morning, but she was feeling especially playful. In a slow and sensual manner, she stood. *What am I doing?* His eyes locked on her hips as she traipsed closer to him, her lips curving upward. *I'm playing with fire.* Once she was in front of him, he peered up at her and leaned back on his hands, confusion apparent in his hazel eyes. Then, with a sinful smile, she placed one leg on the outside of his thigh.

He showed no signs of disapproval, so she continued to straddle him, sitting on his lap. His lips parted slightly, his breathing shallow. The long, hard length of him pulsed against her inner thigh. She couldn't help but bite her bottom lip.

This sense of control over a higher-ranked sentinel was empowering, and she embraced every teasing moment. Gods, he looked good beneath her. Holding his gaze, she placed a hand on his strong shoulder and brought the half-eaten slice of bread to his mouth. "Open."

He didn't even hesitate, taking an alluring bite of the toast. It crunched as he chewed, and then he swallowed, not taking his gaze off her for one second. His eyes were full of . . . something she couldn't put her finger on. *Confusion? Desire? Maybe a combination of the two?*

She leaned forward, grinding her hips into his. He stifled a breath. She reveled in his reaction. Her mouth inched closer to his, and as their lips grazed, she purred, "That was for yesterday." And then she stepped away, leaving him with a frustrated, clueless expression on his features. "We should get going soon." She tossed the small piece of toast into her mouth as if nothing had happened and made her way over to the oak chest where her bags and armor lay.

He just sat there, still processing the moment. Then, finally, he cleared his throat and agreed. "I'll go wake the others." He walked out, closing the door behind him.

Blaise smiled, pleased with herself. He'd get her back though. She wasn't worried about it. Her tumultuous heart still thrummed in her chest. It was strange to think that she had gotten the best sleep of her life with Kaiden next to her. It had to have been because of his warmth. She wasn't used to it.

AFTER SHE RETRIEVED Aero from one of the stable hands on the side of the inn, Blaise settled onto her and watched Audrey walk out before any of the others. "Did you have fun last night?" she asked the redhead.

Audrey looked pleased with herself as she went to retrieve her own horse. She made her way beside Blaise, mounted her steed, and replied, "I thought you'd appreciate some one-on-one time with the captain."

"Actually, I'd appreciate it if you didn't do that again," Blaise said in a firm tone of voice.

"Oh no. You're a virgin, aren't you?" Audrey asked.

Blaise's eyebrows came together. "Not that it's any of your business, but no, I'm not."

"Then what's the problem? You should be used to sharing a bed with him by now." Audrey had a coy grin on her innocent-looking features. Blaise knew her better than that. "What's the big deal anyway? It's just sex," Audrey said.

Blaise's cheeks warmed as the rest of the crew trickled out of the inn. "I'm not interested in him like that," she said, easing Aero toward the main gate of the town, not waiting for her team. If only she hadn't agreed to let Kaiden stay that first night.

Audrey caught up to her. "Liar. He's tall, dark, and handsome, not to mention good with his sword." She let out a giggle.

At that point, Blaise couldn't help but laugh along with her. "You're crazy."

"You really need to loosen up, Sergeant," Audrey stated with a playful grin.

"I think you've loosened up enough for the both of us."

Audrey's smile widened. "I assume you're talking about what happened between me and Mathias last night?"

Blaise gave a curt nod as they passed the small marketplace of Lerwick.

"If you must know, it was great." Audrey lowered the volume of her voice.

"And a one-time thing, right?" At that point, the rest of the men caught up, trailing in pairs behind the women. Isaac had been able to buy another horse from the innkeeper.

Audrey shrugged. "Who knows?"

Blaise decided not to push the issue any further. If Audrey and Mathias wanted to have relations, it wasn't any of her business. Half a mile from the gate, she signaled to the guard ahead to open it, kicking Aero to a gallop. "I'll take point this time."

All six of them sped through the Lerwick gate. There were a handful of straggler revenants outside of the wall that enclosed the small town, but it was nothing the crew couldn't handle. Armed with their swords and crossbows, they took out any monsters that attempted to attack them.

Blaise had heard that Rowena had sent a steel revenant to assassinate late King Elias of Elatora, and it was that creature who had killed her father as well. She had only been thirteen when it happened. Her mother had already passed away. That was the day she and Daniel became orphans.

After they'd spent a few hours riding and fighting, Haven finally appeared in the clearing, a beautiful contrast of white structures decorated with gold. The wall that surrounded the magnificent kingdom appeared taller than Teaos, and the moat was wide and most likely deep as well. The drawbridge was a heavy oak with thick golden chains attached to it.

Once the whole team had ridden through the gate, the Captain of the Haven guard trotted up on horseback and brief introductions were made. Captain Wilhelm confirmed their identities, then escorted the unit to King Theod's castle.

BLAISE TOOK IN the sight before her: an extravagant white castle with accents of gold. The Haven soldiers were dressed in the same colors. The structure had many levels, multiple towers soaring into the clouds, and rows of arched windows. *He must have a lot of staff.*

After Captain Wilhelm escorted the unit into the throne room, he stood next to the platform where the king's chair sat.

King Theod had been crowned when he turned twenty-one. He'd ruled Haven for ten years with a lenient hand and a heavy treasury. He was a simple man with a desire for the simple pleasures life had to offer. There were rumors that another expansion of the kingdom was in the works, but it had been paused due to the lack of resources. He sat on his throne, clad in silken garbs of white and gold, a deliberating expression on his pale features. He ran a hand through his dark blond hair and stood.

The unit formed a row and bowed to the king, and then Kaiden stepped forward.

"Is this the complete unit from Elatora?" the king asked, examining each of them.

"Were you expecting more, Your Majesty?" Kaiden kept his face neutral. "Less?"

"No. No. It's just a contrast compared to the last one my cousin sent into Balam," replied Theod with a curious expression on his face.

"Perhaps that's a good thing." Kaiden glanced at the faces of his sentinels.

"Yes," Theod drawled. "I have two men to add to your group." He gestured to the guards at the entrance, and they opened the heavy doors.

In walked two men clad in black. Why didn't they wear any armor? Weren't they soldiers? Maybe it hindered them. The taller of the two stopped in line with the rest. The shorter one stepped slightly ahead of them. He had short auburn hair. His eyes were like emerald jewels, his skin pale. He didn't appear to be physically endowed with muscle, but Blaise wouldn't underestimate either of them.

"This is akrani satori Zade Blakwall. He has agreed to join you on this perilous mission," said the king.

Blaise met his gaze, and he gave her a knowing smirk. *Hello, Sergeant.* The blood rushed from her face to her pounding heart. Did he know she was one of them? If so, what would he do? Would he tell anyone?

Zade gave a bow to the king, then one to Captain Kaiden and said, "It's an honor." He stepped in line with the others while his counterpart stepped forward.

"This is akrani katai Raijinn Semour. He's one of the best in Haven," Theod said proudly.

Blaise stared at his freckled profile and wondered if he knew how to wield all the elements in all of their forms. If he did, then maybe she could learn from him. Then again, maybe she was getting ahead of herself.

Raijinn had dark brown hair and blue eyes. His skin had freckles on it, and when he turned, Blaise caught a glance at the scar on his right cheek. It appeared to have been a burn mark. It didn't obscure his handsome face; if anything, it added to his good looks. But it made her wonder how much power he possessed.

The king invited them to stay in his castle as honored guests. Kaiden expressed his hesitation about accepting. Blaise understood his concern—he didn't know the king—but after some prodding from the unit, the captain conceded. After all, they had many rough days ahead of them. Who knew when they'd receive this treatment again?

THE KING'S SERVANT led Blaise down a wide corridor of the castle. Gold chandeliers were suspended from the high ceilings. She glanced through one of the many grand windows that lined one side of the wall. It appeared to be a garden with lush greenery and flowers of varying colors. Quite the contrast to Cloveshire Castle. The rest of the unit had been led away to their own suites. She hadn't noticed who went into which chamber. She'd been too taken with the garden outside in the courtyard.

Zade caught up to her and told the servant he would

take her the rest of the way. "What do you think of Haven, Sergeant?" he asked, matching her pace.

Blaise glanced at the white marble floors. "It's very . . ." She thought about saying "extravagant" but refrained. "Beautiful," she finished with a polite grin.

"You know you can say what you think around me."

She really needed to guard her thoughts better. "Maybe you should save your satori for more threatening situations."

A corner of his mouth rose, and then he said, "This is your room, Sergeant Blaise." They stopped in front of tall oak double doors. "But before you go, I must know." He studied her rather uncomfortably. "Do you know?"

She tore away, biting the inside of her cheek. "What in Alymeth are you talking about?"

He kept his gaze on her.

Her mind had betrayed her once more. Like an itch she couldn't scratch, he breached her mind, searching. He clawed deeper. What did he expect to find? She winced at his intrusion. Trying to force him out of her thoughts was like peeling her own skin off. But she tried anyway. She wouldn't let this man, whom she'd only known for a few minutes, into her mind. Something sparked inside her, severing the connection. Her eyes widened.

He rubbed his temples, eyes closed. "How in gehheina did you do that? You're a katai."

"I-I . . . don't know what happened," was all she could get out.

His brow furrowed, and then he muttered, "Curious."

He walked away, but she stopped him. "Did you see something?"

Zade didn't face her as he replied, "I might have," and then continued walking away.

Blaise heaved a sigh, wondering what he'd seen. What did he know, and how had she pushed him out of her mind? She wasn't even an akrani satori. How could he leave her in suspense like that? She suspected he'd done it on purpose. *What an ass.* Perhaps she'd scared him away.

She entered her temporary luxurious chambers, and her mind became devoid of all concerns. Her breath hitched as she stepped into the space and closed the door behind her. There was a white marble floor in which she could see her own reflection. The enormous bed had a burgundy comforter decorated with many plush pillows. Across from there, a warm fire was burning in the granite hearth. On the other side of the room were double doors that led to the spacious balcony. The grand arched windows were covered with sheer curtains that filtered the light of the setting sun. The washroom had a square built-in bathtub filled with steaming hot water. It had the aroma of lavender and eucalyptus. *A bath sounds good.*

She allowed relaxation to envelop her as she cleaned up in the tub, spending more time in the water than she realized. Then she towel-dried her hair, settled into a fitted sleeveless shirt and loose trousers, and walked out onto the cool balcony. The full moon shone high in the dark sky. The gold accents of the darkened buildings in the kingdom shimmered in the pale light, except for a few structures in the distance. It was probably where the king went to satisfy his urges. She'd heard he loved to gamble and satiate his more primal needs. Her eyes went to the guardhouses on the Haven wall. They were lit up as well, and guards were pacing with their weapons. Vigilant. It all appeared so diminutive from where she stood.

As the crisp breeze swept her lengthy damp hair across her face, she heard a familiar deep voice. "Fancy meeting you out here."

She turned her head and let out a breath. "Of course."

Kaiden stood on the balcony next to hers with his forearms leaning on the stone railing.

Why would the king put him in the room next to her? Just her luck. "I bet it'll be different sleeping by yourself tonight," she teased, keeping a straight face.

"I was actually hoping you would join me in my room tonight." He had a devilish smirk on his face, the same one that made her heart race. *Every. Damn. Time.*

Her cheeks warmed despite the cold air against them. She decided to play his little game. He couldn't do much from his balcony anyway. "You better be careful what you wish for." Her lips quirked into an impish grin. "I might just take you up on that offer."

He climbed onto the thick railing and made the short jump from his balcony to hers. They were high up, so if he fell, he would most likely not survive. She stepped back in startlement, hugging her arms against herself.

"Are you crazy?" she blurted out, her eyes wide. Her knees weakened as she stole a glance at how high up they were. *Yup, still afraid of heights.* "You could've fallen, you idiot!"

Kaiden sauntered up to her, barefoot and in nothing but a loose tunic and trousers, and backed her against the cold railing. "I had to find out if you were telling the truth."

She scurried around him. "About what?" He was just getting her back for that little toast incident earlier. Right? *This is ridiculous.* She was beginning to regret it. His sandalwood scent filled her nostrils.

He studied her with a raised eyebrow. "You're afraid of heights, aren't you?"

She glowered. "No." Why'd she made it so gods damn transparent? It didn't help that he wasn't exactly easy to lie to either. Then again, she had always been a horrible liar.

He stepped closer, inches between them, that stupid grin on his handsome face. "You know, the corner of your eye twitches when you lie." His gaze wandered to her bed before he backed her against one of the tall windows of the balcony.

"It does not." She discharged a grunted breath as her eye betrayed her and twitched ever so slightly. *Damn it all.*

"Don't worry. I find it endearing."

The glass panels sent a chill through her body, or maybe it was his close proximity. "Captain." It didn't come out stern like she'd intended. She cursed her traitorous body. It wanted him in a way that would've made the gods blush. She couldn't give in.

"What else are you afraid of?" He placed a hand on either side of her, trapping her between his hard body and the window.

She peered up, meeting his intense gaze. "I'm not afraid of *you* if that's what you're wondering."

The corner of his mouth lifted. "Perhaps you *should* be."

She swallowed. "I'm not playing this game anymore, Captain."

"Who said this is a game?" He wrapped a strong arm around her waist and pulled her body against his. She braced her hands against his chest. He leaned in, letting his lips brush against the curve of her neck.

A breath snagged in her throat, and she bit back a moan. Even though his lips on her neck gave her the best kind of chill, she gathered her wits and pushed him away. "What kind of woman do you think I am? I don't sleep with men I've known for only a handful of days." She wanted to swallow those words after she'd said them.

He kept his distance a few feet from her. "And yet we've been in bed together twice now."

She closed her eyes and inhaled a shaky breath in an attempt to regain some sort of composure. "That's different. We actually slept."

"So, you're telling me that if we shared a bed a third time, we wouldn't sleep?" That cursed roguish grin graced his gorgeous countenance yet again. Her knees weakened for a different reason.

Her cheeks became hot, and she turned away so he couldn't see. "Go back to your room, Captain," she said as firmly as she could. *That wasn't very assertive.*

Warmth emanated off his body as he approached her from behind. "I just want you to know that I would gladly share a bed with you and 'not sleep' all night." His lips grazed the top of her ear, causing gooseflesh to appear on her arms. Then he was gone. He jumped back onto his balcony. Before he walked into his room, he flashed her a crooked grin.

Blaise swallowed. She wanted to scream. She hated how confounded she'd become, how flustered he'd made her with his erotic promises. The thought had aroused her, that much was true, but she refused to let it get the best of her.

That night, as she slipped beneath the silky covers of the enormous bed, thoughts of Kaiden entered her mind. She wondered how good he was at "not sleeping," how his lips tasted and how they would feel against her skin, how his naked body would feel against hers as he plunged into her over and over until they reached their climax. She groaned in frustration as she tossed and turned on the plush bed. *How dare he leave me in such a state!* Next time, if there was a next time, her self-control would most likely be nonexistent.

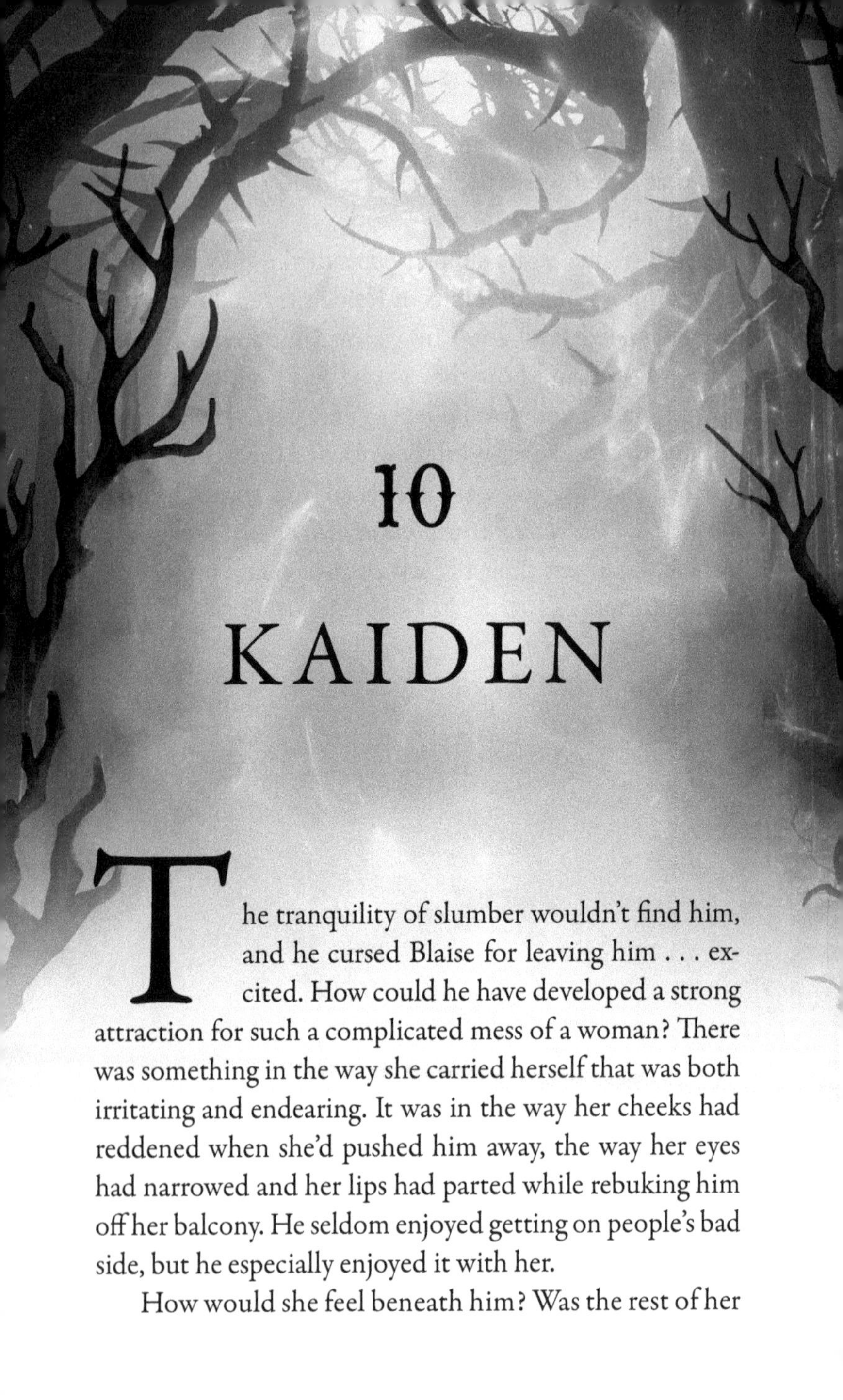

10

KAIDEN

The tranquility of slumber wouldn't find him, and he cursed Blaise for leaving him . . . excited. How could he have developed a strong attraction for such a complicated mess of a woman? There was something in the way she carried herself that was both irritating and endearing. It was in the way her cheeks had reddened when she'd pushed him away, the way her eyes had narrowed and her lips had parted while rebuking him off her balcony. He seldom enjoyed getting on people's bad side, but he especially enjoyed it with her.

How would she feel beneath him? Was the rest of her

body soft like the curve of her neck? *Goddess of chaos, I really need to stop thinking about her.* He sat on the edge of his bed, rubbed his face with his palms, and glanced down at his arousal, which still hadn't gone away. He lay flat on the bed. Closing his eyes, he imagined being on top of Blaise as he took himself in hand and stroked. He envisioned his lips against hers, entering her wet core, penetrating her hard and deep. It didn't take him long to reach orgasm, but he still craved her presence, still craved her touch. He'd never felt so infatuated with someone.

Kaiden walked out onto the balcony after cleaning up and glanced over at Blaise's. She wasn't there, which he'd expected, but he wished she were. Her presence soothed him. Although he would never admit it, the last two nights he'd shared a bed with her were the best sleep he'd had in weeks.

He lay back down in his bed. *I wish I could tell her the truth. She's going to end up hating me. Just think of something else. Anything else.* Did the queen know that his unit of sentinels was coming for her? She'd known every other time. What was so different about this time? What other obstacles would impede their path to Balam?

Beams of sunlight peeked over the horizon and streamed through the sheer curtains of his room. *Great, looks like I'm running on no sleep today.* He readied himself for the day, armored up, and strapped his sword onto his hip, then strode out into the corridor, where twenty of the king's soldiers were rushing toward the grand staircase.

He stopped one soldier. "What's going on?"

"Steel revenants attacking the wall," said the soldier before running away.

Blaise burst through the door of her room clad in full armor, sword on her hip, and she followed the flow of hustling soldiers.

He fell into the organized chaos, scurried through the crowded stables to retrieve Cedric, and made his way to the Haven wall, which stood a couple miles from the castle. Somewhere along the way, he'd lost sight of Blaise. *Shit. Where'd she go?* He scanned through the battalion's formation, but she was nowhere to be found.

By the time Kaiden neared the wall, a few revenants had already made it over the merlons. The Haven soldiers were fighting, attempting to hinder them from going farther into the kingdom. Kaiden leaped from Cedric and ran to help a cornered soldier.

The revenant's arms were steel blades connected to rotting flesh. Its face was deformed and deteriorated like the rest of its body. He'd never seen one before, had only heard of them in the stories his father used to tell him.

Kaiden slid to his knees, slicing at the monster's legs and missing. He recovered, blocking a strike from its bladed arm. He pushed the creature's blade away before rolling across the damp ground. He leaped, swung his sword, and sliced the revenant's head clean off. He had no time to recover from that fight. Arrows flew in his direction. He had enough time to run behind an abandoned wagon for cover. The creature shooting at him had a crossbow for an arm. *Fuck.* He searched for anything that could be used as a shield, found a shallow wooden box of fruit, and emptied it out. With one last breath, he barreled toward his opponent. The arrows pierced his makeshift shield.

When Kaiden was at arm's length from the creature, it swung at his head. Kaiden ducked, spun around, and sliced up, cutting the arm with the crossbow off. It didn't faze the revenant. It kept swinging at the captain. With one final leap, Kaiden plunged his blade into the monster's skull, and it came crashing down.

Kaiden caught his breath as he peered up at the wall-walk. Two steel revenants were stalking closer to Blaise on either side, trapping her. He retrieved his bloodied sword from the skull of the corpse, then found the winding stone staircase and ran up, skipping steps until he made it to the top.

His eyes widened as Blaise outstretched her hands toward both creatures. Azure streaks of lightning emanated from her fingertips. Her chestnut eyes emitted a pale blue haze. She stood there with a determined look on her face. Bands of crackling electricity enveloped the creatures and cooked them from the inside out. The stench of rotting flesh filled his nostrils, causing him to cover his nose and mouth in disgust. Once they'd turned black, skin charcoaled, the lightning ceased. The revenants fell off the wall-walk and shattered into a heap of steel and burnt flesh below.

Kaiden peered toward the Grelan tree line. The revenants were retreating. He turned back to Blaise and ambled up to her. "You have akrani," he stated, not sure how he should feel about her keeping that detail from him. *No.* He decided it upset him and clenched his hands, digging his fingernails into his palms.

She retrieved her weapon from the ground and gazed at her crimson-stained sword. "I'm sorry." She pushed past him, heading toward the staircase. But he grabbed her forearm, pulling her to a stop.

"Why didn't you tell me?" His eyebrows ruffled. It didn't make sense for him to be upset; he had been keeping something from her as well. They were orders though. Anyway, something like that should've been recorded in her transcript. Unless . . . someone had intentionally left it out. That didn't make sense though. People were free to use their akrani. Why did she feel the need to keep it from him? From everyone?

"Why does it matter?" She yanked her arm away and stared at him with narrowed eyes.

"You lied."

"I did not. I just didn't mention it." She crossed her arms over her chest.

"Is there a difference?" He studied her for a moment. "Is there anything else I should know about you?"

"No," she said, rolling her eyes. "Come on, Captain, we all have our secrets. I'm sure there are things you have yet to tell me."

Shit. She's right. He crossed his arms as well. "I just thought we had a better relationship than that." *Why did I say that?* "I mean, a unit is supposed to trust one another." That wasn't what he'd meant to say either. *I'm an imbecile.*

She sighed. "Captain, I don't think it's necessary to be arguing with you about this. We have quite the journey ahead of us, and we're wasting time." Her gaze didn't falter.

"Well, that's one way to start the morning." Mathias came walking down the allure toward them. His brow furrowed. "Am I interrupting?"

Kaiden broke away from Blaise and watched as she walked down the winding slate staircase of the wall before turning to Mathias. "No. We were just talking. Where's the rest of the team?"

"Audrey is helping with the wounded, and George is moving revenant corpses." Mathias scanned the perimeter. "I have no idea where Isaac went though."

Kaiden inhaled deeply, taking in the view of Haven from where he stood. Farmlands were located on the east of the castle, making up a third of the kingdom. On the west were the lavish residential homes and exotic marketplaces. Why King Theod allowed there to be more than one shopping area was beyond Kaiden. A mile in from the wall were the gambling houses, hotels, and brothels.

Commander Stephen had told Kaiden how King Theod had nearly dried up the gald mines in the Azureden Mountains. The king wanted more resources to expand Haven, but the kingdom was already twice the size of Elatora. It was rumored that the king had plans to commandeer Balam's galydrian mines—a valued, scarce commodity in the realm—which were located in the Onyx Mountains.

"Captain," Blaise called from the bottom of the structure.

He glanced down. Two men carried an unconscious Isaac on a stretcher. Blaise knelt at his side with a concerned expression.

"What happened? Is he okay?" Kaiden rushed to the scene.

"One soldier said he fell halfway down the wall-walk steps," Blaise informed him. "I believe he'll be fine. He just needs rest."

The Haven soldiers carried Isaac away on a stretcher while Kaiden and Mathias lingered behind. They walked along the bottom of the wall, clearing debris from the battle. At some point, Blaise had ambled away, though Kaiden didn't exactly know when.

"Where'd Blaise wander off to?" Mathias asked, heaving a big piece of shattered wood over to the pile.

Kaiden shrugged, and a muscle ticked in his jaw. "I'm not sure."

"What happened?" Mathias deadpanned, crossing his arms over his chest.

"Did you not see what she did up there?" Kaiden pointed to the wall-walk.

Mathias stared at him.

"She has akrani, and she didn't tell me. Didn't tell us," Kaiden replied, scanning the perimeter for more debris.

"Eh. I'm not particularly concerned about it," Mathias replied.

"Why not?" Kaiden's eyebrows wrinkled.

"She doesn't seem like the type who'd keep that kind of secret without cause," Mathias said. "Of course, I'm not as *involved* as you are." A smirk crept onto his face.

Kaiden smacked his best friend's shoulder and shook his head disapprovingly. "I'm not involved. Just concerned."

Mathias rolled his eyes. "You expect me to believe that?"

Kaiden huffed, then walked away after saying, "I'm going to go find her before she gets herself into more trouble."

Mathias yelled in a singsong tone of voice, "Someone's in denial."

Kaiden shook his head and said nothing more about the matter. Mathias was just stirring the pot, as he usually did. But there was something in the back of Kaiden's mind, taunting him. It told him Mathias was right. He pushed the absurd thought away as he retrieved Cedric, who'd found a pile of crushed apples. Kaiden grinned at the horse. If only his life were as simple as Cedric's.

I THINK SHE went this way. Kaiden pulled Cedric through the marketplace by the reins. Shops lined both sides of the street, with various wooden stalls scattered throughout. People trafficked the damp streets as the sun reached midmorning.

Kaiden spotted Blaise in the distance. She was talking to an old woman with white hair wearing a long blue dress. As he approached, he caught the end of their conversation.

The old woman's gray eyes were intense and determined. "Your mother was Maxima Everleigh Vinterhale, queen of Balam." She stole a glance at Kaiden, whose eyes had widened.

Blaise had a vacant expression on her face. "That's not possible. My mother was from Elatora." Her knuckles were white as she held on to the reins of her horse. Did she even realize Kaiden had walked up?

"As the sun rises in the east, she will rise," the old woman rasped.

Blaise's eyes widened, and then she shook her head and brushed the old woman off. "You're mad. Please get away from me."

Kaiden assumed the old woman was who King Vaughn had spoken about in their meeting. "Perhaps you should listen to what she has to say," he said, blocking Blaise's path.

She pushed past him without saying a word.

"I'll be in my apothecary when you're ready to hear the truth, child." With that, the old woman disappeared into the crowd of passersby.

Kaiden's eyebrows came together as he followed Blaise, Cedric in tow. King Vaughn knew who she was. Why had he kept Kaiden in the dark about it? It was most likely for Blaise's protection, but still. She was an heir? He couldn't wrap his head around it. "Did you get a name from the old woman?" He fell into step with her.

Blaise appeared to be in a daydream. "What?" she finally said. "I believe her name is Lady Philippa. Why does it matter? She's probably just gone mad and is saying that to everyone."

"Aren't you at least a little curious about what she has to say?" He knew he was. What would this mean for their unit? That they would have to protect Blaise *and* defeat Rowena simultaneously? He let out a breath.

Blaise stole a glance at him. "I was dragged into this unit to complete a mission. That old woman isn't part of it."

Kaiden wondered if he should tell her the truth about ensuring she met with Philippa. He hadn't known she was the heir of Balam. But knowing Blaise, she'd probably blow everything out of proportion. At that moment, he needed her to trust him. "It isn't as though we're leaving anytime soon," he pointed out.

She stopped in her tracks. "Why are you so adamant about this?"

"To be honest, I'm curious as well." He passed her. That was a partial truth.

"Curious?" She'd said it as more of a statement.

He nodded. "What's the worst that could happen? She could either be telling the truth, or like you said, she could just be a rambling madwoman."

"I suppose I could stop by her apothecary after dinner," she muttered.

"Good, it's settled."

Kaiden wanted to stay angry at Blaise for keeping her akrani from him, but that didn't matter at the moment. There was a bigger issue that had to be dealt with: Blaise was the heir of Balam.

King Vaughn had been vague about the reason why he'd wanted Blaise in the unit, and Kaiden hadn't even bothered to ask. He'd just blindly followed orders, as usual. How would Blaise react if she knew Kaiden had been assigned to guarantee the meeting with Philippa? That he was the reason she'd found out her true lineage? That the king of Elatora knew who she was and had still ordered Kaiden to carry out the order? She would never trust him again. He had to tell her the truth; it was just a matter of when.

11

BLAISE

She strode down the wide corridor of the Haven castle, the encounter with Philippa haunting her soul. *As the sun rises in the east, she will rise.* Grams had said that to her before she'd left Elatora. What if it was true? Her whole life would be a lie. Her Grams, her brother, her mother, and her father would not be blood related. Her chest ached and her stomach clenched as she thought about the possibility.

Her mind flashed to when she'd used akrani in that last battle on the Haven wall. She'd had . . . a vision? A memory? She didn't know what to call it, but it had been of Balam, a wasteland with no sign of life anywhere. An overgrowth of black vines had covered the stone fortress in that kingdom.

An unknown entity whispered her name. She didn't know who or where it had come from. The voice sent a shiver down her spine, making the tiny hairs on the back of her neck stand on end. The warmth in her body never returned, and nausea overcame her. *Gods, what's happening to me?* She stopped, leaning against the wall of the corridor for support. Breathing deeply, she snapped back to the present. Turning the corner, she stopped in front of Isaac's room just in time to catch a woman with blond hair and cobalt eyes walking out. That woman was probably a servant.

"Milady." The woman bowed.

"How is he?" Blaise returned the gesture rather awkwardly. She wasn't much of a lady; some might've called her a brute. Her mother used to call her "my little honey badger" because they were fearless animals and would take on opponents twice their size, but she was far from fearless.

The woman replied, "Better. He's wide-awake right now and could probably use the company."

Blaise nodded, and then the woman bowed and walked away.

Isaac's room was much like Blaise's, with an enormous bed and walls covered in white with accents of gold. He pushed himself into a sitting position, shirtless and revealing a bandaged lean torso. His arm had a wrap on it as well, and there were no traces of blood anywhere on them.

Good. He's awake.

Blaise stood at his bedside. "How're you feeling?"

Isaac peered up at her and replied, "Better. I'm sorry for hindering the plan. Is the captain mad?"

"I wouldn't say he's mad."

"But you wouldn't say he's happy either?" It came out as more of a statement than a question.

She paused. "He's just glad you survived."

The corner of his mouth rose. "You're just trying to make me feel better." He gazed down at his hands, which were clasped in his lap, and took on a more solemn expression. "I just feel so useless sometimes."

She shook her head and sat on the edge of the bed. "You're not, Isaac."

"I fell down the stairs, Sergeant." Frustration was apparent in his voice.

Her hand fell on his, and she gazed at him. "The captain chose you to be on this team for a reason."

"Yeah, to be a burden," he mused with a self-deprecating half grin.

"Look, we all have a part to play in the unit. We all have our strengths and weaknesses." She paused. "I think you just need to embrace your strengths more."

He said nothing for a long moment before he finally asked, "Well, what about you, Sergeant?"

She tilted her head. "What about me?"

"It seems you're good at everything."

If only that were true. "Trust me. I have my weaknesses too." She grinned.

"Name a few." He shot her a disbelieving look.

"Well, I'm horrible at hand-to-hand combat, and honestly, I think most of the shots I make with the crossbow are pure luck." She'd said that last part like a secret.

He gazed down at the bedcover in thought.

"Please just try to see this as a learning experience."

After he took a deep breath, he said, "I'll try."

"Good." She pulled her hand away, glad to have lifted his spirits even just a little.

"I saw what you did." He changed the subject. "On the wall."

She sighed, exasperated. "What do you have to say about it?"

He didn't answer right away. "I just want to know. Why keep it hidden from the sentinels?"

With a shrug, she stared at her black boots. "I've been told from a young age that it's dangerous to use in public, so I never have."

"What does the captain think?" Isaac studied her.

"He's upset with me for keeping it secret." It shouldn't have bothered her, but Kaiden had become somewhat of a friend in the time they'd known each other. Her jaw tightened at the thought.

A faint grin crept onto Isaac's dark boyish features. "I wouldn't worry too much. I think he's probably more curious about why you hid it all these years."

Her breathing accelerated, and she rubbed the back of her neck. There was a churning in her stomach she couldn't ignore. "I have to go." She stood from the bed, attempting to control the storm inside her. "I'm glad you're feeling better."

Blaise couldn't breathe in that room. She burst through the door before shutting it behind her, taking deep breaths. Her chest became tighter with each step. She had to calm herself. It was as if someone had placed a boulder on her chest. Her mind raced with thoughts of the upcoming journey, what Philippa had said in the marketplace, and

Kaiden's recent mistrust in her. *Get it together.* Her vision blurred. She placed a hand against the wall to steady herself. Someone approached her.

"Sergeant, is everything okay?" It was Raijinn.

Blaise opened her mouth, but the words wouldn't come out. She fell to the solid marble floor on her hands and knees. Her heart raced a mile a minute, palms sweaty, hearing fading. What was happening? The old lady's voice rang in her head. *Your mother was Maxima Everleigh Vinterhale, queen of Balam.*

"Blaise!" Raijinn's voice echoed in her ears. He bent down and placed a hand on her armored back. "Listen to me. You must slow your breathing."

"I-I . . . can't," she said between quick breaths.

"Yes, you can," he replied.

She gasped, attempting to control herself. *Come on, focus.* Her eyes squinted shut. Her armor weighed heavy on her body. She was sinking.

"What do you hear?" Raijinn asked. "Besides my voice."

She listened closely to her surroundings. "S-servants roaming halls." It hadn't come out as a complete sentence, but she'd tried to get it out between breaths.

"Good. Tell me what you feel." He placed his hand over hers.

She focused on the smooth surface against her fingertips. "C-cold marble." The air in her lungs released slower. Her pulse regulated. A few minutes passed before she peered into Raijinn's blue eyes and said, "Thanks."

He helped her stand. "Perhaps we should take a walk in the courtyard?"

She conceded. Maybe she just needed fresh air. That had never happened to her before, and she hoped it wouldn't be a regular occurrence.

They trundled through the hallway and down the grand staircase of the lavish castle, then turned the corner into another long corridor. They came to double doors that led outside to a beautiful garden.

Oak and pine trees filled the courtyard, there were various colorful flowers, and different species of butterflies fluttered about. Blaise had seen nothing like it before. The king of Elatora had allergies and cared little for flowers and plants. He would rather have spent his gald on his arsenal.

"Wow," Blaise muttered as they walked along the white gravel pathway of the garden.

"Yes. King Theod loves his gardens," Raijinn drawled, and then his face expressed concern. "Now, tell me what caused that episode back there."

She stopped. He followed suit as she replied, "I was thinking."

"About?"

He would find out about it eventually, so she told him the truth. "My akrani abilities and some other events that happened today."

Raijinn grinned and stared at her.

"What?"

"I knew who you were the moment you entered Haven. Zade knew as well," he stated, taking a step closer to her.

She shifted. "What do you mean, you know who I am?"

He slowly bowed and said, "Your Majesty."

Her eyes widened. *It's not true!* It couldn't be true. "Stop. Don't do that." She grabbed his arm, forcing him to straighten. "I am not this queen you speak of, so I'd appreciate it if you would keep this to yourself," she said in a whisper.

"You can't keep hiding who you are, milady." He gently placed his hand on her shoulder. "But if that's what you wish, then I'll honor your decision."

She couldn't help but be suspicious about his motives. "Why? I hardly know you."

"I understand why you don't trust me." He clasped his hands behind his back and walked away.

Her eyebrows came together. "That's it?" She caught up to him. "You're not going to give me reasons why I *should* trust you?"

He glanced at her, then continued into the corridor of the castle after saying, "Why should I tell you when I can just show you?"

Blaise sighed and dragged her hands down her face. These damned men were causing her to go crazy with their vagueness. She wandered back into the garden with her thoughts. How had Raijinn and Zade known of her lineage? Had Zade been able to see who she was with satori? All this thinking gave her a horrible headache.

DINNER PASSED SO quickly that Blaise didn't notice people trickling out of the grand hall. Her mind had been wandering with questions the whole time. She needed answers before they departed for Thessalynne Lake the next morning.

After most of her unit left, she walked out and started toward the main doors of the castle. She spotted Kaiden in the corridor talking to George a distance away. Maybe if she didn't make eye contact with him, Kaiden would leave her alone. She felt his gaze on her.

The captain tore away from his conversation with a grinning George. "Hey, are you going to find Philippa?"

"People are going to get the wrong idea of us, Captain." She stopped just a few feet from the gold-accented double doors.

Kaiden came to a halt as well. "I didn't know there was an 'us.' " He smiled.

Blaise crossed her arms, and her lips formed a straight line on her face. She wasn't in the mood for his . . . Kaidenness.

"I'm not letting you go alone, so I suggest you *deal* with my presence," he said, his smile diminished.

She knew he would argue with her until the sun came up, and she didn't have time for that. "Fine," she huffed through gritted teeth, then continued on her way out of the castle.

Before dinner, Blaise had changed out of her armor and into her casual clothes to blend in better with the Haven folk. Kaiden had done the same, and she wished he hadn't worn such formfitting clothes. They distracted her from her thoughts. Then again, maybe *that* was a good thing. She allowed herself to admire his strong broad shoulders and well-defined biceps. Even his legs were proportionate to the rest of his body, and it was . . . *so annoying.* Her eyes made their way to his firm ass as she walked behind him down the marketplace street. She bit her lip hard and tried to keep her dirty thoughts at bay.

"Which way are we going anyway?" He turned, waiting for her to catch up.

Her cheeks warmed as she averted her eyes, and she hoped he hadn't caught her looking at him in that inappropriate manner. "I think it's this way," she said as she passed him, searching the street. It wasn't congested like it had been when they'd first walked through.

"If you are this queen she speaks of, what're you going to do?" Kaiden asked with a furrowed brow. He fell into step with her.

"I'll worry about it *if* I come to that road." She glanced back at him. "So, what do you think? Do you think it's true?"

He shrugged, not meeting her gaze. "I don't know."

An unreadable expression crept onto his face. Why should she care about his opinion anyway? It didn't matter. She didn't plan to do anything about it. Reclaiming the Balam throne wasn't exactly on her list of things to do. Her eyes continued to scan the streets.

Her pace slowed. "Are you still mad at me?"

He turned, his hazel eyes softening.

Her heart fluttered, and she really wished he wouldn't look at her like that. Every time he did, a part of the barrier she was so desperate to keep up crumbled.

"No, I'm not mad. I just wish you would've told me," he said.

"I know. I'm sorry I didn't," she replied.

They walked beside each other in silence for a moment before a coy grin crept onto Kaiden's face. "So, should I start calling you 'Sparks'?"

"Please don't," she deadpanned.

"Why not? I think it's very fitting," he teased, bumping her shoulder.

"I won't hesitate to punch a high-ranking officer in the face, you know," she said, only half joking.

"Oh, I'm aware." He paused. "Sparks."

She rolled her eyes and walked ahead of him.

Vendor stalls and shops were closing down for the night. *Where is this damn apothecary?* There was only one grand marketplace in Haven, along with many residential homes.

They walked into a cul-de-sac of closed shops. The sun had set. A bite of cold air teased her cheeks. She was surprised the captain hadn't said anything about getting back to the castle. Perhaps it was because he was just as curious as she was about this whole queen debacle.

"I thought you might be back, child." It was the old woman, Philippa. Her long white hair was in a single braid down her back. Her pale gray eyes glistened in the moonlight. The hem of her lengthy blue dress dragged along the dirt road as she walked toward them.

"I suppose you know why I've come." Blaise faced the significantly shorter woman.

"Perhaps you would be interested in joining me for tea?" Philippa led Blaise and Kaiden into her small shop. There were many shelves along the walls of the square space. On those shelves were jars filled with dried plants, flowers, and oils.

They entered a room in the back of the shop. There was a cozy sitting area with a cobblestone fireplace, a plush couch, and an oak coffee table. "Please sit." The old woman walked over to the small kitchen and started boiling water in a pot on the cast-iron stove. She made her way back into the living area before sitting in the plush chair next to the blazing hearth. Staring at Blaise, she said in her grit-filled voice, "You look so much like her."

"My mother was Jocelyn Carrington," Blaise said.

Philippa gave a slow shake of her head. "No. Your mother was Maxima Everleigh Vinterhale, and *she* was the queen of Balam. Jocelyn and Helena protected you. They put protection crystals in the walls of the house so Rowena couldn't get to you with satori." She wrinkled her brows. "Have you used akrani since you left?"

Blaise nodded. "On the wall, when the revenants attacked earlier."

Philippa put a finger to her chin. "Rowena's already sensed your akrani then. I have no protection crystals in my stock at the moment. They're quite difficult to come by, so you'll have to rely on your own mind. Do not fear Rowena. She *will* use it against you."

Rowena had sensed the akrani in Blaise? Protection crystals? Nausea coursed through Blaise. She clenched her fists. "You're lying," she mumbled, refusing to believe any of it.

Kaiden sat beside her in silence, his expression blank.

"I can prove it." Philippa walked into the next room. A few moments later, she walked out with a green, cylindrical crystal in hand. It wasn't a perfect circle and still had jagged edges, making it look more like a half-moon.

Blaise knew of akrani crystals and how different colors held certain abilities. Most of them were good for one use only, except the transformation crystal, which was said to last about a day.

"This holds the memories of your mother." Philippa stood next to the mantel, staring at the crystal. "Only the blood of the true heir of Balam can activate it." She took a needle from the pincushion on the mantel.

Blaise stood with her hands up. "Wait. Blood?"

"Scared of a little prick? Aren't you a sentinel?" Philippa grinned, amusement apparent on her face.

At that point, Kaiden stood, breaking his silence. "How do we know we can trust you?"

He said "we." Blaise's lips curled into a half grin. She couldn't help it. He was looking out for her, and she appreciated that.

Philippa shrugged. "Guess you'll just have to find out." She held up the needle. "So, what'll it be, milady?"

Blaise stood there for a moment, thinking about all the reasons she shouldn't let this woman draw her blood with that needle. None of them outweighed the curiosity of knowing if she was telling the truth. "What do I need to do?" The words came out with a shaky breath.

Philippa placed the crystal in Blaise's upturned palm, then pricked a finger on her other hand, making her bleed. "Put a drop of blood on it," Philippa instructed.

Before Blaise did, she glanced at Kaiden and the concerned look on his face. He nodded, implying he had her back if anything went wrong. His expression went from concerned to protective. It wrapped her in a blanket of comfort as she coaxed a single drop of blood onto the crystal.

It lit up, virescent and magnificently bright. The emerald color crawled up her arm through her veins. She tried to drop the crystal, but it had affixed itself to her palm.

Her vision blurred, then faded to nothing but darkness, and the last thing she heard was Kaiden yelling her name.

Blaise peered down at her palm. The crystal was gone, and she found herself in a foreign place, one she didn't recognize. It appeared to be a bedchamber with many grand windows. Beyond the glass panes, darkness encompassed the sky. Nothing but the stars and the moon shone in the night. A plush velvety bed sat on one side of the space. Many pillows decorated the soft comforter. A bookcase with various tomes sat in the corner, along with a desk and chair. Whose chamber was this?

A woman who appeared vaguely familiar walked over to an oak-framed painting on the wall. It hinged open, leading to a passageway. In the distance, down the hidden narrow path, were two figures holding torches, and they were headed in the woman's direction.

That woman looks so much like me. Blaise stood beside her, but she didn't take notice.

The dark-haired woman soothed the swaddled baby in her arms as two women finally came into unimpeded view. Jocelyn emerged from the darkness, still holding a torch. Blaise's heart dropped at the sight, and she immediately went to touch her. Her hand went through Jocelyn's cheek.

"Mama?" She blinked back tears, and then the dark truth washed over her. She'd known the truth the whole time.

Helena stood behind Jocelyn. Blaise didn't know her capacity for heartbreak and feared it was nearing the point of no return. "Grams. No." Tears poured down Blaise's cheeks as her chest constricted. She stumbled backward. It was true. They'd *both* lied to her. The life she'd known in Elatora had all been a lie.

"Hurry, Rowena is on a rampage with her monsters. You must take Blaise to safety. I'll stay here and stall," said Maxima, handing the baby over to Helena.

All Blaise could do was watch everything unfold before her. She wanted to help her mother—keep her safe, keep her alive—but this was just a memory, a vision of the past. She looked at her baby self and the way Helena gazed at her with such caring eyes.

"I'll not leave you, Your Majesty," said Jocelyn. She brandished her sword, ready to fight.

"Jocelyn, Helena, you've served me well, and now I need you to serve her. You two are all she has now. She is the future of Balam. Of Crenitha." The queen gestured to her baby girl, and then she leaned in and slowly kissed the infant on her forehead. "Now go. I'll provide cover for you to make a clean escape."

"Don't worry. I'll make sure she stays safe," Helena said, gazing down at the baby in her arms.

"I know you will." Maxima's eyes teared up. "I'll provide cover so you and Jocelyn can cross Thessalynne undetected."

"It has been an honor serving you, my queen," Helena said before she turned and rushed down the passageway.

Jocelyn said nothing to Maxima. She just bowed, her eyes glossy, and followed Helena.

Maxima closed the passage. She grabbed her shortsword off the dresser and pulled it from its sheath. Blaise followed her mother's movements. Fear trickled through her as she wondered what she'd witness next.

The double doors burst open, and a woman with long raven hair and gleaming green eyes entered. Four bone revenants accompanied her into the room. "Where is that precious abomination of yours, sister?" Rowena asked, sword in hand. She stepped closer to the queen.

Sister? Abomination? What in gehheina? Blaise's brow furrowed, her core warmed, and the urge to stab Rowena came over her.

"Gone. You'll never find her," Maxima replied, watching Rowena's movements carefully, waiting for her to make the first move. She did.

Rowena swung left, only to be blocked. Then she swung right and was blocked again.

Maxima adjusted her stance and sliced up.

Rowena stepped backward, dodging it. She rushed Maxima, knocking her to the ground, pushing her blade toward her neck.

With a rush of akrani, Maxima summoned a gust of wind to knock Rowena off.

"Are you afraid to fight me without your precious katai, sister?" Rushing her once more, Rowena lunged.

Maxima was quick enough to dodge the attack and counter with her own. Their blades met for a brief moment. "Face it, sister. I have always outmatched you."

A wicked smile crept onto Rowena's face as she said, "Perhaps I just let you think that."

"All this for what? So you can have a crown?" Maxima raised her voice commandingly. "I gave you everything you ever needed!"

"You know *exactly* why I'm doing this." With an unexpected twist of her body, Rowena was able to maneuver behind Maxima, and with one quick thrust, she plunged her sword through her back.

Blaise covered her mouth at the sight of her mother bleeding out on the cold stone floor. How could Rowena kill her sister like that?

In Maxima's dying moments, she used what was left of her akrani to do what she'd promised. A thick mist quickly came upon the kingdom of Balam, providing the cover Helena and Jocelyn needed to get out.

In an attempt to piece everything she'd witnessed together, Blaise gazed into the vacant eyes of her mother, the queen. Why had Rowena wanted a baby dead? Had she really done all that for the crown of Balam? Questions swarmed Blaise's mind as an inexplicable weight fell upon her shoulders. *So, it is true. I am the heir.*

12

KAIDEN

He knelt on the hard wooden panels of the floor cradling an unconscious Blaise in his arms. Kaiden's throat constricted. His thoughts were everywhere, and the urge to yell at Philippa overwhelmed him. Blaise's breaths were becoming shallower by the minute. It set off alarms in his mind as he grasped her cold hand and brought his ear to her chest. It rose and fell, leaving him with a sense of assurance. He held her close, sharing his warmth. *She's breathing. Gods, I shouldn't have let her come.*

"Don't fret. She'll wake soon." Philippa knelt next to him while her eyes scanned Blaise's limp body.

His eyes narrowed, and it took everything in him not to snap at the old woman. "So, you have experience with this?"

She shook her head. "No, this is my first memory crystal."

"Then how can you be certain?" The volume of his voice rose, though he didn't mean to sound so harsh.

Philippa's lips turned up in a soft smile. "You're scared of losing her, and I understand that, but please believe me when I say she'll wake up soon." She placed a hand on his shoulder and gave it a light squeeze.

"No, you're mistaken. I'm not afraid of losing her. I'm just responsible for her safety," he replied, gazing up at the elderly woman before him. Who was he trying to convince? He knew that was a lie. At some point during their time together, Blaise had become something more than just a subordinate, more than just a mission. She'd even become more than just a friend. When had those lines become so blurred?

Philippa let out a breath. "Please, Captain, I have years beneath my belt. I can see clearly what's happening here."

"And what is that?"

"She makes you feel things you've never felt before, and I think that is what scares you the most," Philippa said.

Kaiden glanced at the dying fire in the hearth, then turned his gaze back to Blaise's still frame. He shook his head in disagreement. But if Philippa was wrong, why did the thought of losing Blaise deeply disturb him? Why did her absence leave him with a sense of emptiness inside? Why did the thought of never seeing her smile again make his blood run cold?

Blaise appeared serene. He memorized the lines of her face, willed her eyelids to open. All he wanted to see were those beautiful dark eyes of hers filled with life. That spirited woman who always found cause to disagree with him—he wanted her back.

A few torturous minutes passed. Kaiden placed his forehead on hers, closed his eyes, and wished he hadn't let her agree to doing the memory crystal ritual. He'd just stood there like an idiot, not saying anything. As his eyes reopened, Blaise woke up. His lips parted, and he breathed in relief.

"Are you okay?" he asked, still holding her in his arms, his face inches from her lovely countenance. There they were, those beautiful dark eyes, staring back at him like he was an idiot for worrying about her.

"I'm fine." She pushed him away and rose to her feet, but her knees gave way.

Kaiden instinctively wrapped his arm around her waist, steadying her against his body.

"She's seen the truth." Philippa examined Blaise. "Haven't you?" It was more a statement than a question.

"I need to get out of here." Blaise pushed away from Kaiden once more and stumbled her way through the shop.

Philippa followed. "You must face Rowena and claim what's yours, milady."

"No, I don't. I don't have to do any of it," Blaise said firmly, not looking back at the old woman.

"If you don't, all of Crenitha is doomed. She'll release her revenant army and destroy Haven and Elatora." Philippa sounded desperate. "She'll make the rest of Crenitha a wasteland, just like Balam."

Kaiden wanted to intervene, but he was just as confused as Blaise, so he stayed silent, following her out of the shop into the cold moonlight. The marketplace had closed down, and the streets were empty.

As Blaise distanced herself from them, Philippa stopped Kaiden, grabbing his arm. "You must convince her to face Rowena. Many lives depend on it. The kingdoms depend on it."

All he could do was nod, and then he ran after Blaise.

They made it back to the castle, and it was late. Most, if not all, of the castle had gone to sleep already. Kaiden walked with Blaise in silence down the empty dim corridor. He didn't quite know what to say. She was an heiress, but she was still Blaise. He couldn't wrap his head around it. This had all happened so fast.

He gazed at her profile as they walked, wondering what she was thinking. It couldn't have been easy for her to discover that the life she'd had back in Elatora had been nothing more than a lie. He wanted to comfort her, to tell her everything was going to be okay, but he didn't know that. If she hadn't been someone significant in his life before, she was now.

"Blaise." Kaiden grabbed her forearm, bringing her to a stop.

"I'm tired, Captain." She slid from his grasp and continued toward her room.

He stepped in front of her and demanded, "Just talk to me for a second."

"And say what?" she exclaimed. "That the life I knew in Elatora was a lie? That the people I loved and trusted betrayed me?" Her eyes glistened with tears.

He wanted to wrap his arms around her but knew she

needed space. She needed time to register what had happened, time to decide whether she wanted the throne. There weren't any words he could say to make the situation better, so he let her go. She walked into her room and closed the door behind her. He was left standing alone, helpless.

KAIDEN LAY IN bed with his hands behind his head, unaware of the time that had passed. Thoughts of the past events drowned him, causing a restlessness to stir inside. *I almost lost her.* The memory of her limp body in his arms, her weak pulse, shallow breaths, and cold skin haunted him. *It won't happen again.* Had he confused his sense of duty with another emotion? *No, impossible.*

In an attempt to remedy the maddening disquiet within him, Kaiden opted for a short walk through the moonlit corridor of the castle. He walked up to one of the large windows and stared out at the lovely garden below. The urge to check on Blaise haunted him.

Footsteps interrupted his train of thought. He turned his head and spotted Zade walking up to Blaise's door.

With a furrowed brow, Kaiden approached him. "What're you doing?" It had come out as an accusation, but he didn't care.

Zade's eyes narrowed at the captain. "I heard from a little birdie that the sergeant experienced something traumatic tonight."

Kaiden crossed his arms and leaned against his own suite door. "Might this 'little birdie' be that nosy satori of yours?"

"Okay, Captain, you caught me." Zade raised his hands in surrender.

"If anyone is going to check on her, it'll be me," said Kaiden. He didn't know Zade, and so far, he didn't like him either.

A grin graced Zade's face. "I understand, Captain." He stepped away from Blaise's door. "But we're all on the same team here." The volume of his voice lowered even more. "My only concern is her safety."

Kaiden straightened, not knowing how to respond.

"Nonetheless, I understand your mistrust." Zade turned and walked away. "By the way, you should probably make your way in there soon," he said before walking completely out of earshot.

Kaiden ambled into his bedchamber, a zephyr flowed through the balcony of his suite. He walked out and gazed up at the half-moon. White clouds drifted in front, causing the sky to darken. Then he glanced at Blaise's balcony. She was such a resilient woman, and hearing her sobs caused his heart to ache. He couldn't just stand there and listen. He had to do something.

13

BLAISE

Helena wasn't her grandmother, Jocelyn wasn't her mother, Edgar had never been her father, and Daniel . . . She'd rather have been stabbed with her own sword than experience this pain. She choked down sobs, and tears spilled from her eyes. *Do they all know?* There was no way Daniel could have known, not with the mouth he had on him. She sat on the cold marble floor at the end of the bed, knees to her chest, heart aching. The burdensome truth of what her life was came rushing over her like waves crashing onto the shore. *It's a lie.*

Heat coursed through her body, and her mind raced,

muscles tensed. She could leave, just disappear, but what good would that do? Abandoning her team wasn't an option. She wouldn't do that. She couldn't do that, not to the captain. Her chest constricted, and she drew in short uncontrollable breaths, muscles tensing to the point of pain. *Stop. Please stop.* But it was too excruciating, more intense than the episode Raijinn had helped her with. She couldn't control it.

Come on, Blaise. Just breathe. She didn't have control over her own body. Her hands balled into fists against the white marble as her chest continued to constrict even more. She lay on her side in a fetal position. For some inexplicable reason, warmth trickled up her toes, making its way through her body. What was that? The tension in her body eased but didn't dissipate.

"Blaise?" Kaiden knelt in front of her curled-up body. "What's wrong?"

She gazed up at him but still couldn't speak.

"What do you need?"

No reply. Just stifled breaths.

He picked her up and held her close to his chest. "Try to breathe when I do." He took deep breaths.

The rise and fall of his chest aided her as she tried to match his rhythm. Inhale—one, two, three—exhale. On her second breath, she met his dark gaze, focused on his eyes and the gold specks that seemed to glisten in the moonlight shining through the floor-to-ceiling windows. There was something akin to fear in the way he looked at her. Third breath. Her muscles relaxed. Fourth. The tightening in her chest dissipated. And on her fifth exhale, she regained complete control of her body. "Thanks," she whispered.

He nodded and helped her to her feet.

Without another thought, Blaise wrapped her arms around his lean torso and buried her face in his chest. She became lost in the taste of her salty tears, his sandalwood scent, and the warmth emanating from his body. It didn't matter that she soaked his tunic with her sobs. She let them flow, mourning the life she'd known in Elatora.

He didn't speak a word as he embraced her, holding her close.

She'd never been this vulnerable with anyone, not even her own family. No matter how sad the situation was, no one had ever seen her cry. Yet she didn't care Kaiden was witnessing her in this state.

"I tried to be strong," she said, voice shaky.

"It's a lot to take in. You have every right to feel this way." He brushed his fingers through her long raven hair. "It's late. You should try to get some rest." He led her over to the bed, and she lay down without protest.

"Please." She grabbed his hand before he could pull away. "Stay." Her puffy eyes focused on him. She didn't want to be left alone for the rest of the night, however long that might be. She had no concept of time.

He appeared confused at first, and then his features softened into quiet understanding. He conceded, climbing into bed next to her.

She glanced back at him and smiled.

"What?"

"You left your shirt on this time," she replied as she settled on her back and pulled the covers up around her neck.

He faced her with a curious look. "Would you rather I take it off?"

She rolled her eyes, turning away from him. "Go to sleep."

A few moments passed before his arm slipped around her waist. He pulled her against his warm body and nuzzled into her nape. "Do you mind?" His breath tickled her skin.

"No, I don't."

His arm tightened, pulling her closer against him.

There in his arms, a sense of safety enveloped her, and trust. For the first time ever, she trusted him. "That crystal." She swallowed. "It allowed me to see the last memory of my mother."

"Your mother. Queen Maxima?"

"Yes. She's the reason I'm alive today." Another few seconds of silence passed before she went on. "I just . . . don't know what to do. I'm so conflicted, and part of me wants to just run away from everything."

He stayed quiet.

"Well? Aren't you going to tell me your opinion?" She turned onto her back and faced him.

Beams of moonlight shone through the grand windows of the room, illuminating his face as his hazel eyes locked onto her. That signature smirk crept onto those very kissable lips. "I didn't think you cared about my opinion." He propped himself up on one hand.

"I've learned to live with it." She found herself grinning.

"Well . . ." He paused, tracing the soft skin of her jawline with the back of his thumb. "I know you won't listen to anything I have to say, but I think you should carry out this mission as planned and worry about the rest later."

She huffed and turned on her side away from him. "It's not that simple."

He suppressed a laugh. "You asked for my opinion, Sparks."

"Yeah, I should've known better," she scoffed. "And stop calling me that." Why did Kaiden have to simplify everything? He didn't take into account that maybe she was worrying about "the rest" at that moment. Everything about her life had been manipulated. Had she even earned her place as a sentinel, or had that been planned as well? "Thank you, by the way."

"For what?" he muttered into her hair.

"For never lying to me," she replied.

He didn't respond.

Blaise hadn't expected him to. She didn't want to admit it, but Kaiden's presence had put her at ease the moment he'd entered her room. She couldn't put her finger on why he had that effect on her. She let her thoughts race through her mind, and it didn't take long for them to tire her out, lulling her into a dreamless sleep.

SHE AWOKE WITH his arm around her waist. Her lips turned up in a grin as she shifted to face him. He yawned and blinked the sleep from his eyes before settling his gaze on her.

"Good morning," he rasped in a deep voice.

She returned his greeting, captivated by the gold in his eyes. He drew closer, and her stomach fluttered, breath quickening. "Thank you for staying with me," she said.

His hand still rested on the bare skin of her soft belly. "Why do we always end up like this?" he muttered, lips hovering an inch from hers.

She gulped down a breath, and light-headedness swept over her. "Is it such a bad thing?"

"No, but each time becomes more difficult."

His lips lightly brushed against hers as she whispered, "Difficult?"

Kaiden didn't respond. He gripped her waist while capturing her mouth. His hands intertwined with hers, pinning them against the bed as he worked his way down her jawline, to the curve of her neck, to her collarbone.

Blaise moaned, breathless, wordless, lost in his caress.

His body blanketed hers. He spread her legs with his knees and settled his hips between them. He slid his lips over her skin. Something guttural rumbled in his chest.

When he let go of one hand, she raked her nails down his muscled back and bucked her hips against his stiff arousal. There were too many layers between them; she wanted him inside her. He rubbed himself against the warmth between her thighs. His breaths were shallow as he penetrated her mouth with his tongue. He ground himself against her dampened center, driving her to the brink of ecstasy.

"Fuck, I want you," he growled, caressing the sensitive area behind her ear. She let out a breathless whimper. His hand slipped beneath her shirt, fondling the softness of her breast and the stiff peak that formed.

Her skin prickled against her will. "We shouldn't be doing this," she whispered. Her defiant mouth glided across his collarbone, licking, nipping, sucking.

Approval rolled through his chest. "I know," he agreed, but he didn't stop either.

She arched her back, pushing her chest against his. He caught her mouth again and pulled on her bottom lip.

With one hand on her tailbone, he pressed the hard length of himself against the apex between her thighs, spreading her legs further.

Her eyes met his, lost in the moment, lost in the pleasure of his tantalizing touch, lost in his scent and the way he soothed her with his presence. How had she never recognized it before?

"Do you want me to stop?" he asked, breathing ragged.

She didn't want him to, but it wouldn't be good for the mission if they developed anything more than a friendship. Despite her better judgment, she pulled him down into a kiss. His hand tugged on the waistband of her trousers, and then there was a loud knock at the door.

They broke away from each other. A low groan escaped Kaiden, and they stared at one another for a few seconds.

"I should probably get that," she said.

He nodded with a begrudging look on his face and scooted off her.

Blaise stood, adjusted anything out of place, and walked over to the door. It was Mathias, clad in armor, ready to begin the day.

"Sergeant, have you seen the captain? I just checked his room and—" He stopped midsentence and raised his eyebrows in apparent surprise.

Blaise frowned. She turned to see Kaiden in full view, his hair tousled from their brief moment of intimacy. Her eyes grew wide as she glanced between the two men. How was she going to explain herself? And why was she always getting into awkward situations?

"Oh." Mathias crossed his arms over his chest, his voice playful. "Found him."

Words couldn't be formed in Blaise's brain. She just stood there, lips parted nervously.

"What is it, Mathias?" There was a tinge of annoyance in Kaiden's voice.

"The king would like to see us before we depart from Haven." Mathias smiled coyly. "You have half an hour if you two still aren't finished." He winked at Blaise, and then he took his leave, closing the door behind him.

Despite the dampness between her legs, Blaise walked over to the oak dresser where her armor lay and said, "We should get ready."

"Are you sure about that?" Kaiden hooked an arm around her waist, pulling her back against his pecs. "We have time," he murmured into the side of her neck.

Blaise remembered Daniel warning her about Kaiden and the fact that he was a ladies' man. "I'm sure, Captain." She pulled away, fighting her body's urges.

"I thought you wanted this," he said with an unreadable expression.

"You thought wrong." She continued to pretend to rummage through her satchel.

"I don't understand—"

"I'm not going to be another one of your conquests." She stopped and turned to face him.

He didn't say anything, didn't disagree with her and assure her that she wasn't.

"This can't happen again." She twisted away from him, tucking a strand of hair behind her ear only to untuck it.

"Did I do something to make you feel that way?" he asked, placing his hand on her toned forearm.

She glanced over her shoulder at him. "No, but I've heard things about you."

"What things?" He stepped closer to her, still holding her arm.

She pulled away and whirled around on her heel. "It doesn't matter—"

"It obviously does." His brow wrinkled.

Not wanting to argue with him, she said, "Please, Captain. We both know this"—she pointed her index finger between them—"is a dead end."

Kaiden studied her for a moment before letting out a breath. "You're probably right." His expression was blank. "Maybe it was a good thing Mathias interrupted. He saved us from doing something regretful."

Her stomach clenched at his words. She wanted to tell him that it wouldn't have been regretful for her, but instead she muttered, "Maybe." She only assumed his thoughts were the same as hers on the matter. Better not complicate the mission by starting something with each other. Kaiden would be the type of sentinel who'd choose duty over some silly fling. "It can't happen again," she echoed.

"I know," he said.

She heard the door open and close, and then she exhaled a shaky breath in a failed attempt to release the desire coursing through her veins. She wanted him, and it was clear he wanted her as well. Her lack of self-control around him frightened her. *It can't happen again.*

BLAISE SUITED UP and gathered her gear and bags. She stepped out of her room as Mathias walked by. She fell into step with him, shouldering her satchel. "You won't say anything to the others about this morning, will you?"

A demure grin formed on his handsome face. "I'm not one to gossip, Sergeant."

She loosed a sigh of relief, then corrected him. "Call me Blaise."

He nodded. "Anyway, I think the captain genuinely fancies you for whatever reason."

"How can you tell?" She laughed at his statement.

He shot her a severe look. "I've known him for years, and he's *never* gone out of his way for a woman. Ever. The sentinels and his missions always came first."

"I know he has a strong sense of duty to the Order." She paused. "The last thing I want to do is come between that."

He chuckled. "You already have."

That couldn't be true. She wouldn't let it be. From that moment on, she would keep her distance from Kaiden, and hopefully he would do the same. They walked out to the castle stables to load up their horses before making their way into the throne room where the rest of the team was.

After finding out that she was the true heir to the throne of Balam, Blaise wondered what the people were like. What were their living conditions like? Did the current queen care for the citizens of Balam at all? Blaise assumed not, and although she rejected the idea of confronting Rowena and claiming her throne, something *had* to be done.

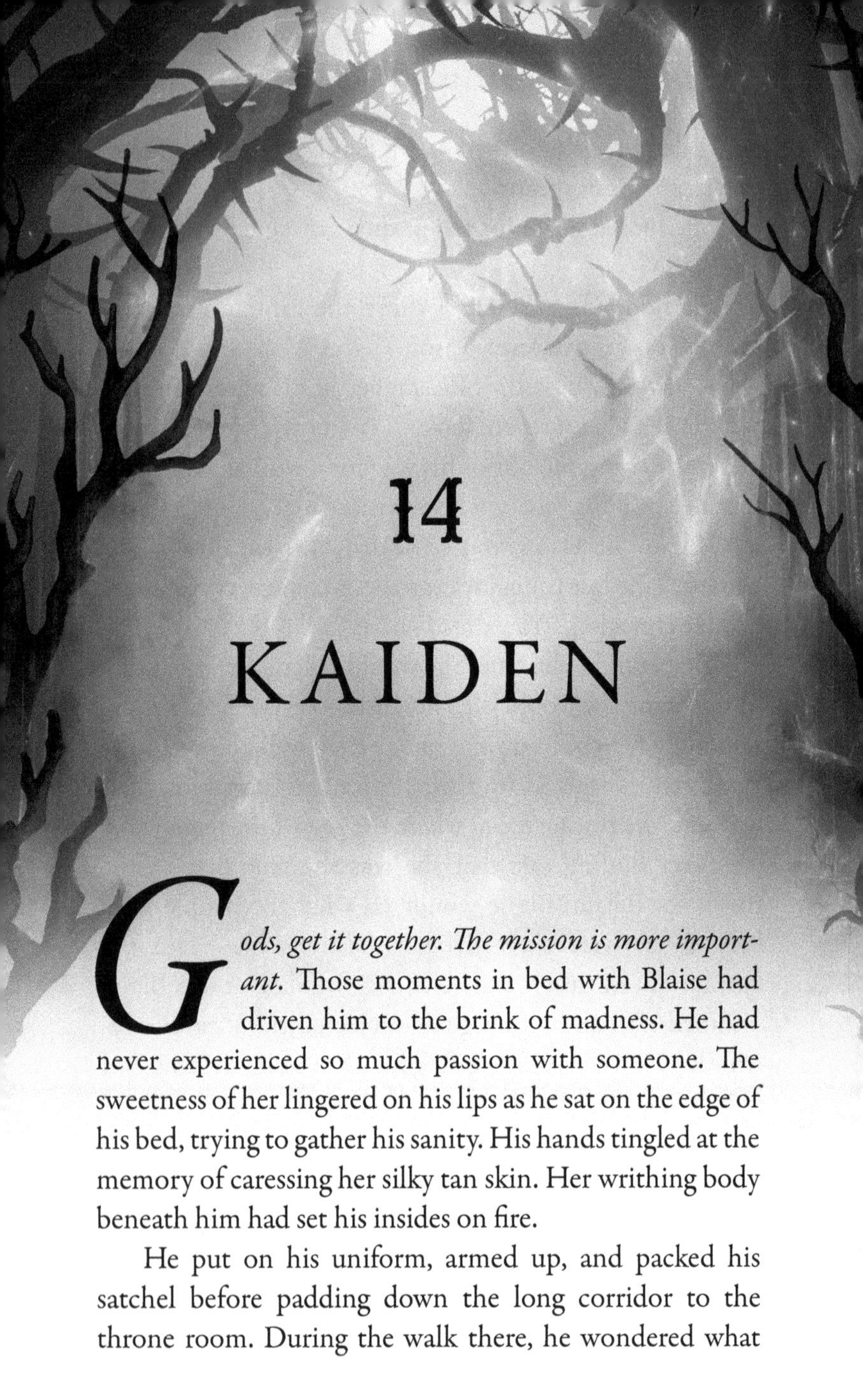

14

KAIDEN

Gods, get it together. The mission is more important. Those moments in bed with Blaise had driven him to the brink of madness. He had never experienced so much passion with someone. The sweetness of her lingered on his lips as he sat on the edge of his bed, trying to gather his sanity. His hands tingled at the memory of caressing her silky tan skin. Her writhing body beneath him had set his insides on fire.

He put on his uniform, armed up, and packed his satchel before padding down the long corridor to the throne room. During the walk there, he wondered what

Blaise planned to do about her awaiting crown. He'd definitely seen potential in her when they'd first met, but he hadn't thought she would be the prospective ruler of a kingdom. What would that mean for their . . . relationship? He didn't know what to call it, but the fact that he could never be with her gradually sank in. It was hopeless. *He* was hopeless.

One thing was certain: the unit couldn't afford to fail in assassinating Rowena—not this time. And to add to the issue, Blaise couldn't be put at risk. Even though she was a sentinel, protecting her meant safeguarding the future of Balam. Kaiden would protect her at all costs. The problem was, she wouldn't make that easy for him to do.

It plagued him that she thought he'd never lied to her. He technically hadn't lied, but he also hadn't told her that he'd been assigned to take her to Philippa. It didn't seem like a big deal. His honor told him otherwise. How would she react? Would she feel betrayed? Everyone in her life—except for maybe Daniel—had lied to her. And to discover that Kaiden had done the same thing? He didn't want to hurt her, but he didn't want to be dishonest either.

The unit awaited Kaiden in front of the throne room doors. He walked in first, and the rest filed in behind him, taking their usual places in front of King Theod, who had an unreadable expression on his face.

"It has been quite eventful since you and your team arrived, Captain Kaiden," said the king.

"Surely you don't think we are to blame for the attack on Haven?" Kaiden hadn't meant for it to sound defensive.

King Theod grinned and replied, "Of course not. A coincidence, I'm sure."

"We're grateful for your generosity and hospitality, Your Majesty." Kaiden bowed, and the team followed. "If you have nothing else for us, we'll take our leave."

"I received a message from King Vaughn. One single scout made it back to Elatora alive. Queen Rowena's army of revenants has become larger than Haven's and Elatora's put together. He predicts she will lead an attack very soon," said the king as he stood from his seat. "Now go. Stay the course, and may the gods protect you."

THE SUN'S RAYS beamed through the leaves of Grelan Forest. Branches of those trees rustled in the gentle balmy breeze. Kaiden noticed there were no revenants around as the unit followed him on the dirt path to Thessalynne Lake. Rowena had most likely called all her monsters back into Balam. He could only assume she'd done that to prepare for the inevitable attack on the two kingdoms.

The information King Theod had disclosed caused an unsettling in his gut. Would the unit be skilled enough to complete the mission? He pushed the thought away. No. The king was right. Kaiden's unit was different.

Cedric's hooves clip-clopped against the dampened ground. Kaiden fidgeted with unease, not used to such a tranquil environment, especially in the forest.

Mathias rode beside him. "I don't like this."

"Me neither," Kaiden replied, scanning behind him. "Where's Blaise?"

"She took the rear with Raijinn."

Kaiden was a bit hesitant about trusting Raijinn with her. But what choice did he have at the moment? He didn't want to cause a scene. "I see," he muttered, his lips forming a straight line.

A grin appeared on Mathias's face. It was that familiar mischievous one. That smirk was often followed by a teasing remark.

Of course, Kaiden was curious about what he was thinking. How could he not be? "Spit it out." He sighed.

"I wasn't going to say anything," Mathias murmured, speeding up slightly.

Kaiden caught up to him. "Yes, you were. I know that look. Just say it."

"It's none of my business."

"And yet somehow you always make it your business," Kaiden retorted.

"I can't help but think about *all* the women who have thrown themselves at you in Elatora, and yet you choose the brutish, most complicated woman in the three kingdoms," Mathias said quietly.

Kaiden continued to scan ahead, keeping watch for any threats. "She's a good listener and friend. That's all."

"You're not fooling anyone but yourself." Then, taking on a more serious face, Mathias said, "Just do me a favor, and don't let your feelings for her get in the way of our mission."

With a short laugh, Kaiden asked, "What are you implying exactly?"

"Admit it. You've grown attached."

"You don't know what you're talking about," Kaiden said in a firm tone of voice.

"Don't I? How many nights have you spent *alone* with her already?" Mathias pointed out.

"One of those nights wasn't my fault." Kaiden groaned.

"And it's not what you think. We honestly just slept." Except for that morning, when Mathias had caught him in her room. Something would've happened had he not interrupted.

Mathias shot him a mischievous look. "Is that what they're calling it these days?"

"Can we just . . . refrain from speaking about this further? Please?" Kaiden was done with this particular conversation. He didn't need to explain himself to anyone—not about Blaise, not about anything. Besides, he and Blaise had already established boundaries, and he would fight tooth and nail to abide by them. Distance was good. Distance was his friend. In the back of his mind, though, he had an urge to be near her, to protect her, to help her claim her throne. *It's my duty. Nothing more than that.* He dismissed the thought and sped up the unit's pace. They needed to get to Thessalynne before the ferry left.

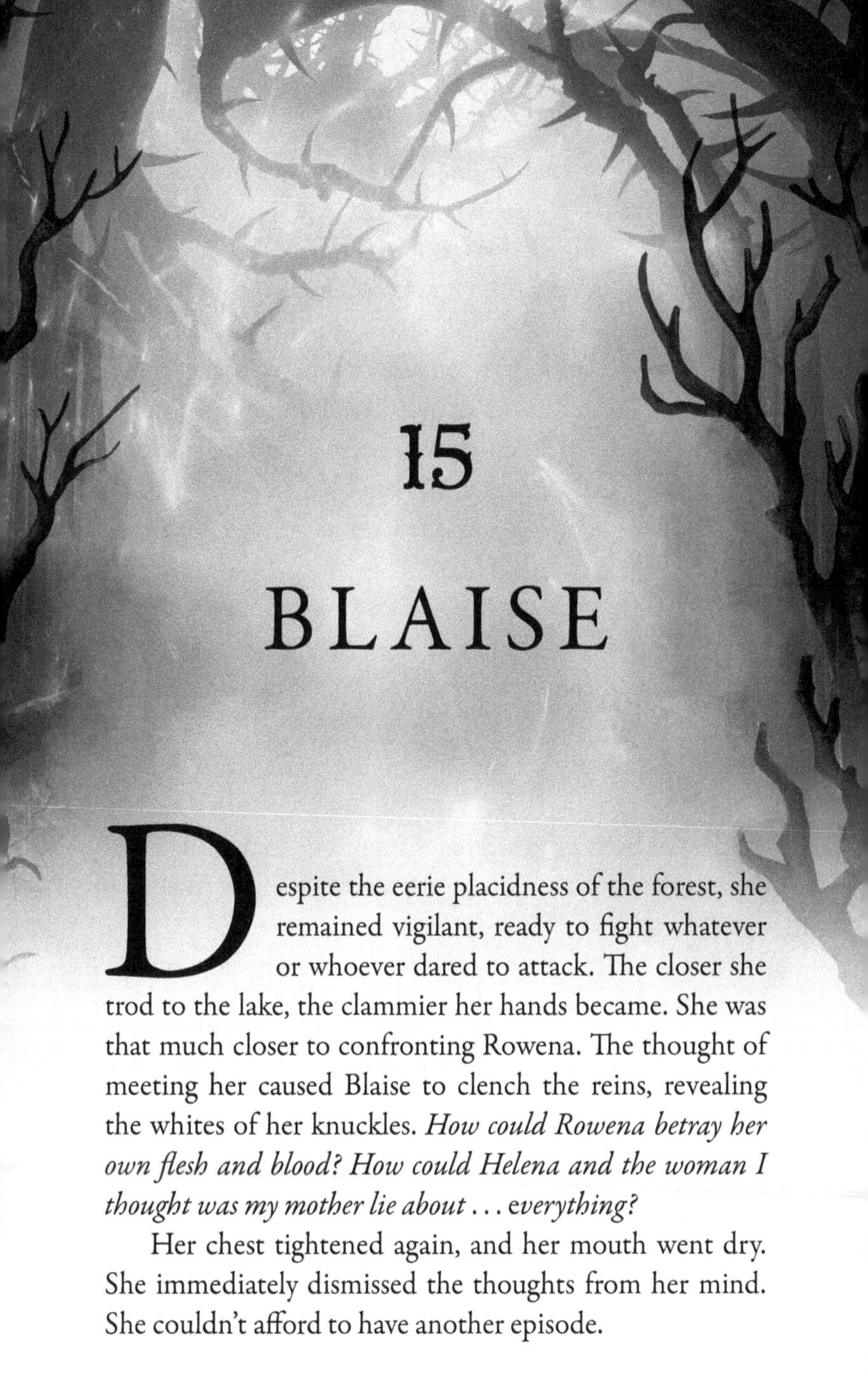

15

BLAISE

Despite the eerie placidness of the forest, she remained vigilant, ready to fight whatever or whoever dared to attack. The closer she trod to the lake, the clammier her hands became. She was that much closer to confronting Rowena. The thought of meeting her caused Blaise to clench the reins, revealing the whites of her knuckles. *How could Rowena betray her own flesh and blood? How could Helena and the woman I thought was my mother lie about . . . everything?*

Her chest tightened again, and her mouth went dry. She immediately dismissed the thoughts from her mind. She couldn't afford to have another episode.

"Are you okay, milady?" Raijinn asked, riding closer to her.

Blaise didn't look at him. She kept her eyes on her surroundings—colorful wildflowers and rhododendron shrubs—and dodged a low-hanging branch. "I'm fine." She expected him to back off. Unfortunately, he didn't.

"You don't seem fine." He stared at her.

Aero's pacing hooves sounded in the stillness of the forest. In fact, the horses' steps were about all that could be heard. Leaves rustled above as rays of sunlight shone through them, touching the Grelan floor.

"What's wrong?" he prodded, not minding her annoyance.

"What do you want me to say? I just found out my entire life is a lie." She'd said the last part in a whisper. Her eyes had become watery again. No. She had to keep it together.

He scanned the area. "I understand why you're perturbed."

"Perturbed?" she scoffed. "I am *not* perturbed. I am beyond that. I'm . . ." The words weren't coming to her. "I don't know what I am." She loosed a breath.

A grin formed on Raijinn's handsome face, which caused her to frown at him.

"Something about this amusing?"

"You're not seeing the entire picture, milady. Everything they did, all the lies they told, was to ensure your protection," he stated.

"Why does it matter to you if I claim the throne anyway?" she asked, shooting him a sidelong look.

He appeared caught off guard by her question. "It's complicated."

"It can't be more complicated than my situation."

There was a brief silence between them before he finally replied, "My father served the late queen of Balam—your mother. We helped an infant princess cross Thessalynne Lake with her newly appointed guardians."

Her eyes widened as realization washed over her. She'd never fathomed that many people had risked their lives so she could live. It made her stomach ache. "You couldn't have been that old."

"I was seven." He continued to scan the surroundings.

Zade and Isaac were ahead of them and out of earshot. Blaise couldn't risk anyone else finding out about her *little* secret. At least not at that moment. She waited for Raijinn to continue.

"I made a promise to my father before he passed away not too long ago. I promised I'd find you and help you claim your throne," he said, glancing at her.

"I just don't understand how you knew I'd be in Haven."

Another grin graced his features. "Philippa told me that if I was patient, fate would bring you to me, and she was right."

"And where does Zade fit in all this?" she asked.

"He's been there for me since I moved to Haven, and we've served the king together. We've gone on many missions for him," Raijinn replied. "Zade wants nothing more than to end Rowena and see the rightful heir on the throne of Balam."

Blaise nodded. Even Zade expected her to take the throne from Rowena.

"I don't suppose you would know anything about my father, would you?" she said with hope in her voice.

Raijinn pursed his lips and shook his head. "I'm sorry. The king passed away before you were born. My father gave me no more details about it."

"I see," she murmured, gazing into the distant path.

"The fortress archives," he blurted.

She cocked an eyebrow. "What?"

His stare softened on her. "You'll learn more in the archives of the Balam fortress."

"I doubt I'll have time to search through tomes once we've arrived there." She was half joking.

He rolled his eyes. "After, obviously. And that's only *if* we make it out alive."

That was definitely a big if. What had her father looked like? Had he been a good king to his people? How had he died? Her life had been filled with so many unanswered questions lately. She'd figure out the answers one at a time, but first things first: get to Balam.

Thessalynne Lake came into view. It was a massive body of water so large that the other side of the shore appeared nonexistent. The next thing that came into her view was the ferry—on fire, sunken halfway into the murky waters.

Kaiden leaped off his horse and walked closer, appearing to comprehend the sight before him. Blaise couldn't see his expression, but she assumed he was in disbelief and likely in deep thought about an alternate route. Without thinking, she dismounted Aero and walked beside him.

She stared at the burning barge for a moment before saying, "We can go around. Either way we go, we'll have mountains to pass."

"Then we'll go around Azureden and follow the lake path. It'll be the shortest way," Kaiden muttered, more to himself than to her as he climbed back up on his horse. She followed suit, and the unit formed up, making their way toward the tall mountains in the distance.

BLAISE WASN'T LOOKING forward to the two-day journey ahead, mostly because she didn't know what to expect. Would she confront the creatures Grams had told her about in bedtime stories, like the horrible mountain trolls that only came out at night and lived in groups of three? And what about the kynarah? A chill ran down her spine as she shunned the thought from her mind.

The sound of horse hooves against the forest floor sent ripples of contentment through her body as they followed the obscure path toward the Azureden Mountains. The sea breeze caressed her high cheekbones and wisped stray strands of hair across her face. Her eyes combed through the thicket of trees. In the clearing on her left was a small stone building with no doors and open windows. Green vines grew over the unkempt structure. The gabled roof had collapsed into itself. Blaise was well aware that the people of Crenitha used to worship the gods.

Isaac rode up next to her. "I've only read about temples in tomes." He had a look of awe on his face. "I'm guessing that one belongs to the goddess of chaos, Jynx, according to the symbol above the doorway."

She had to squint her eyes to make out the symbol: a circle with eight arrows pointed outward, almost like a star. "You're right," she said, glancing at the young sentinel. "I never had much interest in the gods growing up."

He appeared disappointed at her response.

Her gaze focused on the path ahead. The mountains still appeared to be at least a few hours away, and she had grown tired of the silence. "But what else can you tell me about them?"

His brown eyes seemed to brighten as he straightened in his saddle. "Well." He placed his index finger to his chin. "The temple of the high god, Amasu, is said to be five times the size of the other gods' temples."

"Really?" Blaise raised a brow. "Where is his temple located?"

Isaac tilted his head toward the clear blue sky. "I believe it was located in Balam. Not entirely sure if it's still there though."

"Who's your favorite of all the gods?" she asked, scanning the trees for anything suspicious.

He waved his hand and said, as if there were no competition, "Amasu, of course. He's the father of akrani, father of the gods. From what I've read, there are many theories regarding the reason they disappeared."

"And what are those reasons?"

"Amasu's children, the minor gods, were becoming too involved in the affairs of us realm dwellers, even going so far as taking away our free will, so the high god came up with a set of rules they all had to follow," he said. "But their rules aren't in any of the tomes I've read."

Her eyebrows rose; she was impressed with his knowledge. "One of them is probably to leave us alone to our own devices."

He nodded, a grin on his handsome face.

"And look where that got us," she mused. "It seems abandoning us did no good."

If the gods hadn't had those rules, would Crenitha be in this situation? Would her mother still be queen? They were questions she would never know the answers to.

After another few hours, Kaiden stopped the unit a mile from the base of the mountains. The balmy evening breeze turned cold as the sun made its descent. They'd come across a circular clearing in the forest.

"We'll make camp here. George will take the first watch tonight," Kaiden said.

There were many tall pine trees surrounding them, which made for suitable cover. As Blaise helped set up her and Audrey's tent, she thought about what life would be like if she were queen of Balam. She didn't even know how she would go about making any decisions regarding that kingdom.

Blaise then noticed a sly grin on Audrey's face. "What?" Her eyebrows came together.

"I know you're hiding something," Audrey whispered, leaning closer.

With wide eyes, Blaise stuttered, "I-I don't know what you're talking about."

"I saw him leave your room this morning, Sergeant." Audrey raised the top of the tent and braced it in place.

Blaise anchored it down with rope and stakes. She was a bit relieved to hear *that* was the secret Audrey was talking about. "Oh, that." She sighed.

"What did you think I was talking about?"

"Nothing happened," Blaise said, entering the tent with her bedroll.

Audrey fumbled inside, bedroll in hand. "You keep saying that."

"It's true." Blaise shrugged, making her bed on the dirt. "I'd be lying if I said otherwise." And she was lying, but she'd never hear the end of it if she admitted to almost having sex with the captain.

At that moment, Kaiden bellowed for Blaise. With one last glance at Audrey's smug grin, she made her way outside. Raijinn and Zade had started a small fire. Isaac sat close with a book in hand, using light from the flames to read. George was leaned up against one of the tall pines, keeping watch, his hand on the pommel of the broadsword that hung from his hip. Mathias was probably resting in his tent.

Starlight cascaded across the night sky as firelight shone on Kaiden's handsome face. He waited for Blaise next to a fallen tree trunk, away from prying ears.

With an inhale, she walked over with her arms crossed. Audrey had joined the others, and it looked like Isaac had started talking to her about the book he'd been reading.

"What is it?" Blaise hoped she didn't sound too nervous.

"I want to help you," Kaiden said with a breath.

Her arms fell to her sides. "What?"

"You're going to do it, right?"

She put her hand up, palm facing him. "What're we talking about right now?"

"You're going to claim your throne, right?" He pulled her behind a thick tree trunk and lowered the volume of his voice.

She averted her gaze, trying not to focus on his closeness or his woodsy scent. "I can't do it."

"What do you mean you can't do it?" He leaned closer, inches from her face.

She inhaled, attempting to gather some courage before she met his hazel eyes. Gods dammit, they were beautiful. "It means I can't do it, Kaiden." After distancing herself from him, she said, "This is your fault."

His brow furrowed. "How's this *my* fault?"

"If it weren't for you, I wouldn't even be on this ridiculous task force." She turned away from him.

"You would've found out eventually, and it doesn't change the fact that you are the rightful heir." He stepped closer to her. "I know you're scared, but think of all the good you could do in Balam if we were to succeed in overthrowing Rowena."

She scoffed, still not looking at him. "You really have that much faith in me?"

"Of course. I saw something in you, Blaise, and it was more than what you were doing on Teaos." He chuckled and went on. "I have to admit, I didn't think you'd be the long-lost heir of Balam."

She pinched the bridge of her nose before confronting him, meeting his gaze. "So, what then? I go to Balam and fight Rowena? I'll probably need to learn more about my akrani before then."

"Doesn't Raijinn have katai? I'm sure he'd be willing to help. And you won't be alone in this. I'll be with you every step of the way," he promised.

"And the akrani alchime? We still need to rescue him from the dungeon." She couldn't wait to hear his answer to that.

"We can multitask." Kaiden shrugged.

Why did he make everything sound so simple? Blaise's breathing accelerated just thinking about being in the presence of Rowena. Would the unit be skilled enough to defeat the queen? Blaise didn't want to disappoint anyone. That had been part of the reason she'd stayed on Teaos in the first place. *I can't do this . . .*

"Look, I don't want to put pressure on you, but I think Philippa is right. Balam needs you." Kaiden ran a hand through his dark hair. "Just think about it."

She gave a nod. "I will. Am I dismissed?"

"Yes." The word had come out cold, as if nothing had happened between them in that bed back in Haven.

It was fine, she convinced herself. That was exactly what she wanted. Then why did her heart sink at his response? Why did her stupid body respond to his close proximity? Why did she want to taste his lips again? She shook her head, ridding herself of those thoughts.

Blaise ambled toward the warmth of the fire. Isaac and Audrey were still engulfed in their bookish conversation while Zade lay on his side, eyes closed. Raijinn sat with his legs outstretched, ankles crossed, leaned up against a log.

She walked up to Raijinn. "Can I talk to you?"

He peered up at her, his blue eyes glistening in the firelight. "Sure."

"Privately?" she said through her teeth.

Zade opened one eye, a curious expression on his face.

She pointed her index finger at him. "Don't even think about prying into my thoughts again."

"And I thought I was the only mind reader here," Zade drawled, the corner of his mouth raised.

Raijinn studied her before standing. He followed her away from the campsite. Once they were out of hearing range, Blaise asked, "You can control your akrani, right?"

He raised an eyebrow. "Yes," he said slowly.

She let out a quick breath. "I need your help."

"With?" He curled his fingers and looked at his nails.

"You're really going to make me ask?" She rolled her eyes. He knew what she wanted.

With his arms crossed, he waited for her to continue.

"Fine." She sighed and cleared her throat. "Raijinn, will you teach me how to control my akrani?" It was difficult for her to ask for help. She wasn't used to it and would most likely never get used to it.

He stepped closer.

Their eyes met again, and she lost herself in an ocean of cobalt. She caught a sliver of silver around his irises, like a storm was brewing inside him. It intrigued her. Did her own eyes look like that? Stormy?

"Okay," he said.

Her eyebrows came together. "What? That's it?"

"Would you prefer it if I said no?" He took a step closer.

She swallowed, unsure of what was happening between them. "What? No. I'm just—"

"Surprised?" he interrupted.

She nodded.

"I'm more surprised that you asked for my help." He grinned.

"This wasn't my idea," she admitted, folding her arms over her chest. "But I'm going to trust you to help me with this."

"And I won't betray that trust, milady." He placed a hand on her forearm and squeezed before he headed back to the campfire. Something about his gesture put her at ease.

He'd been so nonchalant about his answer. He'd known what she'd wanted when she'd first called him over. Blaise's hands clenched briefly as she stared at Raijinn for a moment with narrow eyes. There wasn't much she could complain about though. He'd agreed to teach her, and she was thankful to him for that. She walked back to her tent and listened to the sound of the men quietly conversing amongst one another.

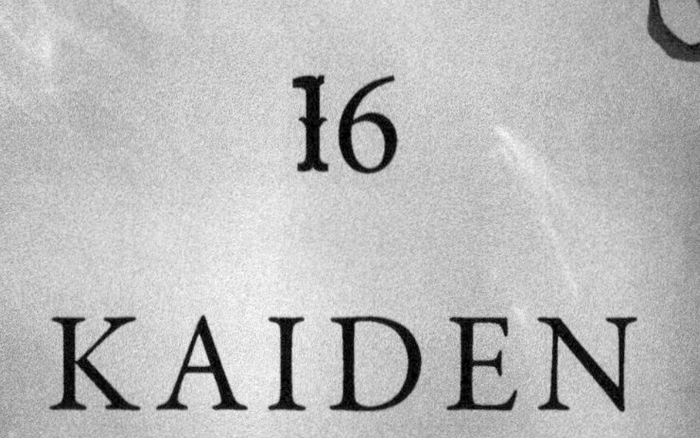

16

KAIDEN

A wave of dizziness swept over Kaiden as he slipped out of the tent while everyone slept. Why he'd felt that suddenly was beyond him. He'd probably just stood from his bedroll too quickly. On the way to relieve George from guard duty, he passed the smoldering campfire. Three hours had passed without incident, which sent a quiver of unease through his stomach.

George had been leaning against a thick tree trunk. He appeared to be nodding off when Kaiden walked up to him. "Hey, go get some rest."

The burly man's head jerked back, and his eyes widened at the captain's quiet voice. George rubbed his eyes, and before he walked away, he asked, "What's been going on with Sergeant Blaise, Captain? She seems on edge lately. The others have noticed and are concerned as well."

Kaiden couldn't tell him the truth. Not yet. For one, he didn't know if he could trust *everyone* on the team, except for Mathias. And second, it wasn't his secret to tell. She had to be the one to break the news to them. At the same time, he hated lying. He'd always believed that a good unit trusted one another, yet he couldn't bring himself to tell George the truth. "I'm a little upset with her about keeping her akrani a secret." It was a half lie.

George's brow furrowed. "That's hardly fair, Captain. I'm sure she's had her reasons for not tellin' you. For not tellin' us."

Kaiden didn't reply.

"I've been thinkin' about my wife lately. I didn't leave her on good terms." George changed the subject. "And now, I realize I may never have another chance to make things right."

The captain studied the burly man before him and said, "You'll get your chance. I'll make sure of it."

George appeared surprised by Kaiden's words, but he said nothing. Perhaps it was because he didn't believe the captain, and it probably wasn't Kaiden's place to promise such things, but he couldn't help it.

Twigs and branches snapped in the distance. Kaiden shushed George and heard heavy steps nearing their camp, and not just a set of steps. They sounded like long-strided ones. Something massive was headed their way.

Kaiden had to warn the others. Without further hesitation, he brandished his sword. His legs carried him in the direction of the tents. He woke Zade and Raijinn while George alerted Mathias and Isaac.

He didn't get to the girls' tent in time. They'd set up the farthest from the men, which he assumed had been Blaise's idea. The monsters that were causing those earth-shaking footsteps emerged from the darkness of the thicket: trolls that dwelled in the Azureden Mountains. They were five times the size of an average man and had pale green skin and hairy manes. Their teeth were razor-sharp, and they had beady black eyes.

George rushed in, broadsword swinging at one of them. He kept it at bay as the other two trolls attacked Audrey and Blaise's tent. Sword in hand, Kaiden ran over to help them only to be backhanded against a tree trunk by one troll. He coughed, the wind knocked from his lungs. He searched for his weapon and recovered from that hard blow, but it was too late. One of the trolls had an unconscious Audrey tossed over its large shoulder. All three trolls disappeared into the forest a moment later. Raijinn and George followed the monsters. A few flashes of light occurred in the distance amongst the trees. Kaiden assumed Raijinn had used his katai.

"Fuck," Kaiden exclaimed, searching for the rest of the team in the light of the moon.

"They took Audrey." Blaise ran up to him after climbing over a fallen tree trunk. She had an upset look about her. "It's my fault. I hesitated. I had a clear shot."

George propelled himself through the foliage, whacking away at anything impeding his path, and after a few seconds of catching his breath, he said, "The damned trolls snatched Isaac too. I lost Raijinn, but I think they went into the cavern pass."

Zade walked up in that moment with his sword in hand.

"Where's Mathias?" Kaiden asked, scanning the destroyed campground before him.

"He was right behind me, I thought," said George, his hands on his knees.

At that moment, they heard a loud moan coming from the trees nearby.

Kaiden rushed toward the sound and searched for a few seconds before finding his best friend in a sitting position, holding his head in pain.

"You okay?" Kaiden asked, reaching a hand out.

"I'm fine." Mathias grabbed his best friend's hand and used it to pull himself to a standing position. "How's everyone else?"

"They took Audrey and Isaac," Blaise informed him.

Mathias frowned. "We have to go after them."

Raijinn pushed through the tree branches and came into view. "They escaped into the mountain. I didn't want to risk a cave-in."

"What're they doin' up at this time of year? I thought trolls hibernated durin' harvest?" George remarked, a befuddled look on his bearded face.

"They probably didn't get the message," Blaise deadpanned.

"Trolls are known to cook their meat before they eat it. We'd better act quickly if we want to get to them alive," Kaiden stated. They wasted no time packing up and leaving their camp on horseback.

THE UNIT RODE through the wide entrance of the Azureden cavern pass. A crisp humid breeze disturbed the torches they held as they rode farther into the mouth of the cave. Kaiden rode beside Raijinn, though not by choice. It wasn't that he didn't like Raijinn. He just didn't trust him, especially with Blaise.

"I get the feeling you don't care for me much, Captain." Raijinn broke the silence.

Kaiden glanced back. Mathias and George were directly behind him, and Blaise was directly behind them riding beside Zade, out of earshot. Good. "You're new to the unit," Kaiden said, voice firm.

"I assume you were able to comfort Sergeant Blaise that one night." One side of Raijinn's mouth quirked.

"What are your intentions with her?" Kaiden's insides burned, and his stomach clenched. He was being stupid. He had no claim on her, no right to ask Raijinn such a question. But it couldn't be helped. He needed to know.

Raijinn shot him a sidelong look. "What are *your* intentions, Captain?"

Kaiden's nostrils flared, but his response was calm. "To keep her safe."

"Then we have that in common."

The ground quaked. Small rocks crumbled from the ceiling, but they didn't injure anyone. A cloud of dust drifted toward them. It caused all of them to erupt into a coughing fit. Once it had cleared, Kaiden peered behind them and saw the entrance of the cave blocked by huge boulders. They had to find another way out.

"That's just great," Kaiden muttered, shaking his head.

"This cavern should lead all the way to Meliwe Forest.

We just have to take the correct passage," Raijinn said as they continued.

There was a glimmer of firelight reflecting off the gray stone wall up ahead. Audrey's scream echoed throughout the cave, followed by Isaac's muffled cry shortly after. Kaiden couldn't quite understand what they were saying. At least their cries didn't sound pained.

"Perhaps it'd be wise if one of us stayed back with the horses," Zade said, lowering the volume of his voice so that it didn't echo.

Kaiden agreed. "Mathias and Zade, stay behind. The rest of us will go after Isaac and Audrey."

Blaise leaped from Aero and prepared her crossbow. George and Raijinn came down from their steeds and readied their weapons as well.

"Let's go." Kaiden led the way toward the sound of grumbling trolls. He signaled Raijinn to scout ahead while he, Blaise, and George stayed behind.

After a few minutes, Raijinn returned and told them there were three trolls. Audrey and Isaac were tied up in the farthest corner of that cavern.

"George and I will cause a diversion. Blaise and Raijinn, attack the trolls with akrani. And for the love of the gods, try not to cause a cave-in," Kaiden said.

A look of worry mixed with fear crept onto Blaise's dirt-covered face. Kaiden grabbed her hand and gave it a gentle squeeze. "Everything will be fine. Just follow Raijinn's lead." He hated saying it but knew it would be the best thing given the situation.

She gave a curt nod, and then they quietly made their way around the corner, hiding behind boulders and using the shadows as cover.

Their stealth and quickness impressed Kaiden for a moment. He threw a large rock at one troll and leaped out into full view. That troll chased after him while George popped out from behind a boulder and lured the other one away. Kaiden didn't know where the third one had gone, and at that moment, it didn't matter.

Kaiden mustered up all the strength he had to run from the beast. He glanced behind him.

Blaise trailed the troll, her hands streaming with crackles of blue. She pointed two fingers at her ginormous target. With panic apparent on her face, she conjured up more lightning and fired at the giant. Some of the electrical current bounced off and hit Kaiden by pure accident.

Kaiden's body tensed as the power surged through him. He realized Blaise had pushed him out of the way of the falling troll as it came crashing down beside him. The next thing he saw was her blade embedded in the creature's head.

Blaise fell to her knees beside him. "I'm so sorry."

Remnants of her akrani rippled through his body as he gradually rose to his feet. "I'm just glad that most of it hit the troll." He grunted, falling to one knee.

She caught him, slinging his arm over her shoulder. "I really need to learn how to control it better," she said, more to herself than to him.

"That would be great," he remarked half-jokingly.

A loud roar echoed throughout the cave.

"Can't you go any faster?" Blaise prodded as she helped him along.

He shot her a narrow-eyed glare. "I'd like to see you run after getting hit by a bolt of lightning."

"Most of it hit the troll," she mocked, a corner of her

mouth rising in amusement as they continued toward the fight.

By the time they arrived at the scene, Raijinn had stunned one of the trolls. It fell backward into the firepit. George had made his way over to the corner of the cave where Audrey and Isaac were tied up, the last troll trailing behind him. A streak of blue flames escaped Raijinn's fingertips and engulfed the giant. Its arms flailed about, trying to extinguish the fire. That gave Blaise enough time to retrieve her crossbow and shoot it. The arrow whizzed through the air before hitting its target in the back of the head. The monster fell forward, landing a few feet from George. A halo of crimson formed around the creature's head soon after, its skin charred from Raijinn's katai.

"What took so long?" George exclaimed as he worked to untie Audrey's binds.

Blaise had walked back over to help Kaiden. "We had a minor accident," she said, examining the captain, making sure he was still in one piece.

Raijinn made a pushing movement with his hand, and a gust of wind shot from his palm, putting out the small flames on the dead troll. He then walked up to Isaac and untied his restraints.

"What happened?" Raijinn asked. "Did you hit the captain with katai?" It was meant to be a joke.

After George unbound Audrey, they walked closer to the rest of the group.

Kaiden just knew he wouldn't hear the end of it. At least Mathias hadn't witnessed it. He'd have been laughing his ass off—after he'd made sure his best friend was okay, of course. Kaiden stayed silent, gazing at his hands folded in his lap.

An outburst of laughter echoed and bounced off the rough formations of the cavern.

Blaise didn't laugh, but she looked like she wanted to as Kaiden said with a furrowed brow, "It's not funny." The memory of the jolt caused him to grimace. "It was quite painful, in fact."

"Hey, Captain, was it a shocking experience?" George laughed uncontrollably. He had one of those contagious laughs, warm and genuine, and Kaiden couldn't help but to chuckle along with him.

Mathias caught up to them amidst the laughter. He'd left poor Zade alone with all the horses. "Well, glad to see you all having fun without me." He crossed his arms. "What's so funny?" He glanced at Kaiden's frazzled appearance with a raised eyebrow. "What happened to you?"

George wiped a tear from his eye. "The sergeant hit him with her katai."

Mathias glanced at Blaise with an unreadable expression. "I can't believe I wasn't there to witness that." He cracked a smile and guffawed at his best friend's misfortune, pointing his index finger at Kaiden. *Immature asshole.*

Blaise eventually gave in and joined the group. It was the first time Kaiden had seen her laugh. The sound of her giggling did something to him; it sent a sensation of tingles throughout his body. He hadn't thought she could be more beautiful, but he'd been wrong. This was the side of her that he wanted to see more of, even if it was at his own expense.

Kaiden let them indulge in a few more seconds of laughter before he said, "Let's go. We have to find another way out of these caverns."

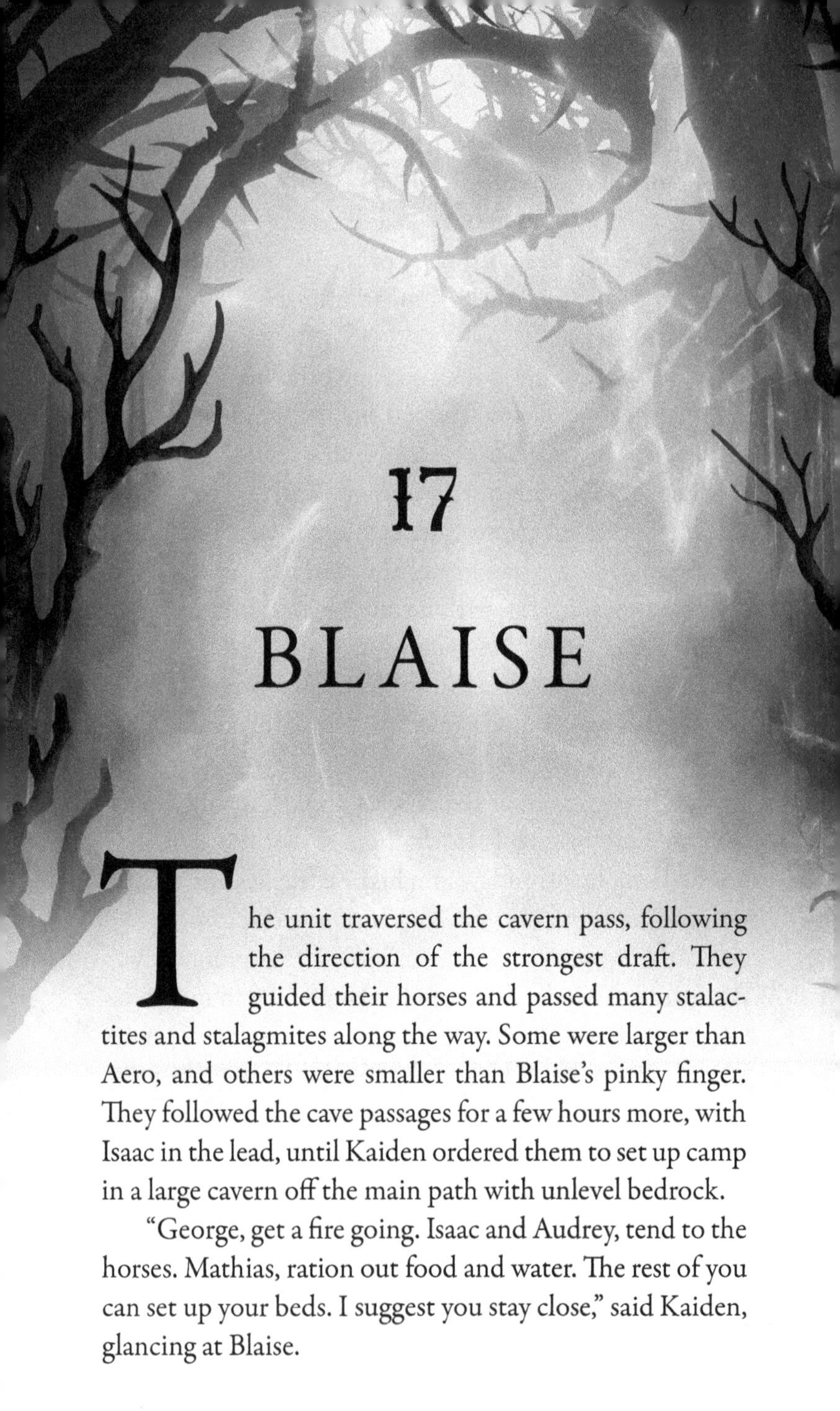

17

BLAISE

The unit traversed the cavern pass, following the direction of the strongest draft. They guided their horses and passed many stalactites and stalagmites along the way. Some were larger than Aero, and others were smaller than Blaise's pinky finger. They followed the cave passages for a few hours more, with Isaac in the lead, until Kaiden ordered them to set up camp in a large cavern off the main path with unlevel bedrock.

"George, get a fire going. Isaac and Audrey, tend to the horses. Mathias, ration out food and water. The rest of you can set up your beds. I suggest you stay close," said Kaiden, glancing at Blaise.

Had he been talking to her indirectly? She glared at him as she unhooked her bedroll from Aero's saddlebag.

"It's a bit cold over here. You sure you don't want to be closer to the fire?" Raijinn asked, walking up to Blaise as she picked one of the flat rock formations about ten feet from the campfire.

She shot him a blank expression. "I'm fine here."

Raijinn had his own bedroll slung on his back. "Well, I'm sure you wouldn't mind if I joined you, right?" He dropped it a few feet from her.

She narrowed her eyes. "I suppose not." Then she caught sight of Kaiden, who had set up his bedroll a good distance away. Good. Distance was good. He gazed at her with a glint of what Blaise assumed was jealousy. She couldn't tell, but then again, why should she care? *Distance is good.* But part of her wanted to be closer to him, and not just in the physical sense. Talking to him was easy; she felt like she could trust him with all her secrets, like she could tell him anything and everything—when they weren't at each other's throats. Her breath hitched at the thought. What did that mean? It didn't mean anything. She *refused* for it to mean anything.

"Perhaps I should find another spot," Raijinn said.

She sat, legs crossed, on her bed. "No. It's fine." It would probably be better if she was near someone anyway.

"Great!" He knelt and set up his bedroll. "I was thinking we could do a bit of training tonight."

She echoed, "Tonight?"

"Now." He straightened.

"Now?"

He nodded and cocked an eyebrow. "Are you going to repeat everything I say?"

"It's not like I have anything better to do," she muttered as she rose to her feet.

"Let's go to a more private area. Shall we?" He took her hand and pulled her over to another section of the cavern behind a grouping of stalagmites. Firelight shone through the cracks of the formation.

She had her suspicions about Raijinn and his motives. Did he really want to help her unlock her katai? She kept the thought in the back of her mind and followed him.

"This looks sufficient enough." Raijinn stopped, letting go of her hand.

"Now what?" she asked.

He studied her before reaching for her hands once more.

She pulled away. "What're you doing?" Her brow rose.

"I need to get a sense of why you can only summon a portion of your katai. Trust me." His lips quirked.

She didn't, but what choice did she have? With narrowed eyes, she conceded and placed her hands in his cold ones.

"Relax. Close your eyes." He did the same.

With much hesitance, she followed his directions. How was he going to sense why she couldn't tap into her other katai abilities? She'd been holding his hands for a few minutes and didn't feel anything unusual. Warmth emanated from his hands, then crept its way through her forearms. It was such a strange feeling, like insects crawling under her skin. Her whole body was soon enveloped in that unusual sensation. Beads of sweat fell down her temples as her temperature rose, which set off alarms within her.

"Raijinn," she murmured, throat constricting. Her insides were on fire. Her mind's eye flashed bright white.

The Balam fortress, covered in thorny black vines. Another flash. A rectangular slate pool. It's inky waters formed a vortex, liquid spilling over the rim. Her heart pounded, and her jaw clenched. She couldn't let go of his hands.

"I'm almost finished," he replied calmly.

The burning inside her had become unbearable. She willed her body to listen and forced herself from his grasp. "Shit." She fell to one knee. Her hands trembled as she whispered, "What in gehheina?"

He helped her up. "Blaise."

She straightened, releasing a tired breath. Her eyes met his concerned ones. He looked like he might have seen a ghost. "What is it?"

"You"—he stepped within inches of her—"are more powerful than you think."

That statement caused a chill to trickle down her spine. She'd been afraid of akrani for most of her life, had been taught that it was dangerous. All that power. All the possibilities. She had been happy in her ignorance, but now she wanted answers.

"I don't know how it's possible, but the akrani I felt in you is similar to Zade's," he said, his eyebrows wrinkled. "But it is also similar to mine."

Had he just told her she had satori and katai? But how in the five gods could she have more than one akrani? Could it be a mistake? Had the goddess of chaos and the god of peace meant to gift her with both? Dizziness rippled through her, and she lost her balance. Raijinn gripped her forearms, steadying her.

She inhaled, then exhaled. "How is that possible?"

He stared at her. "From what I know, it's unheard of."

"What now?" she asked. "Can you still train me?"

His expression softened. "Of course, but you'll most likely need to train satori with Zade. That akrani is quite complicated. There are so many forms you can learn that it's quite difficult to master and exhausting as well."

Katai was probably just as draining, if not more. She took another breath. "Okay. Well, let's start then." She allowed him to take her hand and place it in his with her palm up.

"Allow it to flow through your hand," he said with an inhale.

The warmth sparked from the center of her palm and spread outward through her fingertips. Tingling arose in her hand once more, bearable for the moment. She didn't know how much longer she could tolerate it. The muscles in her hand cramped as the heat intensified. Then a blue flame slowly materialized and hovered just above her palm.

"Good." Raijinn had a pleased look on his face. "Very good."

She smiled and became entranced in his silver-blue eyes for a few more seconds. A sensation of ease overwhelmed her. What had she opened herself up to?

Someone behind Blaise cleared their throat. She turned to see the captain with a firm expression on his features and his arms crossed over his chest. "How's training coming along?"

Raijinn stepped away from Blaise and dropped her hand. "We're making progress."

She nodded, jaw ticking in annoyance.

"Now I know what we need to work on, but that'll be enough for the night." Raijinn grinned at Blaise, then walked past the captain toward the rest of the team.

Kaiden and Blaise stared at each other before she finally said, "Why'd you interrupt us like that? We were onto something."

"My apologies," His voice dripped with sarcasm. "It didn't look like he was training you to do anything important." He stepped closer to her, arms still crossed.

Realization hit her like a ton of rocks. Her eyes narrowed, and the corner of her mouth rose. "Wait," she said slowly. "Are you jealous?"

"Of him? Don't be absurd." His gaze didn't falter.

"Oh, *I'm* being absurd?" She placed her palm on her chest.

Kaiden closed the distance between them. He brought his face inches from hers and lowered the volume of his voice. "I know what you want, Blaise." That roguish grin crept onto his face. "And it *isn't* him."

She challenged him, leaning even closer, hands on her hips. "That's quite an assumption, *Captain*. Anyway, I'm not in the mood for"—she gestured to his whole person, her palm up—"this right now."

"Come now." He nibbled on his bottom lip before continuing. "If Mathias hadn't interrupted us that morning, you would've let me have my way with you."

"You arrogant bastard." With a huff, she started to walk away, but he grabbed her arm and pulled her flush against his body. His grip on her was firm, possessive.

He placed his index finger beneath her chin and tilted her head, bringing his lips within a hair's breadth of hers. "I'm going to kiss you, and you're going to let me."

Her heart pounded against her rib cage as she attempted to pull away. "This can't happen," she whispered, more to herself than to him.

His hand roamed to the small of her back, and he pressed his hips against hers. "All you have to do is tell me to stop."

The hardened length of him twitched through the threads of his trousers against her inner thigh. *Dammit. Just say it. It's one word.* She couldn't get it out. The word lingered in her throat like an annoying itch.

He brought his lips to hers in one gradual motion. Her breath hitched as his mouth worked against hers. With ease, he pushed her back against the boulder and caressed the curve of her neck.

Why couldn't she say no to this man? Why did it feel so good when he put his hands on her, when he nibbled on her skin, when he worked his tongue against hers? She'd never felt so attracted to a man and had always been able to demonstrate self-control, but she couldn't do that with Kaiden. He caused a fire in her, a craving for his lips, his touch, his presence. She could never admit that to him though.

His movements slowed to a stop, and he lingered on her skin for a while before he let out a frustrated sigh and buried his face in the crook of her neck. "I'm sorry." He stepped away, and his gaze met hers, the glint of longing still in his eyes. "You're right. That shouldn't have happened."

She couldn't place all the blame on him. After all, her lips had moved against his willingly. It had all become so confusing. Here she was, the lost heir of Balam, and here he was, captain of the Sentinel Order, son of the second-in-command.

Kaiden could never be with someone like her—a stubborn, scared woman incapable of making important decisions. She couldn't even control her own katai. Besides, Commander Stephen most likely had a wife picked out for the captain, someone who could make him happy. She would be a high-class model citizen of Elatora who carried herself in such a way that other men would want her and other women would want to *be* her.

Blaise could never be that woman for him, and she needed to come to terms with that fact, as saddening as it was. *It won't work. It'll never work.* But she still fought the urge to wrap her arms around him and bring him in for another kiss.

"I . . . can't seem to get enough of you." He brushed the stray hairs from her face.

She chewed on her bottom lip.

He changed the subject. "Did I really interrupt something important?" His features expressed some guilt.

She grinned. "No. I was in need of a break anyway."

"Good," he murmured.

His close proximity intoxicated her. She cleared her throat, stepping farther away from him. *Distance is good.*

"You mentioned you two were onto something." Kaiden crossed his arms and leaned his back against the wall. "Mind telling me what you were talking about?"

Should I tell him about possibly having a second akrani ability? She mimicked his body language. "Why do you want to know?"

His eyes locked onto her. "No secrets, remember?"

She figured he'd find out sooner or later. "He sensed an unfamiliar akrani in me."

His gaze fell to the ground as if he was trying to make sense of what she'd just told him. "And?" was all that came out of his mouth.

"He thinks it's satori," she replied, pushing off the wall and letting her arms fall to her sides.

Kaiden looked at her, a wrinkle in his brow. "But how's that possible? It has to be a mistake."

She frowned. Had he just called her a mistake? Her face warmed. "Why does it *have* to be a mistake?"

He stilled as if realizing what he'd just said. "No, I didn't mean it like that. It's just unheard of for someone to be blessed with two abilities."

"You don't think I know that?" The volume of her voice rose. "I'm just as confused as you are about all this. I wish the gods would come out of whatever hole they're hiding in and give me some answers." Her voice reverberated throughout the cavern.

Kaiden closed the distance between them and enveloped her in his arms.

Her eyes widened at his sudden gesture, but his warm embrace sent ripples of ease coursing through her body and into her core. Why? Why did he have this effect on her? She cherished the moment, closing her eyes and laying her head on his shoulder.

"We'll figure it out," he said into her hair. "Right now, you need to decide what you're going to do."

She hoped he wasn't talking about her crown.

"About taking the throne," he finished, pulling away.

"I don't want to talk about that right now."

"Well, you can't keep avoiding it."

Blaise lifted her chin and looked into his gold-speckled eyes. "I'm not fit to rule a kingdom," she muttered. "And we don't even know if we stand a chance against Rowena and her army."

A glimmer of what looked like amusement appeared in Kaiden's eyes. "You're thinking of too many things at once."

She stepped back, out of his arms. "I guess this is why you're the captain."

He grinned. "I guess."

"Thank you." Her lips curved up. "You seem to know how to calm me down."

One of his eyebrows rose. "Really? And here I thought I was doing the opposite."

"Well, you have your moments." Silence ensued between them as she fidgeted beneath his stare. "What?"

He averted his eyes and shook his head. "Nothing."

"Tell me. Granted, it'll probably upset me, but I think I'm used to it by now." She'd said it in a half-joking way, leaning her weight on one leg, holding her arm.

Kaiden rolled his eyes and let out a short laugh. "Every time I think I have you figured out, something else comes up. It's quite . . ."

He'd better not say anything stupid. Blaise waited for him to come up with the word.

"Maddening." He huffed. "I can't remember a time when I've been this flustered by a woman. Not even my own sister."

She didn't know if that was meant to be a compliment or an insult. "I'm sorry, I think?" she said with much hesitance in her voice.

He crossed his arms and tilted his head. "Are you really though?"

Her smile widened. "No, not really." He flustered her, caused a flutter in her stomach. And she couldn't seem to make it go away, not while in his presence.

Blaise made her way back to the rest of the group with Kaiden, knowing nothing could ever come of the feelings she had for him. Whether or not she claimed her throne, they could never be together. She would always come second in his life because of his duty and commitment to the king and the Sentinel Order, and yet she couldn't help but hope.

18

KAIDEN

His eyes focused on Blaise's resting body. He couldn't see her face; her back was facing him. The corner of his mouth rose as he leaned against the wall of the cavern. While beautiful, strong, and courageous, she wasn't without fault. She was stubborn, indecisive, and insecure, but something about her made those qualities endearing. His stomach fluttered as he thought about her gorgeous smile and the way she pursed those very kissable lips when in deep thought. Gods, he was utterly and completely taken with her.

Kaiden brushed his fingers through his dark hair, watching over the unit as everyone slept. Isaac had made his bed closest to the firepit, while George slept the farthest away. Zade slept on the flat rock formation right below Blaise's, and Raijinn slept a few feet from her. Mathias snored across from Isaac on the other side of the fire. And Audrey slept next to Mathias, her snore inaudible compared to the rest of the unit.

A few hours passed, and the fire reduced to nothing more than embers in the pit. It would be Mathias's turn to take the next watch. Kaiden's eyes were heavy, but he kept them open and remained as alert as possible. From the corner of his eye, he saw a figure sit up. It was Blaise. She stood and walked into the darkness of the tunnel.

"Blaise." He tried to get her attention without disturbing everyone's sleep.

No response.

He wondered if he should wake someone, just in case. No. He could handle her. Kaiden quickly lit a torch from the hot coals and quietly ran after her. Where had she gone? She couldn't have gotten far. The flame from the torch sparked as he swung it left and then right in search of her.

He continued down to another cavern and made out Blaise's figure in the darkness. *Where is she going?* He squinted, looking ahead. She appeared to be standing next to a large cave shaft.

She faced him as he stepped a few feet from her. That was when he noticed her eyes were a shade of green. *Wait.* The problem was her eyes were never that color. They were brown. *What in gehheina?* She closed her eyes, and a gust of wind caught her long dark hair. Her face was void of any emotion. She stepped back into the abyss.

"Blaise! No!" He rushed toward her and caught her

by the wrist as she fell over the ledge. The torch fell down the deep, dark shaft. "Blaise!" His heart thrashed in his chest, and he held on to her wrist with both hands. How had he moved that fast? That didn't matter at the moment. What *did* matter was finding the strength to pull her onto solid ground.

She gazed up at him with those eerie emerald eyes and blinked a few times. Her eyes changed back to their original chestnut color, and realization washed over her face as she screamed, gripping tight to his hands. "Oh my gods!" She wriggled, eyes wide and filled with fear.

His muscles burned as he struggled to hang on to her. "Blaise," he groaned, adjusting his grip on her wrist.

She looked down into the darkness below and continued to scream.

He could hear the panic in her cries.

"Stop squirming." His grip had begun to slip. Her eyes began to emit that pale blue haze he'd seen on the Haven wall as small waves of electricity flowed from her hands into his. She produced actual—

"Sparks, look at me." It took all his willpower and strength to hang on to her despite the dimming pain of her katai thrumming through him.

Her gaze focused on him. She hung there in his grasp.

"I have you." His eyes bored into hers. His arms ached, but he wouldn't let go. He would *never* let her go, even if it meant falling in with her.

She swallowed and appeared to calm in an instant, and her katai gradually subsided.

He mustered all the strength he had into pulling her up. His muscles were on the brink of fatigue as she braced her feet against the vertical rock formation. She used her legs to push herself up. The aching in his arms didn't subside. He ignored the burning in his legs, and with one final heave, he hauled her to the safety of the cavern floor.

They collapsed to the ground, and she wrapped her shaky arms around him.

Kaiden, though confused, tightened his arms around her trembling body. Had she been sleepwalking? There was definitely something off. He sat up and held her body between his legs.

"Thank you." She lingered in his arms, and he didn't dare move.

"What happened?" he whispered into her hair.

"I . . ." She trailed off. Her quivering lessened.

"You know you can trust me."

"I know." There was a brief silence before she went on. "I think it was Rowena. I could feel her clawing her way into my mind when we first left Haven. I had a moment of weakness."

"What do you mean?" In the darkness of the cavern, his embrace tightened, and he pulled her more completely against him. He was thankful to the gods—if they were even there—that he'd had the strength to pull her up. *Thank the gods she isn't wearing her armor.* He still didn't know where that burst of strength had come from.

She didn't answer immediately. "I first felt her in Haven after I used my katai on the wall. I think that's why my mom never wanted me to use my akrani in public growing up."

Fuck. Philippa had warned Blaise that might happen when they were back in Haven. He couldn't imagine what it was like trying to fend off Rowena's satori. Perhaps that was why Blaise didn't sleep well at night. He'd noticed that bags had formed under her eyes. Although he and the rest of the unit hadn't been getting much rest either, Blaise looked as though she was getting none at all.

"Captain?" A familiar voice echoed throughout the cave.

Kaiden told Blaise to hold on to him after they stood. He outstretched his hands and took a few steps before coming into contact with the rough wall. "We're here!"

Blaise tugged on the back plate of Kaiden's armor as he guided them toward Mathias's voice.

Torchlight came into Kaiden's line of vision.

"What in gehheina happened? I heard screaming." Mathias came into full view.

"I—" Blaise started.

"We'll discuss it later with the rest of the unit," said Kaiden. He didn't realize he was holding her hand until Mathias looked.

"Or maybe it wasn't the type of scream I thought it was." The corner of Mathias's mouth lifted.

Kaiden had words at the tip of his tongue when Blaise interjected, "Don't be an idiot." She grabbed the torch from Mathias and started back to the rest of the group.

With his arms folded over his chest, Kaiden beamed, a sense of pride washing over him at her remark. Maybe she could handle herself. He shot Mathias a glance and shoved him forward. "You heard the woman. Don't be an idiot."

"You may be the captain"—Mathias pushed his best friend back with a grin—"but I respectfully request you shut up."

The two ambled down the cave path and followed Blaise as they continued to roughhouse each other.

Kaiden was thankful for the distraction. After that scare with Blaise, he needed a little lighthearted banter. What had happened with her stayed in the back of his mind, along with so many questions. He hated keeping things from Mathias. But he couldn't risk anyone discovering that Blaise was the lost heiress of Balam. He'd distanced himself from his best friend, and that wasn't the worst part. Blaise still didn't know that she'd been part of his little side mission. He'd never had any trouble following orders in past missions, but with her . . . She complicated everything. He was scared to lose her. Scared to have her. Scared to admit the truth to himself.

What is the truth?

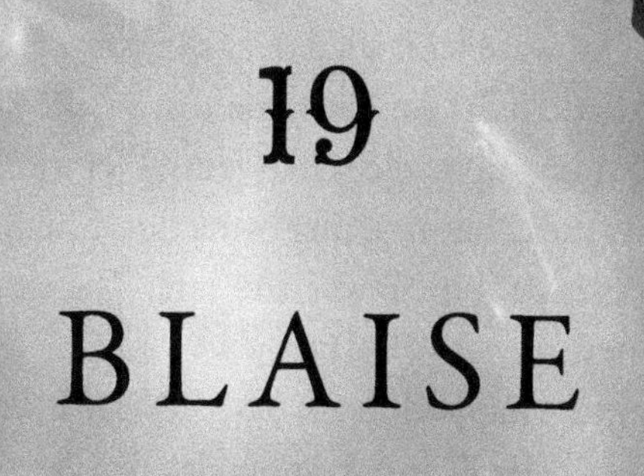

19

BLAISE

She hadn't told Kaiden everything. Yes, Rowena had bypassed Blaise's mental barriers and gained control of her, but in contrast, Blaise had glimpsed a part of the queen's plans. Rowena was going to unleash her army on Elatora within the week, and they wouldn't be ready for the attack. She wondered if she should tell Kaiden about what she'd seen. What if it had just been some demented dream? Had Rowena shown Blaise her plans on purpose?

Despite everything, Blaise had also dreamt that night, which was odd because she'd been sleeping like shit lately.

In the dream, she had been in a room with no windows.

There was an open balcony on the far end, but it was dark out. Not even the light of the moon dared enter that place. Black iron wall sconces lit the area, though barely. In the center was a rectangular pool. She walked up to the dark waters and peered in, expecting to see her own reflection. Instead, she saw Rowena. Her menacing emerald eyes glistened with baleful intent, and a cold and devious smile crept onto her face. *Abomination.*

The dismal waters crawled over the stone ledge toward Blaise. The little hairs on her nape rose at the sight of the inky liquid sliding up her legs like veins. Her mouth opened to let out a shriek, but nothing came out. She flailed in an attempt to escape, but it was too late. The darkness had consumed her.

Her mind snapped back to the dank cavern. She packed up her bedroll and strapped it onto Aero as Kaiden walked up leading Cedric by the reins. A strong draft hit them, which meant they were getting close to the exit of the pass. *Thank the gods.*

"How're you feeling?" he asked, meeting her tired gaze.

She loosed a breath. "I'm fine."

"You want to talk about last night?" he asked, petting Aero.

"I . . ." She inhaled and debated whether she wanted to tell him about Rowena's plan and if she should tell him about that dream. Would he even believe her? He *had* saved her life. *I should at least tell him about the army of undead.*

"Blaise?"

"You know how Rowena got into my thoughts last night?" She lowered the volume of her voice and leaned closer to him.

He gave her a slow nod. "Yes?"

"Well, somehow—don't ask me how—I saw her plan of attack." She pursed her lips, awaiting his response.

His eyebrows knitted. "How's that possible?"

"Last night, I accessed her mind while she was controlling me. She's going to attack Elatora before the week is over, and then Haven. She's basically going to wreak havoc on Crenitha." Blaise searched his face for a reaction, but he remained annoyingly calm, as usual.

Mathias walked into their conversation. "Did you just say Rowena plans to attack Elatora before the end of the week? That only leaves us five days to travel." His azure eyes went to Blaise. "Also, how do you know this information?"

"Queen Rowena was able to get into my mind with her satori. In short, she tried to kill me last night." Blaise noticed Mathias appeared more concerned than Kaiden. She really wished she could read the captain better. "What should we do?" She directed the question at both of them. By this time, the rest of the group had encircled them, and the captain filled them in on what they had been talking about.

"Wait a minute." Audrey's eyebrows came together in confusion. "Why does Blaise have such a strong connection to Rowena in the first place?"

Blaise, Zade, Raijinn, and Kaiden exchanged glances.

"You've been keeping secrets from us, *Captain*." Mathias's lips formed a straight line as he crossed his arms.

Kaiden winced, shooting him a faint smile, then looked to Blaise as if expecting her to explain things.

She stared at him for a moment before giving him a slight conceding nod. "I know this sounds crazy, but—"

There'd be no going back after she told them. "I'm the lost heir to the throne of Balam."

Audrey's jaw fell open. George still appeared somewhat confused, and Isaac's and Mathias's expressions were unreadable.

"Wait a minute. *You're* a princess?" George's voice reverberated against the cavern walls.

"This isn't good at all," Raijinn remarked, shaking his head.

"I'm sorry. I thought I was diligent in shielding you," Zade said, looking down at his feet, a sad look forming on his youthful face. "She must be using some kind of amplifier."

"Amplifier?" Blaise cocked an eyebrow.

Zade said, "Yes, there are a few things that can strengthen and enhance akrani—"

"Which I can explain later," Raijinn interrupted.

Blaise chewed on her bottom lip, asking no other questions about it. She did want to know more about the complexities of her power, but there were more important things to worry about at the moment.

"We can head back to Haven and have the king send a messenger to Elatora," Mathias stated.

"We can't turn back now. What about the mission?" Raijinn argued.

Mathias shot him a severe look. "My people are in trouble."

"*Our* people are in trouble," Audrey added, folding her arms over her armored chest.

Blaise's eyes swept over each of their faces, and she knew what had to be done. "We split up."

Kaiden's brow furrowed. "No. We're stronger in numbers."

"This isn't about the strength of our numbers, Captain. Lives are at stake here. What choice do we have?" Mathias interjected.

Raijinn said, "She's right. It's the only way we can accomplish both tasks."

"Mathias, Isaac, Raijinn, and I will go to Balam and complete the mission," Blaise said.

A brief silence ensued before Kaiden pulled her away from the rest of the group. "What're you doing?" he asked once they were out of earshot.

"What do you mean?" Her eyebrows wrinkled as she crossed her arms over her chest. "I'm obeying orders."

"I'm the lead on this mission. *I* should be the one to go to Balam," Kaiden stated.

"And what about King Theod? What if he asks about you?" She shook her head. "No. It would look better on you as the lead to go to Haven. They're also more likely to believe you than me."

He glanced over at the team, who were talking amongst themselves. "It'll take us a day to get to Haven, two days at the most. Will you at least wait to regroup?"

"She's unleashing her army in *five* days, Kaiden. We've already lost precious time in this gods damned cave." Blaise leaned against the rough wall of the cave and studied him. Did he doubt her capabilities? She looked at him with squinted eyes. "You don't think we can do this."

"I didn't say that."

"You don't have to. It's implied." She straightened and took a few steps closer to him.

"That's not it, gods dammit!" He didn't falter.

"Then what is it?" Her voice echoed throughout the cave pass. The team quieted their banter to stare at Kaiden and Blaise. Just as he was about to reply, she cut him off. "We don't have time for this. We're splitting up, and I'm going to Balam to complete the mission. There's nothing you can do to stop me." She then went to regroup. "How much longer until we're out of this cave, Isaac?"

He appeared caught off guard by the question. "Uh . . . another fifteen miles, give or take," Isaac replied as he scanned the formation and observed the direction of the draft.

"Okay. Once we find our way out, we'll split up," she said.

Blaise wanted to confront Rowena and hear the truth about everything. Then Blaise was going to kill her—for her mother, for Crenitha, and for herself.

THE UNIT CAME to a cave spring, and Kaiden ordered the unit to get a few hours of sleep before they reached the surface. They watered the horses; thankfully, the path in the cave hadn't been too steep or treacherous for them. After Blaise washed up in the icy liquid, she set up her bedroll behind a large boulder away from everyone, especially the captain.

Why had Kaiden been so hesitant in agreeing with her plan to split up? Where had his sense of duty gone? Had he become attached to her? *No. He just wants me to think that. Don't be stupid.* The sound of George snoring echoed through the cave, causing her to toss and turn even more.

Flames illuminated the gray walls near her, gradually becoming dimmer as the hours passed. She accepted that she wouldn't be getting any sleep for a while after exiting the cave. She sat up, rubbed her eyes with her palms, and then stood and padded around the boulder to check on the unit.

Audrey always slept closest to the fire. Her hands were folded on her stomach, and her auburn hair was sprawled across her pillow in all of its wavy splendor. She almost never snored—only when she'd had too much ale.

George's big body was asleep near the mouth of the cave, his sword clenched in his right hand as he lay on his stomach. If snoring were a competition, Blaise was pretty sure he'd win. She couldn't help but grin at the thought.

Raijinn, Zade, and Isaac were spread out, hidden behind large stalagmites. They were all sleeping soundly, and Blaise envied them. Then a thought entered her mind. *This may be the last time we're all together like this.* Her heart sank into her stomach as realization hit her. *I may never see any of them again.*

Mathias geared up and relieved Kaiden of guard duty.

Kaiden soon tiptoed up to her. He'd been standing watch near the entrance of the cave. "Hey." He rubbed the back of his neck with his palm.

Blaise folded her arms across her chest. "Hey." She leaned against the boulder.

"Can we talk?" he murmured.

"I have nothing to say to you, Captain," she replied.

George snorted loudly in the distance, then turned onto his side in the fetal position and continued his peaceful slumber.

"Fine. I'll talk then." Kaiden walked behind the huge rock.

Blaise followed, taking a deep breath. She stood next to her bed, hands on her hips, determined to keep her distance.

He stood across from her in the small space and leaned against the vertical formation behind him, face illumined by the firelight. "I know things haven't exactly been agreeable between us—"

She scoffed. "That's an understatement."

"Would you let me speak?" He stepped toward her.

His proximity sent a comforting tingle down her spine. She didn't falter and gazed into his dark eyes. "Fine."

"Could we forget about what's happening around us for a moment?"

She managed to step around him, maintaining at least a foot of space between them. "That's a bit difficult considering our pressing situation."

His eyebrow rose at her sudden movement. "You said you weren't afraid of me. Did you lie about that, Sergeant?"

Her eyes narrowed as she hugged her arms against herself. "No." She struggled to find the words. "I just . . . Things happen when we get close to each other."

He smirked, inching closer to her once more. "Is that such a bad thing?"

"I thought we already established this would result in a dead end?" Her throat had become dry, and her hands had gone clammy. So incredibly annoying.

He had her backed against the cold stone of the cave wall. "*You* established this would be a dead end. I never agreed." His index finger brushed away the strands of hair framing her face.

With that devilish grin on his face, he took one last step toward her. "I wish I were more eloquent with my words, but I'm not. I'm more of the actionable type."

She inhaled a sharp breath as he wrapped his arm around her waist and pulled her against his warm body. The remnants of self-control she possessed were lost when his lips pressed against hers in a familiar kiss she'd secretly longed for. His tongue penetrated her mouth, and he pressed against her while one hand reached beneath the hem of her tunic and roamed the softness of her skin. She massaged his tongue with her own, eliciting a guttural moan from him.

It took all her willpower to pull away. "We need a clear mind, and this isn't helping." She gazed into his eyes as her chest heaved, lips plump from his caress.

"My mind hasn't been clear since the day you came into my life." He captured her mouth once more, silencing any argument she had. Breathing labored, he pulled her flush against his warm body.

She snaked her hands up his muscled pecs and around his neck. Her tongue slipped into his mouth, exploring it. He let out a growl and hoisted her up by the waist. Her legs encircled him, and through the threads of his trousers, his long, hard arousal rubbed against the apex of her sex.

He set her down and pulled away, the gold specks in his eyes glistening in the dim firelight. "Do you want me to stop?"

She shook her head and whispered, "No."

They made their way over to Blaise's bed. She took off her trousers and undergarment before she lay on her back.

He yanked off his tunic and threw it to the side. "Are you protected?" His defined chest heaved in anticipation.

It took her a moment to realize what he'd meant by that. "I take an elixir every month. It temporarily prevents me from ovulating," she assured him.

His eyebrow rose. "Is that . . . safe?"

"Of course. I wouldn't take it otherwise." Her heart fluttered at his concern.

He knelt between her legs, running his hands up her thighs to her waist and ending at the stiff peaks of her breasts. "I can't get over this. Don't think I ever will."

She arched into his touch with a sigh, drunk on his sandalwood scent. "Get over what?"

He leaned over and caressed her neck before whispering into her ear, "The way you irritate me. How you feel the need to disagree with everything I say." He traced kisses along her jawline before he continued. "Your smile, your laugh. How brave and strong you are. How breathtakingly beautiful you are."

"I thought you said you were bad with words." Her lips turned up, and she met his hazel gaze.

A grin formed on his handsome face. "But most of all, I can't get over how much I want you." His fingers slid down her soft stomach and past her navel to the folds of her warm core. "You're so wet already." He smirked, bringing those two fingers to his mouth, tasting her. It drove her crazy. He brought his finger back between her legs and plunged into her, eliciting a gasp. Before she could settle, he pushed another into her.

She moaned.

He covered her mouth with his free hand and whispered, "We have to be quiet. Wouldn't want to wake the others." His fingers worked in and out of her, pushing her closer to her release.

She fidgeted beneath him, felt the pulsing hardness of his length against her thigh. He moved his hand and captured her mouth with his own before sliding his lips down the softness of her neck. His name came out on her breath, and she felt his lips curve in a smile against her skin.

He pushed himself up on his forearms, and their eyes met. His dark gaze told her how much he worshiped her. That he would do anything for her. That he would stop his own heartbeat for her.

"I think I'm ready," she whispered.

"Are you sure?" His voice was low, full of desire.

She nodded. "Yes."

He pulled his trousers down to his thighs and freed himself, then positioned his arousal against her, sliding it up and down her folds a few times.

She pursed her lips, a moan caught in her throat. He slid into her. She flinched, brow furrowed in delicious, fleeting pain. Gods, he was well-endowed. It took everything in her body not to make a noise. Her back arched, and her chest rose against his as he filled her, as he stretched her.

"I'm sorry. Do you want me to stop?" he asked.

"No, I'm fine," she assured him.

Kaiden kissed her and continued to gradually ease into her to the hilt. He stayed there for a moment, letting her get used to him.

Once she gave him a nod of approval, he began to move, slowly at first. Then his movements became more primal. Passionate. His lips moved against hers as he penetrated her wet core. Their breathing was labored, their skin moist with perspiration. He placed his forehead against hers and ravished her mouth. His hips moved against hers faster, and she bucked against him. The movement caused him to stroke deeper into her.

"Fuck," he hissed. "You feel so good."

"Harder," she demanded breathlessly.

He positioned one of her legs so that the back of her knee lay on his shoulder. With each thrust of his hips, she struggled to keep quiet. He maintained his hard, quick pace. Her hands braced against his pecs as he pumped into her. His lips caressed her neck, and he intertwined his other hand with one of hers, bracing it against the thin mattress.

Gods, she was close. So close. Her eyes locked onto his as she reached her climax. Her back arched, and her head fell back against the pillow. Her walls pulsated and tightened around him. With a few hard, quick thrusts, his body tensed, breath hitching. He throbbed inside her as he filled her with his sweet release. Then he traced light kisses along her jawline before collapsing beside her.

Blaise glanced at Kaiden, catching her breath, mind swirling with thoughts. What did this mean to her? Had it been an itch she needed to scratch? That was all it could be, but her heart said it was something more. She couldn't have fallen for him. He was arrogant, bossy, stubborn, and just downright difficult, not to mention he was the son of the second-in-command. And to make matters worse, she was the heir of Balam. Even knowing all that, there was no denying it anymore.

Kaiden stared into her eyes as his own breathing regulated, a soft smile on his beautiful face. "What's going on in that head of yours?"

"Just thinking about tomorrow," she lied.

"Don't."

She sat up and dressed. Her eyebrows came together. For a moment, she'd forgotten about Rowena and her impending attack upon Crenitha.

"Just be with me." He pulled his own trousers up and buttoned them. "Let's get some sleep."

Her features softened. She conceded and lay next to him. He drew her body close to him. It killed her, lying in his arms. Why did he give her a sense of comfort? Why did his presence cause her heart to thrum in her chest? But the question that irritated her most was why did he feel like home? She pushed the thoughts away and lay in his arms until sleep enveloped her.

20

KAIDEN

Glad to finally be out of the cave, Kaiden examined their surroundings and noted the cypress trees. Grelan Forest only had pine trees, which meant they had made it into Meliwe Forest. The warmth from the afternoon sun caused sweat to trickle down his temples.

Kaiden thought about the previous night. He'd shared intense moments of passion with Blaise. Part of him wanted it to mean nothing, wanted it to be a means of letting out frustration, but he'd have been lying to himself. Whether he wanted to admit it or not, he'd given a piece of his heart to her, something he could never take back even if he wanted to. The thought of separating from her made his stomach turn. There was a good possibility he would never see her again.

Zade interrupted his thoughts. "We can follow the lake back to Haven."

Kaiden agreed with a nod before turning to Mathias. "I need to speak with you in private."

The two men made their way out of earshot, walking into the thicket while staying alert in their surroundings.

"You do know what's at stake here, right?" Kaiden asked. He studied the unreadable expression on his best friend's face.

Mathias nodded. "She's the future queen of Balam. I know."

Kaiden paused. "It's imperative that you protect her at all costs."

An amused expression formed on Mathias's countenance. "Has it ever occurred to you that she might not need protecting?"

It had, but Kaiden had to be sure. He glanced in Blaise's direction. She sat upon Aero, patiently waiting for Mathias to regroup. Kaiden didn't respond. He just wanted her safe. Alive. The sun shone through the leaves of the trees above as the crisp breeze caressed his face.

Mathias walked up to Kaiden and placed a hand on his shoulder. "That's not the only thing bothering you, is it? Look, I know what happened last night. You're not *that* discreet."

Kaiden cocked an eyebrow. "It didn't mean anything," he lied.

Mathias rolled his eyes. "We both know what's going on here. *You* are just being a stubborn ass." He crossed his arms. "Just tell her how you feel. Tell her the truth."

Kaiden shook his head slowly as a moment of silence passed. "The truth," he scoffed. "The truth is King Vaughn tasked me with making sure Blaise arrived in Haven safely. I didn't understand why at first, but then she discovered the truth about her lineage."

A heavy sigh escaped Mathias as he glanced over at Blaise before turning back to his best friend. "You have to tell her, or you may not get the chance later."

"I will." Kaiden inhaled. "Just tell me you'll keep an eye on her. I don't want what happened in the cave to happen again."

Mathias muttered, more to himself, "That ruthless bitch." He shot Kaiden a reassuring look. "Of course. Now, I'm going to send her over so you can tell her how you feel."

Kaiden nodded as Mathias made his way toward Blaise. *This is the right thing to do. She deserves to know.* He just didn't know how to tell her. His communication skills were exceptional when in the line of duty, but when it came to the opposite sex, he was more like a bumbling idiot. Perhaps that was the reason he was still single.

Blaise walked up, hands on her hips, a firm expression on her lovely face. "You wanted to see me?"

She's so beautiful. He pulled her behind a large tree trunk and met her gaze. "I... wanted to tell you something."

Her eyebrows ruffled. "Okay." She waited for him to continue.

His hands trembled slightly. He could slice off the heads of revenants and conquer any enemy with his sword, yet he didn't know how to go about telling this woman the truth. He turned his back to her, took a deep breath, and then faced her once more. "I just wanted to tell you to be safe." Mentally, he palmed his forehead. *That's not what you wanted to tell her, idiot.*

A befuddled look came over her countenance. "Is that all?"

"No." The volume of his voice rose abruptly.

She appeared taken aback by his sudden response. "Is this about what happened last night?"

"I'm sorry. No, it's not about *that*," he said, glancing down at his clammy hands. Why was it so difficult to tell her? He met her gaze. "Not that it's not important—"

"Would you spit it out already?" she prodded impatiently.

"King Vaughn ordered me to take you to Haven, but I didn't know you were an heiress until you met Philippa," he blurted, then studied her as she processed what he'd just said. It was like a load had been lifted off his chest. He was glad to finally tell her the truth, but he was pretty sure she was going to give him a well-deserved punch in the face.

Her eyebrows came together. "Wait. What?"

"King Vaughn ordered me to ensure the meeting between you and Philippa happened. She technically found you though," he replied, pointing his index finger at her.

She stared at him, holding her arm, seeming to process everything.

"I'm sorry. I didn't have a choice," he said.

"You lied to me," she stated, her expression unreadable. "Of course. *Everyone* else has."

"King Vaughn ordered me not to tell you about anything." He stepped closer.

She backed away. "Were you ordered to fuck me as well?"

His breath hitched. Her words were like a dagger to his chest. "How could you say that?" He backed her against the thick tree trunk. "Was that all it was for you?"

"How could it be anything more? You blatantly lied to me." She didn't meet his frustrated gaze. "You made me think you were the *only* person I could trust." Her voice was strained.

He inhaled, and his chest tightened. What could he possibly say to make this situation better? "You can *still* trust me. They were orders. *You*, of all people, should understand that."

"Because gods forbid you disobey orders." She met his gaze as the volume of her voice rose.

"Would you rather I kept lying to you?" he asked, trying to be the calm one. But his patience was waning.

"Why didn't you?" She turned her back to him.

"Because I'm a man of honor," he said. Was he *really*? If he was truly a man of honor, then why did he keep this secret from her for so long? His stomach churned at the thought.

"Right," she muttered. "And it has nothing to do with the fact that we may never see each other again."

He didn't know how to respond.

"Do you even truly want to be with me?" Her glossy eyes bored into his. "What did last night mean to you?"

The night before had meant so much to him, and of course he wanted to be with her. He'd wanted to be with her since the day he'd dueled her, oddly enough. But was that something she needed to hear before going to face

Rowena? He didn't want her mind anywhere else but the mission.

She looked at her boots in the silence. "It's okay. It's better this way."

A lump formed in his throat. She didn't deserve this. He could only imagine how alone she felt.

"We've wasted enough time here." Her lips formed a straight line.

Everything that had come out of his mouth wasn't even close to what he'd wanted to say or how he'd wanted to say it. "I'm sorry," he murmured.

"At least you've proven one thing," she said. "You *are* a dutiful captain." She tore her icy stare from him and walked away.

She'd managed to make something that should've been a good trait sound so negative. His throat tightened, and his lungs constricted. He leaned against the trunk for a few seconds to collect himself. *That was a disaster.* He rested his head against the bark and closed his eyes. She was right. He should've told her sooner rather than later. His shoulders slumped as if a huge weight had been placed on them, but it didn't compare to the sudden ache in his chest.

Finally, he straightened and took one deep breath before walking up to Mathias, Raijinn, and Isaac. Blaise had already started riding ahead. "You'd better catch up to her," Kaiden told the three. "Stay the course." Then he watched as they all rode away.

"Captain, we should get a move on as well. It shouldn't take us long to get back to Haven," Zade stated.

What if that had been his only chance to tell her how he felt about her? Kaiden mounted Cedric and led the way in the direction of Thessalynne Lake. He pulled on the reins, signaling his horse to turn around, and rode in the opposite direction of where he was supposed to go.

"Captain, where are you going?" Audrey shouted.

Kaiden shouldn't have left things that way between him and Blaise. He should've just told her how he felt, told her that he wanted her, needed her even. Kaiden continued down the path, his heart racing as Cedric's hooves kicked up dirt. With his head on a swivel, he glanced back. He gained some distance from Audrey, Zade, and George. He needed to stop wasting time and turn around. *Haven.* He had to get to Haven. Then he'd go to Balam and help Blaise defeat Rowena. And not because of orders. He was going to do it for *her*. With a determined spirit, he turned around and headed back toward his group.

"SOMETHING ON YOUR mind, Captain?" Audrey interrupted his thoughts, riding up beside him.

Kaiden gazed at the dirt path ahead. "Huh? What makes you think something's on my mind?" He found it peculiar that Audrey would be concerned. They hadn't spoken much on the journey thus far. He glanced back at Zade and George, who followed closely at a slow pace.

"You just seem a bit distant since we split from the others," Audrey said as they closed in on the path between the Azureden Mountains and Thessalynne Lake.

He hadn't realized that much time had passed since they'd separated. Had he been that lost in thought? "I'm just . . ." He inhaled.

"You're worried about Blaise," she stated.

His eyes stayed on the path ahead. "Don't get me wrong. I worry for all of them."

"I understand. Trust me. You don't have to explain anything to me." Audrey's grin diminished as she looked away.

It was then that Kaiden realized she was probably worried sick about Mathias. Did Audrey's feelings run deep for his best friend, or was it completely platonic? Could she relate to how Kaiden felt about Blaise? Unfortunately, Mathias had a problem with commitment. Kaiden used to share the same problem with him. Lately, the only person he pictured himself with was Blaise. "You have nothing to worry about," he assured her. "I'm sure they'll all keep one another safe."

"Thank you for saying that, Captain." That kind gleam reappeared on her lips as they continued down the path.

The lake shimmered in the sunlight, and gentle waves hit the shore on the left of the team. Massive mountains with snow-covered peaks were on the team's right side. Below the snow line were different shades of gray slate. Kaiden came to realize this would be the last peaceful moment before the inevitable revenant attack.

21

BLAISE

Being a sentinel meant taking orders, and that was all Kaiden had done. She'd let her emotions get the best of her. But she had every right to be upset. Why would the king task him with helping her discover the truth? How in gehheina did the king of Elatora even know about her? This whole situation made her head and her heart hurt. If King Vaughn knew about her, did King Theod know as well? Her nostrils flared just thinking about it. Some choice words would be said to them—if she survived the mission, that was.

"Shall I start calling you 'Your Majesty'?" Mathias rode

up beside her with a smirk on his face. It almost looked like the same insufferable one Kaiden always flashed her.

She glanced at him and shot him an amused grin. They'd been riding in silence for a few hours. "Very funny," she drawled.

He gazed ahead, a serious expression on his face. "Who said I was joking?"

"I'm not fit to rule a kingdom. That's absurd. Could you honestly imagine me on that throne?"

Mathias studied her with kind blue eyes. "Yes."

Her brows rose at his response.

"Kaiden sees something in you, Blaise. Although I couldn't see it at first, I can see it now." He stared her. "Speaking of him, what did he have to say when you spoke?"

She scanned their surroundings. The wind had picked up, and the leaves overhead rustled as she replied, "The truth."

Mathias glanced up at the blue sky with a sigh and muttered, "I see." He proceeded to look at her. "And what did you have to say about it?"

She let out a breath. "I told him I couldn't trust him."

He glanced at her with much disapproval in his eyes. "He was only following orders, and at least he had the integrity to tell you."

She understood that but still didn't like being lied to. "Right," she muttered, staring at the path ahead.

"Of course, that doesn't make it right," he said. "But we're sentinels. We took an oath, remember? Loyalty to the king, commitment to the Order, and service to the people of Elatora."

She rolled her eyes. "Yes. I know."

"Do you?"

"I just . . ." She trailed off, scanning the green trees around her. "I thought he cared for me more than that."

"Oh, believe me, he does," Mathias said, and her eyes snapped back to him. "In fact, I think he *more* than cares for you, if you know what I mean."

"Are you saying he—" Blaise couldn't get the words out. It was too soon. She and Kaiden hardly knew each other. Mathias had to be mistaken, but then again, he was Kaiden's best friend, and Mathias hadn't lied to her about anything thus far. Why would he lie about this? She shunned the thought from her mind. "That's ridiculous."

"If you say so." He shrugged.

The question lingered on her tongue as a rogue arrow punctured the ground next to Aero's hoof. It spooked her, but Blaise was able to get her under control within seconds. Then her attention went to the dozen hooded figures surrounding them.

She went for the grip of her sword.

"Wait." Raijinn stopped her. "They're refugees of Balam."

Blaise's eyebrows came together. It hadn't dawned on her that some of the people wouldn't want to be under Rowena's rule. It made sense though. She raised her hands in surrender. "We mean no harm."

One of the dark-clothed figures stepped forward and pulled off his hood. He was much younger than Blaise had expected, younger than Daniel even. "Detain them," he ordered.

Before they could lay a hand on Blaise, Mathias unsheathed his sword and swung at one of the refugee soldiers.

"No, stop!" Blaise shouted at him as she leaped from her horse only to be tackled to the ground by two men. They jerked her arms behind her back, immobilizing her. The last thing she remembered before her vision filled with darkness was an arrow plunging into Mathias's chest. He fell off his horse's back, and a plume of dirt silhouetted him as he collapsed to the dampened ground.

VISION BLURRY, IT took her a few seconds to focus on her surroundings. She was bound and tied to a wooden post in a standing position, and it appeared she was being held captive inside a cabin. Nothing but embers smoldered in the cobblestone fireplace. A bone-chilling wisp of air slithered through her body. The top half of her armor had been taken off, leaving her in the dirty fitted tunic she'd been wearing for days. *Where am I? Is Mathias okay? Where're Raijinn and Isaac?* Blaise struggled against the thick ropes tied around her wrists.

Before she could even attempt to escape, the wooden door swung open, and that same young man from earlier stepped in. "You're awake." He entered alone and approached her, hands clasped behind his back.

The first thing she noticed about him was his bright green eyes beneath his shaggy brown hair. "Who are you? Where are my companions? What happened to Mathias?" she asked, struggling to keep the calm in her voice.

"The name's Ollie, and don't worry about your friends. They're being held in another cabin nearby. They're alive, for the most part." He stood in front of her.

"Why are you keeping us here? All we want is passage through Meliwe," she bit out.

He circled her like an animal would its prey. "How do I know you're not one of Rowena's followers—what do they call them? The Wayward. We've been in hiding since she ascended the throne. How do I know you're not her spy set on revealing our location to her?"

She just stood there in silence, refusing to tell him about the mission. "How do I know *you're* not from the Wayward? And you've seen my armor. You know damn well where I come from."

A smirk formed on his boyish features as he inched closer to study her.

The door flew open again, and in strode an older man with long hair that was pulled back into a ponytail. His beard was short and matched the brown on his head. "Don't toy with our guest, Ollie." There was a tinge of boredom in his voice.

A muscle in Blaise's jaw twitched. "Guest?" she scoffed.

The man waved Ollie aside and gazed at her. Then he asked in his deep, rough voice, "Who are you?"

"Who are *you*?" she retorted. Her gaze didn't falter. They weren't getting any information out of her. If they were going to torture her, then so be it.

"My name is Piers. I'm in charge of security here." He took a step back.

She glared at him. "Where's *here* exactly?"

"That information isn't relevant at the moment." Piers then retrieved Blaise's gold necklace from his trouser pocket and held it up. "Where did you get this?"

She didn't answer.

"One of your men has made quite the accusation

about you. I'm going to ask you one more time." Piers inched closer to her face. "Where did you get this?" His steely tone rattled her.

But she still didn't respond.

"This crest belongs to the Vinterhale family." He continued to stare at her. "You do know they're royalty, right?" When she didn't respond, Piers turned to Ollie. "Cut her loose."

Her eyes widened. "What?"

"Would you rather stay bound to this post?" Piers's voice dripped with sarcasm.

With much hesitance, Ollie unsheathed his dagger and obeyed.

"I've heard rumors that you were still alive," Piers remarked as he placed the necklace in the palm of her hand. "There's hope for us yet."

She placed it back around her neck and tucked it into her fitted tunic. "Where am I?" She stole a glance at the shortsword on Piers's hip.

"Calun," Ollie interjected.

"Why don't we give Her Majesty a tour?" Piers suggested.

"Please don't call me that," she insisted. "And how is it you know who I am?"

Piers started for the front door. "One of your companions entrusted us with that information. Willingly, I might add."

Dammit, Raijinn. Blaise followed him and said, "I'm not going to Balam to claim the throne."

She stepped out of the cabin and was struck with awe. The village was enclosed by a massive cavern. It didn't appear as dark and bleak as it should have; there were many torches lining the path of the small village. The homes and businesses were a combination of slate and wood, and they even had a river flowing through the community. It was surprisingly cool in the cavern, unlike the one in Azureden. She admired the resourcefulness of these people and their will to survive. The passersby had nothing but cheerful expressions on their faces. These were her mother's people.

"Why are you traveling to Balam, then, if not to claim your crown?" Ollie inquired as he followed her closely.

"I just want to stop Rowena from releasing her army on the land," Blaise replied as she followed Piers down the slightly steep road. "After that, I'm going back home to Elatora."

"In other words, you don't care about your people or your kingdom." Piers turned and faced her.

Her chest tightened at his remark. "I just found out about my lineage a few days ago, and now I'm suddenly expected to rule a whole kingdom?" she snapped. "I used to be a guard on the Teaos wall. I hardly qualify as 'ruler' material."

"It doesn't matter what you *used* to do. It doesn't even matter when you discovered the truth. What matters is what you will do *now*." Piers came to a stop and confronted her. "You won't just be taking over a kingdom. You won't just be claiming a throne and putting on a crown. You'll be taking over a legacy—your mother's legacy."

Blaise blinked. She had no words.

"But maybe you're right. Perhaps it would be better to let a regent take over in the meantime." Piers turned and continued to lead her down the dirt path.

She hadn't expected that answer from him. Her stomach churned as she closed her eyes and inhaled. "I'm sorry," she said. The topic of the throne and Balam was too heavy. She needed to change the subject. "Why did the people flee Balam?" she asked, immediately wanting to palm herself in the forehead for bringing up another touchy subject.

They passed the tiny marketplace, which only consisted of three wooden carts.

Piers stole a glance at her. "After Rowena overthrew her sister, she started to harvest the people for her precious army."

Blaise cringed and felt as though her skin were crawling. She knew Rowena was using the akrani alchime to create the revenants but was unaware how. The dead were created from the living. Perfectly good lives were being taken, and it made her want to vomit.

"Did you not know how her monsters are created?" Piers asked with a cocked eyebrow.

She shook her head, and a wave of sadness overcame her. "Do you know why Rowena turned against her own sister?"

"She isn't of the Vinterhale bloodline," Ollie said abruptly. "The late king adopted her years before your mother was even born."

Piers nodded. "She wanted the throne, plain and simple. She did whatever was necessary to secure it."

Blaise wanted to ask more questions but refrained and let Piers finish showing her around the underground village.

When the three made their way back to the cabin, Isaac and Raijinn walked up to Blaise. Her eyes widened, and her heart skipped a beat as she gave them each a long hug. "So glad you two are okay."

"We're fine, but Mathias took quite the beating," said Raijinn with an amused grin.

"Where is he?" she asked.

Isaac gestured to the cabin down the way.

"Go and check on him if you'd like," said Piers.

Blaise strode down the path and into the warm cabin. Mathias lay on a cot with bandages wrapped around his muscled chest where the arrow had punctured him. He looked at her with a blank expression as his clasped hands rested on his stomach.

"Don't look at me like that," he said as she sat on the edge of the cot.

"Like what?" She paused. "Like you're an idiot?"

One corner of his mouth rose.

"I know you don't trust Raijinn, but he obviously knows a lot about this land. You should've stood down." She shot him a severe look.

"I know," he replied. "I just . . . panicked for a moment."

Her eyebrows came together. "Why?"

"I made a promise to Kaiden that I'd protect you, and I couldn't imagine telling him I'd failed." He looked away from her.

Blaise didn't know what to think, didn't know if she should be angry with Kaiden or glad that he cared for her safety. "Why would he make you do that?" It was a stupid question, but she needed to hear Mathias's opinion.

He sighed and grimaced from his healing wound. "You already know why."

She shook her head slowly and swallowed.

"If you don't return what he feels for you, don't let him hope." He gave an unyielding expression.

How *did* she feel about him? She'd experienced innocent love as a young girl, but nothing like this. It was all very confusing and downright scary, more so than the troll she'd saved Kaiden from in the Azureden Mountains. How was that possible? How could this feeling be more terrifying than trolls? *You're ridiculous.*

At that moment, a brown-haired woman walked in. Her long wavy locks cascaded down her shoulders to her waist. There was something about this woman's cobalt eyes that gave Blaise a sense of warmth and welcome despite the rest of her stoic features.

"Blaise, this is Nira. It's because of her that I'm alive," Mathias said with a grin.

"Thank you for saving this big lug." Blaise stood and bowed politely.

"It was a struggle at first. He wouldn't lie still while I was working on the wound," Nira said as her lips tipped up, expressing a hint of amusement.

Mathias frowned and grimaced. "It was more like a painful massage."

"You have gitros," Blaise stated.

Nira nodded. "His wound drained my akrani a bit, and I had to recuperate." She glanced at Mathias and said, "I think one more session will have him as good as new."

He looked at Blaise with pleading eyes.

Blaise grinned. "Well, I shall leave you to it then." She walked out. It wasn't long before she began to hear his pain-filled cries. A cringe rippled through her because she knew the process all too well. Her mind flashed back to when she'd trained as a squire. Her shoulder had been sliced open while sparring, and an akrani gitros had come to her aid. She remembered the searing agony of kneading hands as her wound closed up. It was something she'd prefer not to experience again.

Where had Isaac and Raijinn gone? She assumed they'd gone to the tiny tavern for food. The thought made her stomach grumble. Mathias's cries finally subsided, and Nira walked out, closing the door behind her.

"He's resting now. There's a small scar where his wound was, but nothing too noticeable," Nira said.

Blaise stood next to the window of the cabin. "Thank you again."

"Would you like to join me for the evening meal?"

"Yes. I'm starved." Blaise didn't hesitate to answer. "Do you know where Piers and Ollie went? They're okay with us wandering about the village?"

"After discovering who you are, of course they're okay with it." Nira started to walk down the path to the small structure about a quarter mile away. "Your Majesty," she whispered.

"Please don't call me that," Blaise replied, reducing the volume of her voice.

"Is it not true?" Nira frowned.

"It's not that it isn't true," Blaise replied, matching her slow pace. She struggled to decide whether she should tell Nira her thoughts.

"You must feel completely overwhelmed."

Blaise sped up her pace as she replied, "I'd say that's entirely accurate."

"Can I just say"—Nira stopped in her tracks—"that your mother was a great woman."

"You knew my mother?" Blaise hadn't expected her to know the late queen.

Nira nodded. "As a young girl of nine, I served in the castle as a handmaiden-in-training. Queen Maxima was incredibly kind."

"Do you know why Rowena turned against my mother?" It was strange calling a woman she'd never known her mother.

Nira's face turned melancholy. "Many believe she felt it was her right to claim the throne despite not being a Vinterhale. She did everything she could to win the favor of the king, but in the end, he picked your mother. I believe there's more to that story than meets the eye."

Blaise's eyebrows wrinkled. "Why do you say that?"

Nira let out a breath. "Oh, don't mind me. I'm just making assumptions, like I usually do." Her blue eyes met Blaise's as she said, "Anyway, Rowena isn't the true queen. You are."

Letting out a heavy sigh, Blaise turned around. "I don't even know if we can defeat Rowena."

"So, that's your mission then?"

Blaise nodded, facing her once more. "Yes, and if you ask me, it's suicide."

"And yet you're still going to fight?" Nira raised an eyebrow.

"Yes," Blaise said. "I know if I don't try to stop her, I'll regret it for the rest of my life, however long that may be."

Nira stared at her for a few seconds. "You have to believe you're going to stop her. Don't doubt yourself."

"How can I not? I used to guard a wall in Elatora, and it wasn't exactly teeming with activity. What can I do? I can't even control this cursed katai!" Blaise paced a few feet ahead of her.

Nira caught up to her. She stopped her from going any

farther and said, "All that may be true, but it doesn't matter if you don't have faith."

"In what?" Blaise scoffed with an eye roll.

"In yourself." Nira paused. "Your mother was a great queen because she had faith in her people and faith in herself."

Blaise rolled the tension from her shoulders. She didn't know what to say, but a lot of what Nira had said made sense. Though they'd only just met, Blaise valued Nira's opinion for the simple fact that she'd known her mother.

"Forgive me," Nira said after a while.

"No." Blaise glanced down and held one arm. "Don't apologize. I think that's exactly what I needed to hear."

Nira smiled. "Come along now." She hooked her arm through Blaise's and led her the rest of the way to the tavern.

22

KAIDEN

He hated being away from her, hated the way they'd parted. An emptiness filled him from the top of his head to the tips of his toes. And the fact that he hadn't had the guts to tell her how he truly felt made things much worse. It had been a day since he'd separated from Blaise and the others, but it felt like a lifetime.

Kaiden glanced around at Audrey, George, and Zade, who were tentative in scanning their surroundings. The sun had begun its descent, which somewhat worried him. He'd heard about the Azureden Mountains and the creatures that dwelled in them.

A calming breeze caressed Kaiden's cheeks as the lake glistened beneath the setting sun. The path they trod veered into the mountains, which funneled into Grelan Forest. That pass was narrow, but that was the least of his worries. A sharp pain coursed through his mind. He leaned forward, holding his head.

"Captain? Are you all right?" Audrey rode up beside him.

Kaiden didn't know what was happening. It had never happened before. And for the first time in his life, he didn't know what to do or how to make the throbbing go away.

"Captain?" George's voice seemed to echo.

When Kaiden had finally worked through whatever *that* was, his three comrades were circled around him, concern on their faces. He cleared his throat and gripped the reins. "I'm fine. I just . . ." He examined each of them. "I'm fine. Let's go."

Zade stopped right before they entered the mouth of the mountain pass. "Perhaps it would do us well to make camp before we travel through."

"We've already lost enough time. If we're going to regroup with the others, we can't stop," Kaiden said, keeping his pace and continuing onward.

George passed Zade and asked, "What's the matter? Afraid?"

"If you knew what was through that pass, you'd be afraid too." Zade followed Kaiden.

Audrey lingered back as she asked, "What's in those mountains?"

"They're called kynarah," Zade said. "They're horrible creatures with the head of a woman, sharp talons, and strong wings. They only come out at night and dwell in these mountains alone. They have an appetite for anything that breathes."

George mused, "So, in other words, they're not picky."

"It's not a laughing matter," Zade said firmly.

"I suggest you load your crossbows." Kaiden drew his own weapon, which had been hanging on Cedric's saddlebag.

Once the sun had set, the pale blue light of the moon brightened their path. There was an eeriness to the silence between them. Kaiden readied his crossbow and his mindset. It would only be a matter of time before the kynarah attacked.

"I've never encountered them before," Audrey whispered.

"Count yourself lucky," Zade replied.

George's horse whinnied and threw him off its back. He landed hard on the ground as the horse galloped away down the path. Kaiden, Audrey, and Zade froze, scanning the moonlit sky.

"Fuckin' horse," George muttered as he dusted himself off, and then he picked his crossbow up off the ground with a grunt.

A creature with white skin and wings like a bat attacked George. It had long onyx hair and bared its pointed razor teeth at him. Its face was contorted in a vicious hunger for blood.

Thank the gods, George was able to move his bulky body fast enough to avoid the kynarah's sharp talons.

Kaiden rode toward George, shooting at the kynarah, but it was too damn quick. It flew straight up and disappeared into the shadows of the mountains. "Get on with Audrey!"

A high-pitched shriek echoed in the pass as George mounted Audrey's horse with her sitting in front.

Five white-skinned kynarah swooped down from the sky and attempted to grab the sentinels with their razor talons. Their shrieks echoed in the night.

"Go!" Kaiden signaled Cedric into a gallop. He stayed behind Audrey, George, and Zade as the kynarah continued their attacks. The screeching sound reverberated in his ears as he shot at the winged things. An arrow hit one in the chest, causing it to flail and plummet into the side of the rocky formation. Zade shot one, and it barreled down to the ground, barely missing Kaiden. Dust swirled about upon its violent impact.

"Grelan! Up ahead!" Audrey pointed at the end of the narrow passage. George shot at the kynarah, succeeding at keeping the razor-toothed creatures at bay.

With the opening to the forest so close, Kaiden pushed Cedric to his limits. First, Audrey rode out, followed closely by Zade. *We're going to make it!* As the thought came into his mind, a kynarah dove down. It dug its claws into Kaiden's shoulder, pulling him off Cedric. He reacted fast, pulling his emergency dagger from its sheath and stabbing the creature right through its heel. Another loud shriek filled the sky as Kaiden fell ten feet. Thank Karasi it hadn't flown him too high. His vision blurred as he hit the ground, gasping for air.

"Get up, Captain!" He heard George approaching, then that high-pitched shrieking again.

When Kaiden's vision cleared, he realized that he'd been slung over George's large shoulder. "I got you, Captain!" George said, panting heavily.

Audrey and Zade covered George, picking off a few

more kynarah with their crossbows. George—in full sprint—hauled Kaiden to the safety of the thicket. He leaned the captain against a tree trunk and collapsed to the damp ground, heaving loudly.

Kaiden reached over, wincing in pain, and patted him on the belly. "You did well, George. Thank you." He was extremely grateful for the team in front of him. Maybe this mission wasn't hopeless after all.

"Either I'm out of shape or you need to lose a few pounds, Captain," George wheezed, a tinge of amusement in his voice.

"No offense, big guy, but I think it may be the former," Zade said.

The loud shrieks of the kynarah faded back into the Azureden pass. Zade and Audrey joined Kaiden and George on the forest floor.

"Do they not like the forest?" Audrey sat with her legs crossed.

Zade shook his head. He sat against a thick tree trunk with roots sticking out from the loose dirt. "They stay in the mountains. The forest is difficult for them to maneuver in, plus it's dangerous for them to wander far from their home."

"Why is that?" she asked.

"They can't be in the sun or they'll catch fire," Zade replied as he rested his eyes.

Audrey just nodded and said nothing more about it.

Kaiden winced as he sat up. "Come on. Let's get moving."

"What about the horses? They need rest and water," Zade said.

"What about us? We need rest," George added, still

sprawled out on the ground. "I may seriously consider retirement if I live through this," he murmured.

"Even if we get a few hours of sleep, it won't hurt our arrival time. We'll still get to Haven by noon, Captain," Audrey said.

They were right. Everyone needed to rest, though he didn't want to. Kaiden was determined to get to Haven, have the king send a messenger to Elatora, and then turn right back around and travel to Balam. *I have to see this mission through.*

Kaiden allowed everyone—including himself—to rest for a few hours before they headed back on the path to Haven. Fortunately, they didn't run into any more obstacles while in Grelan Forest. They couldn't afford any more mishaps, not with Rowena being on the verge of releasing her army.

The heavy Haven gates rattled and clanged opened, and the sentinels were met by Captain Wilhelm. "Back so soon?" the dark-haired man said, his hand resting on the grip of his sword.

"I have urgent news for the king," Kaiden said, bringing Cedric to a halt. "Queen Rowena will attack Elatora in just two days' time. Then she'll continue her rampage into Haven."

Wilhelm furrowed his brow and crossed his arms over his broad armored chest. "How do you know this?"

Zade then said, "Forget how he knows it, Captain. Let us see the king."

Kaiden shot Zade a warning glare.

"Have you forgotten your place, Sir Zade?" Wilhelm asked.

"Please, Captain, let us have an audience with the king," Kaiden said, hoping Wilhelm would disregard Zade's impatience.

A few more moments passed before Wilhelm said, "Fine. I'll escort you to him personally."

They waited for Captain Wilhelm to mount his steed, then followed him down the road to the castle.

KAIDEN DID MOST of the explaining once they were approved to see King Theod. George, Audrey, and Zade stood next to him. It gave him a sense of satisfaction that he'd been a good leader to them. That he'd gained their trust.

The king sat on his extravagant gold throne and appeared to ponder the information Kaiden had just told him. There was an uncomfortable silence that made Kaiden think there were bugs roaming his bare skin. He wanted the king to take immediate action and send reinforcements to Elatora, and that was exactly what he'd requested after explaining Rowena's attack.

"How do you know Lady Blaise's vision is credible?" King Theod asked with clasped hands resting in his lap.

Kaiden had no choice but to tell him the truth. "Rowena established a connection with her somehow. Blaise was able to see Rowena's plans because of this."

"Why exactly does Blaise have that connection with Rowena?" Theod asked with a curious look on his face.

"Because Blaise is the daughter of the late Queen Maxima. Blaise is the true heir of Balam," Kaiden stated. It sounded so surreal. Queen. Blaise would be queen if they completed the mission.

The king looked to Zade as if asking for truth in what the captain had just told him.

"It's true, Your Majesty," Zade said, stepping forward.

"Well, where are she and the rest of your team, Captain?" the king asked.

"She and half of our team are traveling to Balam to try to stop the attack from happening," said Kaiden. He grew impatient; there wasn't time to waste. "Please, Your Majesty. Send a messenger to Elatora. Tell King Vaughn to ready the sentinels."

The king sat there for what felt like a lifetime before finally saying, "I'll do more than that." He called Captain Wilhelm into the room and told him to gather a small company of soldiers. "Go to Elatora and warn King Vaughn of the attack, and then help defend that kingdom."

Wilhelm nodded, but before he walked out, he shot Kaiden a short unreadable glance.

"Thank you, Your Majesty," Kaiden said. A wave of relief came over him. It didn't last long as his concern went to Blaise and the rest of the unit. He wondered how far they'd gotten and if Mathias had kept his word.

King Theod interrupted his thoughts. "I assume you four will be going back to Balam to regroup. I know how you sentinels are. Loyal and dutiful to a fault."

"I don't think we'll get to them in time to assist," Kaiden stated, glancing down at his clasped hands. "It's at least a three-day journey from here. The only ferry is at the bottom of Thessalynne."

"I have a way for you to get to Balam in a day and a half

at most." A grin crept onto the king's face as he said, "Take my boat. It hasn't been used in a long while. I was saving it for an emergency, and getting to Balam is certainly an urgent matter. For us all."

With a grateful heart, Kaiden took a knee, and his three companions followed suit. "Thank you, Your Majesty," Kaiden said, his spirits lifted. *This plan might work. We might arrive in Balam long before Blaise and the others.*

ON FOOT, THE four traveled through Grelan Forest to Cleree River and found the king's barge. It was hidden beneath an old fishing dock on the widest part of the river. Kaiden stepped into the sturdy old oak boat first. Audrey then cautiously hopped her petite body in, followed by George's massive body and Zade's lanky one. Everyone traveled with a small satchel strapped to their back and carried their weapons, along with oars the king had given them before they'd left Haven.

"He wasn't lying when he said it hadn't been used in a long while," Zade remarked, gesturing to the weathered wood of the boat.

"At least he was kind enough to offer it to us." Audrey had her oar laid on her lap.

Zade didn't reply.

"Well, isn't this nice," George stated, breaking the long tense silence.

Audrey nodded. "Yes, quite nice."

"Raijinn and I know this river well. He would practice his katai around these parts, bidding the Cleree to do his will. It takes much akrani to do that, or so I've heard," Zade said as he took the helm, guiding them down the calm part of the river.

"So, you can see the future, right?" George asked, holding tight to the oars on his lap.

Zade grinned. "Satori isn't quite that simple, but in short, yes."

"Can you explain it?" Audrey asked, glancing back at him.

Kaiden sat up front in silence, thankful for their conversation. It took his mind off Blaise for the time being.

"Well," Zade started, "satori draws the akrani from the earth. If I focus enough, I can see memories of how this realm was formed, but that takes an incredible amount of akrani."

George then asked, "Do you draw akrani from the realm as well to see the future?"

"Essentially." Zade nodded.

The boat came into more turbulent currents. It bumped and rocked as Zade steered, trying to avoid capsizing from the rough waters.

"It's going to get worse before it gets better," he yelled through the rushing sounds of the river. "I suggest you hold on!"

The boat dipped, then popped up, nearly tossing Audrey from her bench. George managed to grab hold of her before she fell out. It dipped and popped up again, then rocked right. All four of them leaned left to keep the boat from flipping over, only to have to lean right.

Zade steered through more tempestuous waters, avoiding large boulders and rocks for a few minutes more before the mouth of the lake came into view.

Kaiden and the others had gotten soaked from their ride down the river, but it was much better than sinking. Then, just as the boat was about to funnel into Thessalynne Lake, something large made a thud.

"Fuckin' revenant!" George blurted, unsheathing his sword and striking at the limbs of the creature.

It was a revenant hybrid and had a crossbow for one arm and a spiked mace for the other. The creature shot at Zade, but he deflected it by summoning an invisible shield.

"I didn't know you could do that!" George swung his sword in quick succession at the monster.

"You never asked," Zade replied, a smirk apparent on his features.

Audrey attempted to use her pressure point technique on it only to be knocked off-balance. Luckily, George caught her wrist, saving her once more.

Kaiden swung to cut off the revenant's crossbow arm. He missed, striking the steel part instead. He dodged the strike of its mace and sliced below the knee, cutting the creature's leg off, but it was still mobile despite the missing limb.

A circle of light appeared in Zade's hands. It grew bigger by the second. "Get down," he exclaimed once the shield had grown to the size of his hands. He thrust it into the back of the revenant, causing the monster to fly off the boat. It sank into the depths of Thessalynne Lake.

Kaiden plopped tiredly onto the bench. He caught his breath and took a small canteen from his satchel. After taking a swig of water, he eyed Zade. "I didn't know satori had that ability."

"There's a price I pay when I use it." Zade stumbled forward, and Audrey caught him, letting George steer the boat. As she helped him sit on a bench, he said, "Every time I use it, I lose some of my own memories. Sometimes it's temporary, but a lot of the time it's permanent."

"Do all akrani satori have it?" was Kaiden's next question.

"No," Zade responded.

"I wouldn't relax just yet." George gazed out onto the shimmering water.

Kaiden studied the water, and there was nothing at first glance. But then he saw it. A large sea-green fish tail splashed. "Shit," he hissed.

"What is it?" Audrey asked, her voice dripping with concern.

"Pull up your oars," Kaiden ordered, pulling his own out of the water. The waves had become rough and were rocking the barge heavily. He spotted two more of those fish tails. They were closing in. "Zade, can you tap into their minds?"

"Will someone tell me what's going on?" Audrey inquired once more.

"Sirens," George whispered.

"I thought they were a myth." She lowered her voice.

Zade answered Kaiden's question. "No, I can't. They're stubborn, strong-minded creatures."

From what Kaiden remembered in the stories his father had told him growing up, all sirens looked similar and were equally deadly. They had white hair, pale skin, and onyx eyes. Their tails and talons were incredibly powerful, and their songs enchanted victims into a trance so they could drag them into the depths of the water.

A high-pitched ethereal sound came into earshot. Kaiden covered his ears. "Don't listen! Cover your ears!"

But it was too late. He looked back at the three, and their eyes had turned completely white. Dropping his hands, he discovered the beautiful melody had no effect on him, to his surprise. Not a moment passed before a claw popped up from the water and grabbed hold of Audrey.

Kaiden leaped, grabbing her other arm. He unsheathed his sword only for it to be knocked out of his grasp. *Gods dammit.* He reached for his crossbow, which was more than an arm's length away. *Just a little farther.* A finger touched the handle of the weapon, then another finger, and then another. His grip on Audrey slipped. "No!" Leaning over the cap rail, he reached into the water and attempted to grab her. But it was too late. The creatures dragged her into the depths. "Fuck!"

Kaiden didn't know why their song wasn't affecting him, but he was thankful for that. Another one of the creatures reached for George. Kaiden brandished his sword and cut off its arm. She screamed and swam away, soaking him in lake water. The boat stopped rocking.

"Zade, snap out of it, dammit," Kaiden whispered, awaiting another attack.

The waves became tempestuous once more as a flurry of sirens surrounded the boat, grabbing for him and his companions. He swung his sword, slicing off limbs, taking whatever shots he could with his crossbow. There were just too many. He barely managed to keep them from bringing anyone else under.

One of the sirens wrapped her arms around Kaiden's neck and pulled him down. He grabbed the edge of the boat, using all his strength to stay out of the water. Another talon shackled around his arm and dug into his skin. A pain-filled shriek escaped him. He looked over at Zade once more and said, "Dammit, I know you're stronger than this." His arms weakened by the second. He didn't know how much longer he could hold on.

Zade's eyes dilated as he broke out of the trance, and then he lunged for the crossbow and shot an arrow straight through the siren that was wrapped around Kaiden's neck. A shriek escaped her, and her black blood stained the lake.

Kaiden wasted no time. He grabbed his own weapons and shot at the cursed creatures who leaped from the water. With a few more swings of his sword and a few more arrows, the sirens retreated. The waves ceased, and the lake stilled.

George's eyes returned to their original color as he came to. "What happened?"

Kaiden sank onto the bench in the front of the boat and sighed tiredly. He didn't feel like explaining the past events to them at that point, so he looked to the akrani satori at the helm expectantly. "The sirens."

"Audrey," Zade murmured, staring into the water with a melancholic expression on his face.

George lowered his head. "May she rest in nehveina."

What was he going to tell Mathias? Kaiden cupped his face in his hands. "I should've had a better grip on her." His mind flashed back to the hold he'd had on her. If only he hadn't tried to reach for that stupid crossbow. He should've seen it coming. His mind wandered back to Blaise. He would never forgive himself if something happened to her. It should've been Kaiden in her place.

"It's not your fault, Captain." George placed a heavy hand on Kaiden's uninjured shoulder.

"She was a good sentinel and did her job well," Zade added, looking out toward the glistening water. "Fare thee well, sister in arms." The orange glow of the setting sun reflected off the still waters of the lake.

Kaiden grabbed Audrey's sheathed sword and leaned over the side of the boat. He let it hover above the water before dropping it, watching the blade sink into the depths of Thessalynne. "Fare thee well."

"Shit," Zade muttered as they approached the Balam shores.

"What now?" George asked, running a hand through his beard.

Zade looked toward the shore and said all too calmly, "Ambush."

23

ROWENA

They were trying to stop her. They'd *been* trying to stop her, but all she wanted was a united Crenitha with her as the queen empress. She gazed into the pool in front of her, pacing over the dark marble floor of the sanctum in the Balam fortress. The black water of the square pool glistened with promise. Her akrani flowed from the top of her head to the tips of her toes.

Her existence used to revolve around peace in the realm, peace in Crenitha. But she didn't want to conform to the expectations of her kind. She didn't want to bring peace to these inferior realm dwellers. After all, why should a being such as herself be subjected to serving *them*?

Rowena had charmed her way into the Vinterhale family to prove herself worthy, to do what *he* hadn't been able to do. But she'd failed.

This is your second chance to make things right. She gazed at her reflection in the pool. It wasn't the first time these waters had spoken to her. Rowena said, "I will not fail you this time, my lord."

A different, deeper tone of voice entered her mind. *As the sun rises in the east, she will rise. As it sets in the west, you will fall.*

Rowena screamed and struck the water. Her breathing was rapid, panicked, and filled with fear of the premonition. It couldn't be true. She wouldn't let it come to fruition. *I will kill her this time. She will not get away.*

"Your Majesty?"

She froze, her dark dress and onyx hair drenched. Straightening in a gradual motion, she turned to the sound of the voice. One of her bone revenants had entered. She kept a handful of them in the fortress to serve her. "What is it?"

"The akrani alchime is ready for the bonding ritual," said the creature, gazing down at its deformed feet in fear.

Rowena swept her wet raven hair behind her and nodded.

The revenant just stood there staring at her.

"Is there something else?" she barked indignantly.

It shook its head. "No, my queen."

"Then get out!"

IN THE DEPTHS of the dark damp dungeon, she kept her akrani alchime safe. Andreas had created the revenants for Rowena before she'd decided to kill her sister. It'd taken him twenty years to create the numbers she'd demanded, but it would be more than enough to take Crenitha. Elatora and Haven didn't stand a chance.

Rowena entered the torture chamber of the dungeon. She'd remodeled it into working quarters for Andreas to create her abominations. He'd been fortunate to finish her army without running out of fresh flesh. Many of the people in Balam had fled once they'd discovered what Rowena had been doing.

"It's about time, Andreas." Her harsh voice penetrated the silence.

The man stood at a stone table in the middle of the room next to a freshly alchemized revenant. His shoulder-length blond locks were pulled back in a low ponytail with strands framing the prominent, rugged features of his face. "Careful." He shot her a warning glare.

She ignored his harsh tone and asked, "Is this the last of them?"

He nodded, appearing quite annoyed, as if she were disturbing *him*. His dark-colored robes had bloodstains, and his hands and face were tainted crimson from years of creation, years of murdering innocent humans for his warden queen. In his hand was an onyx dagger he often used to carve his symbol onto the bodies of his creations, giving them life. He pierced about half an inch into the revenant's torso and dragged it, using akrani to breathe life into the soulless thing. Its chest rose and fell as it took in the world and the two people in the room.

"Form up with the others," Rowena ordered, and the revenant padded out of the room. "Finally, I will have their loyalty. It will be through their loyalty that I will become queen empress."

Andreas placed the dagger on the table.

Rowena studied him for a moment, then searched his mind to see if he had been telling the truth. It appeared he had been. "Give me your directions."

"I must mark you with my dagger," he said. "Unfortunately, there are some consequences."

She shot him a piercing glare. "What consequences?"

"If you die, they will all die." His facial features were unreadable, as usual. "Your akrani will be tethered to theirs."

"Well, we won't have to worry about that then." If anyone was going to die, it would be Maxima's daughter. She cursed herself for not realizing she'd been alive all these years, for not sensing her sooner. Helena and Jocelyn weren't fools. They had likely been shielding Blaise. The thought of her name made Rowena convulse in disgust.

"Lie here, my queen." Andreas patted the table.

She used the step adjacent to the table, then lay on the cold surface. The long skirt of her dress draped over the edges as Andreas stepped closer and told her to lie on her side and expose her shoulder blade. She obeyed.

"This is going to hurt," he remarked.

A soft gasp escaped her as he dug into her pale skin. Pain was all she could think about as the tip of the blade carved deep, causing drops of blood to run down into the expensive material of her dress. "Fuck," she gasped. "Are you almost done?"

It took him a few long seconds before he withdrew the dagger from her skin.

In those moments, a surge of energy entered her, overwhelmed her. She'd never felt anything like it before, even with her own akrani. Comparable to water, the energy flowed over her body, and if she hadn't known any better, she would've sworn she was glowing. It stole her ability to speak.

"Don't worry, this is only temporary. It takes a while for the akrani to settle."

She stopped fighting it and let the new power settle where it may. This was it. The beginning of the end, and it would start with the death of Blaise.

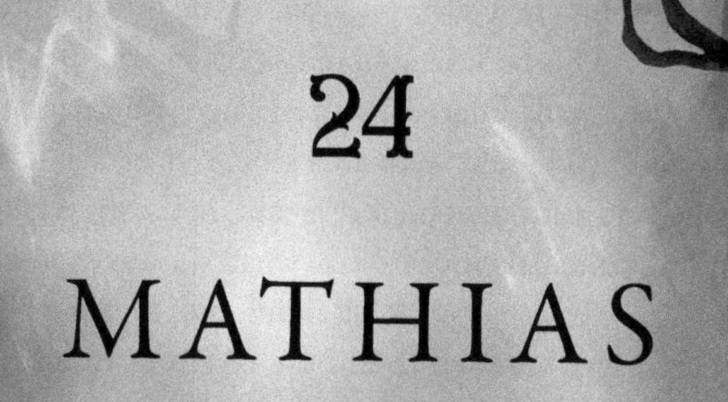

24

MATHIAS

The healing sessions had taken much energy from him, but he was thankful. His wound had been healed completely thanks to Nira and the abilities her akrani provided. She hadn't needed to help him, but she'd done it anyway. The sunlight beaming through the dome of the large Calun cave had disappeared. Mathias had slept most of the day, so he was wide-awake.

As the village slept, lights from the dying streetlamps shone dimly through the window of his cabin. He glanced around the large room and took a head count.

Raijinn had taken the couch. He lay on the cushions with his hands clasped on his stomach, snoring softly. Isaac lay sprawled on a brown wool blanket next to the warm hearth. Then there was Blaise. Where had she gone?

Panic swept over him as he stood from the cot to search the room more thoroughly, then the rest of the cabin. "Wake up! Blaise is gone!"

At that moment, a shriek erupted from outside, followed by the sound of a fight breaking out. Mathias had no time to put his chest plate back on. All he managed to do was throw on his boots and brandish his sword.

A battle had erupted in the village. Revenants had discovered Calun and were attacking, but how had they known? Mathias fought bone revenants in the street, slicing their heads, their arms, their legs, whatever was exposed.

"This is Rowena's work," Raijinn said, fighting beside Mathias, using his katai to kill the creatures running toward them.

Mathias thought of nothing but Blaise. Where had she gone? Had she known the revenants would attack?

Isaac soon joined the fight but was caught between two revenants a distance behind Mathias and Raijinn.

Lightning hit one revenant, cooking it from the inside out. "I can't use too much of that." Raijinn sliced off its head. "Wouldn't want to cause a cave-in."

"Yes. Wouldn't want that." Mathias grunted, spinning and swinging his sword toward a steel revenant. This one had an armored chest. He sliced its arm off and lunged his sword straight through its brain, leaving it incapacitated. The revenant fell in a heap to the ground, but the fight was far from over.

Isaac had finally caught up. "I saw Blaise. She was headed in that direction." He pointed to where the revenants appeared to be manifesting from.

"Shit," Mathias said. "I'll go after her. Help the townsfolk!" In saying that, he took off. While fighting through the creatures, legs aching and heart racing, he caught sight of her. She appeared to be in a trance, walking toward the exit of the large cave. "Blaise," he bellowed after her as he drove his blade into the skull of a revenant and donkey kicked another to the ground. *Rowena must have gotten into her fucking head again.* Feet from her, he reached for her arm, but something grabbed his leg, causing him to crash onto his back, knocking the air from his lungs. His eyes blurred as he gazed in her direction and watched her walk out of the cave. He cried her name one last time. It was no use; she'd become Rowena's puppet. A gut-wrenching ache entered his body. He'd failed his best friend. It was the one thing he'd been tasked with, and he'd failed.

Mathias scanned the area. The revenants weren't killing the people; they were capturing them, and he'd become one of their prisoners as well. Dragging him by one arm, the creatures threw him into a wagon with steel bars. There were numerous others filled with Balam refugees.

"Mathias."

He turned to see Isaac and a group of others in another carriage. "Where's Raijinn?"

"He's still in there," Isaac replied, pointing to the cave opening.

A rumbling came from the earth, followed by a crashing sound, and then a furious cloud of dirt erupted from the entrance. Once it cleared, Mathias's stomach tightened at the sight of a pile of boulders blocking the opening. "Dammit, Raijinn." He banged his palm against the steel bar.

"He could still be alive," a soft female voice said.

Mathias turned. "Nira, you made it." He glanced around at the other dozen people in the carriage, frightened and curled into themselves. One woman was cradling her newborn baby. "Why did they capture us? Why not kill us?"

Nira gazed down at her dusty brown boots. "*She's* going to bring us to the akrani alchime. He'll kill us, then turn parts of us into revenants."

"What the fuck," he said slowly as the bile in his stomach rose. "I'm not going to let that happen." The carriages began to move. A bone revenant took the reins of the wagon. Isaac's carriage moved ahead of them.

"There's a reason we've been hidden away for over twenty years, Mathias," Nira said, a despairing look on her lovely features. "She even defeated the military force, the Alchyra, and turned them into steel revenants."

Mathias shook his head. He didn't want to lose hope. "We still have Blaise."

"The queen is a cruel woman, and I know she'll torture Blaise to within an inch of her life, then simply take it." Nira gripped the bars so tight that the whites of her knuckles appeared.

He didn't know what he would say to Kaiden if he ever saw him again. Even though Kaiden would never admit it, Mathias knew Blaise's death would most likely shatter him. His chest tightened just thinking about it. More importantly, he'd failed the refugees as well. He'd joined the Sentinel Order to protect people from terrorists like Rowena, but he couldn't even protect himself from her. Here he was, her prisoner, about to be turned into one of her disgusting revenants. Hopelessness began to set in when he realized his fate. Nira was right.

Mathias stayed silent after that and observed his whereabouts. The weather turned bone-chilling. They were approaching Balam faster than he'd anticipated. It wasn't a smooth carriage ride, but that was the least of his concerns.

There were no farmlands. How had she sustained herself and her fortress all these years? Perhaps she had revenants for those tasks as well, or a private garden in her courtyard. Still, the Balam he remembered hearing about wasn't anything like the wasteland before his eyes. He stared out into the dead lands as they neared Rowena's towering fortress.

"What happened?" he asked, thinking out loud.

Nira replied, "There was no one to upkeep the farms, and Balam is a dry land to begin with, so when we all fled, the life from the land dissipated as well."

"She takes no pride in her dwelling. She cares for nothing but power over Crenitha," Mathias stated bitterly. "My hope is for Blaise to cut that bitch down where she stands and reclaim this land."

"There is still so much fear and doubt in her heart. I've felt it, and as much as I want to think that she is our saving grace, I can't bring myself to believe it," Nira remarked with a solemn, unapologetic expression on her face.

Mathias looked away from her once again to stare at the colossal structure they were approaching. It was magnificently built yet poorly kept. The fortress had a drawbridge with an empty moat, which they crossed. There were black vines on the outside of the fortress, clinging to the gray brick. It had many jagged edges and arches, with the potential to be beautiful. At the moment, everything appeared dark, despondent, and dead, like the rest of Balam. Dead, like the hope of the refugees.

25

BLAISE

How had she even gotten here? The last thing she remembered was falling asleep in the cabin back in Calun. Her chest tightened. What had become of Mathias, Raijinn, and Isaac? Had Rowena ordered her revenants to kill them? What about the refugees? What had become of them?

A tear fell from her eye to the dirt floor of the prison cell. Darkness encircled her, the iron cuffs snug around her wrists.

What is this place? Chains spread her arms, and the tension caused her to think one of her arms might have dislocated. She was on her knees, resting her back against the cold stone wall. *This is all my fault. I shouldn't have brought them. I shouldn't have stayed in Calun.*

"There's no use in thinking such things," said a sultry female voice from the darkness.

It could only be one person. It had been *her* akrani Blaise had sensed back in Haven, and she'd sensed it again when she'd entered Meliwe Forest. If only she had the willpower and mental strength to kick Rowena out of her mind, but she was too powerful. She'd forced her way into Blaise's past, into the memories she'd made with Helena and Daniel, with Jocelyn and Edgar. "Why are you keeping me here?"

A cackle rang through the cell as footsteps approached. Queen Rowena stepped into the ring of light surrounding Blaise. Her sharp features matched the roughness of her voice—regal and strong and proud. The hem of her long maroon gown dragged across the floor with each stride she took toward Blaise. Long wavy onyx hair framed her pale oval face, and an ominous grin crept onto it as she stared. "Oh, darling, it's nothing personal. Just orders."

Blaise scoffed, "Orders?"

Rowena struck her cheek, causing her to jolt back into the wall. *You really don't know. It seems they've done a good job in shielding you from everything.*

Blaise used her akrani to try to force Rowena out, but it was no use. It was like attempting to move a mountain. She tugged arduously to take back control of her mind, but the ringing pierced her ears to the point of pain.

"You're strong, I'll give you that, pet." Rowena gripped Blaise's chin between her index finger and thumb. "I suppose I could tell you the truth. Your death is inevitable at this point."

"Why not just kill me and be done with it?" Blaise asked, pulling away from her grasp. "What do you have to prove by doing this?"

"I like to make statements," she crooned. "Just like I did with your mother, and just like I will do to your precious unit."

Blaise's eyes widened. "They're alive?"

"For now. Until my akrani alchime turns them all into revenants," Rowena replied.

"You can't—"

"Oh, but I can, and I will," Rowena interrupted, leaving the light for a moment. She walked back with a nine-tailed whip. The tails had shards of glass and steel embedded into them.

Blaise's heart pulsed faster as she approached. "You're sick," she hissed.

Rowena ordered the revenant guards to flip Blaise so that her chest was against the wall. Blaise's arms were stretched so far that she thought they might pull from her sockets.

"You have been a pain in my ass since before you were born," Rowena seethed, drawing back and snapping the whip against Blaise's back.

The shock of pain made Blaise wince, but she didn't cry out.

"You are the reason I was sent here in the first place, so I suppose I should thank you for that." Rowena struck again.

Blaise shrieked, her breathing labored, mind going blank, losing all the questions she'd had for Rowena.

"This is all because a premonition came true." Rowena threw another blow.

The shards embedded into Blaise's rib cage area, and when Rowena pulled back, it tore skin from meat.

Blaise's cry echoed throughout that level of the dungeon. She gathered herself, grimacing through the astringent pain, and thought about what Rowena had just said. One of the gods had a vision? Rowena had been sent to Crenitha? What in gehheina was she talking about? "Get to the point," she ground out. Her nerves screamed, blood dripping down her side.

With a sadistic grin on her face, Rowena leaned close. "You," she sneered, "are the daughter of a god."

"What?" Blaise let out a shaky breath. "How? I . . . No . . . That can't be. The gods abandoned us decades ago."

Rowena took a step back. "It's simple really. Your father fell for your mother, Maxima, and their love brought you into the realm. But . . ." She swung the whip. *Crack.*

Blaise grunted, grinding her teeth in an attempt to hold back a scream.

"The horny bastard broke a rule. And guess who was sent to fix the mistake?" Another swing, and a crack reverberated through the space.

More skin tore, more flesh mutilated. Light-headedness washed over Blaise, and she fell, kneeling in crimson liquid. She was a half god. But which one had fallen in love with her mother? Was it Amasu, the high god? Teival, the god of death? Or was it Colvyr, the god of peace? That last one made the most sense. That would explain her satori. It wouldn't explain her katai though. "W-who . . ." Blaise struggled to get the word out.

"Who is your father? Afraid I can't tell you, child."

Blaise gazed down into the pool of her own blood, and her head began to spin.

"Now, I can't have you unconscious while I torture you. Stand up straight!" Rowena's hard-hearted voice echoed through the damp cell.

She couldn't. Blaise had become too weak. There was no way she could stand, but she tried anyway, only to fall, hanging by the chains on the wall. Blood trickled down her back, and her vision blurred. She didn't even want to look at the damage Rowena had done.

"Did you really think you could defeat me?" Rowena grabbed a handful of Blaise's hair and pulled her head back, exposing her neck. "You're weak and worthless, just like your pathetic mother." Rowena straightened and said nothing more before exiting the cell.

Blaise's mind spun with so many questions. Rowena had been sent to kill her? One of the gods had broken a rule and fallen for her mother? What in gehheina was Rowena? A servant of Colvyr? An ellorian? Or a servant of Teival? A grysill? It didn't matter either way. Her lungs burned as crimson continued to seep from her body. Her life ebbed, and she knew death would soon come for her. But that would mean that she'd failed her unit, failed the refugees, failed Crenitha. A tear formed in the corner of her eye and trickled down her bloodied cheek.

BLAISE WANTED TO be back in Elatora with Helena and Daniel. Why had things happened this way? Why had she agreed to join this stupid task force? If it weren't for Kaiden, she'd have still been blissfully unaware of her true lineage, happy and content on the wall and out of Rowena's radar. But had she been happy? Had she been content doing the bare minimum? It didn't matter. The stench of death crept nearer by the minute, and there was nothing she could do about it.

The cell door unlocked and creaked open. Rowena came into Blaise's peripheral.

"Back for more so soon?" Blaise spat bitterly.

"I've come bearing gifts."

"I don't want any of your gifts." Blaise coughed, and blood spewed from her mouth.

Rowena grinned. "I have a feeling you'll want this one."

At that moment, a steel revenant entered and threw someone in front of Blaise. It took her a moment to recognize the person. Her heart dropped as realization hit her like a ton of rocks.

"Kaiden," she choked out. He couldn't be there. It had to be some demented dream. She looked upon his beaten and bruised body. He struggled to his feet and turned to meet her gaze, leaning on the wall across from her.

"Blaise." He appeared just as startled at her appearance as she was with his. The steel revenant punched Kaiden in the face, knocking him down. He spat up blood as he pushed himself up.

Blaise flinched. "Stop!" Despite Kaiden's lie, she didn't want that for him. He didn't deserve it. A ringing in her ears ensued as the monster delivered blow after blow, first to Kaiden's side, then to his stomach. The revenant picked him up and tossed him against the stone wall next to where Blaise knelt in chains.

Kaiden just lay there, motionless.

"I'm going to fucking kill you," Blaise bit out. The pain of seeing him on the ground overshadowed her own, and a surge of warmth ignited within her core.

Rowena bent down and examined Kaiden. She swiped her index finger across his bloodied face and licked it. Her eyes widened, and then a look of amusement overcame her pale features. "Did they really think that sending a half blood with you would help?"

Kaiden had regained consciousness by then. "What the fuck are you talking about?" he spat, pushing himself up to his hands and knees.

"I'm talking about the ellorian blood running through you, weak fool." Rowena kicked him back down.

He coughed up more blood.

Blaise stared at him, a mixture of emotions rolling through her. It made sense. His strength and speed were exceptional. And she almost always felt a sense of peace with him, except for this moment, when he was beaten and bloodied. His energy was weakening with every blow delivered. She could feel it. She could feel *him*. All the pain in her body didn't matter. She just wanted him safe, alive, and as far away from her as possible.

"You said you were sent here. What or who are you?" Blaise asked, hoping to divert Rowena's attention.

Emerald eyes pierced Blaise's chestnut ones. Rowena stepped closer. "I'm a full-blooded ellorian, a servant of Colvyr, the god of peace. I've lived for centuries—and not just in this realm."

"So, what? You're wreaking havoc on Crenitha all because of me?" Blaise asked, arms aching, wrists chafing from the cuffs. Her eyes drifted to Kaiden, who had a bewildered look on his face. She could only imagine what he felt. All she wanted to do was embrace him and tell him everything was going to be all right.

"Stupid girl," Rowena drawled. "Do not think so highly of yourself. I'm doing this as punishment for your mother's sin."

"Is taking my life not enough?" Blaise winced from the open wound in her side.

"No, it's not," Rowena snarled. "An example must be made of you realm dwellers."

Blaise's brow furrowed. "Aren't you ellorians supposed to be peacemakers of the realm?" She wanted nothing more than to drive her sword into the false queen.

Rowena placed a hand on her hip. "What do you think I'm doing?" She waved. "But enough talking. I have an army to release upon Crenitha." She glanced at Kaiden, then the revenant. "Bring him."

"What're you going to do to him?" Blaise hadn't meant for it to sound so desperate. But she was. Her heart ached at the sight of him so weak, so vulnerable. "It's me you want." Her voice was strained. "Release him!"

"Oh, I plan on releasing him," Rowena replied, a snide grin curling upon her thin lips.

Blaise tapped into what was left of her akrani and manifested lightning to her fingertips. A streak of electricity sparked toward Rowena, but she leaped out of the way.

The desire to spill Rowena's blood coursed through Blaise with the power she wielded. Her heart pulsed in her ears, her throat parched from dehydration as the energy flowed. A mental rope pulled her back from the beyond, dimming the azure lightning crawling across her skin. It faded to nothingness.

"I admire your diligence, pet." Rowena entered her mind and blocked her akrani.

Blaise sank into the chains, the cold wall against the side of her face. The revenant hauled Kaiden out of the cell as she whispered, "I'm sorry."

"Frankly, you should be thanking me. His death will be quick, unlike yours." Rowena took a step closer. "You're going to die in this cell. Your body will rot and become food for the rats and insects that dwell down here." Before Rowena walked out of the cell for the second time, she said, "Take comfort in knowing that death is near. Now, if you'll excuse me."

She was left alone with her sorrow, with her tears, with her hopelessness. Blaise looked to the shadows around her. Even the halo of light that encircled her had dimmed significantly. It was only a matter of time before she became enveloped in complete and utter darkness, and no one was coming for her.

Blaise's chest ached on her inhale. Her heartbeat had slowed immensely, and death trailed on her heels. She exhaled and found herself back home in Elatora. But how could that be? Maybe it was her satori. Bewilderment overwhelmed her as she walked through the seemingly empty house.

"Grams? Daniel?" she called and turned the corner into the kitchen.

There Grams stood, beneath an open cabinet, reaching for a mug. Blaise immediately walked over to assist her grandmother. She retrieved a mug from the shelf and placed it on the counter.

With a smile, Grams said, "Thank you, Pooka."

"This isn't real," Blaise murmured, her brow furrowed.

"What're you talking about?" Grams mixed her herbal tea before she brought it to the table and took a seat.

Blaise sat across from her. "I'm not supposed to be here."

Grams sipped the liquid and stared at her for a few seconds. "Where are you supposed to be?"

Blaise glanced down at herself and noticed she wasn't wearing her armor. She met Grams's kind gaze and replied, "In Balam. Dying."

Grams's eyebrows rose, and worry crept onto her features. "Why are you still doubting yourself?"

Blaise's gaze diverted, her surroundings melting away. The cozy house she'd once called home was replaced with the cold dank walls of the dungeon cell.

Grams's voice echoed, "Come back to me, Pooka."

Faces appeared in her mind's eye—first Daniel's, then those of the sentinels she'd stood watch with. Audrey and her perky personality came to mind. George and his bruteness. Raijinn with his assertiveness and loyalty to Blaise. Zade and his intrusive cockiness. Isaac, who reminded her so much of her brother.

She thought of all the refugees who'd made a life for themselves in Calun. They didn't deserve to flee from their land. They didn't deserve to be turned into revenants.

Finally, Kaiden came to mind, the newly appointed captain. She'd let her pride get in the way of admitting the truth to him. Did he feel the same for her? Could they have a future together? She would never know if she didn't find a way to escape this cell.

Despite her weakened state and all the blood she'd lost, Blaise summoned akrani once more. Instead of fueling it with rage, she let the calm neutrality of her mind take over. It flowed from her core to the tips of her fingers. The blue lightning surfaced around her wrists and pulsed against her restraints. With one final push of energy, she broke free from the chains and fell to the ground. Her legs throbbed with pain, but she managed to lift herself from the floor and summoned the katai once more. The cell door burst open. It flew across the corridor, and she limped out of the cell, leaning against the wall for support. She had to find Kaiden before it was too late.

26

KAIDEN

His head throbbed, and his body ached as he awoke. He thought he'd heard his name as his vision cleared. Kaiden lifted himself up and leaned against the wall. The pain in his body had decreased immensely. Confused, he scanned his surroundings. A beautiful woman with long brown hair came into view.

"Hey, how're you feeling, Captain?" she asked, checking the pulse in his neck.

"How do you know who I am?" He realized the dim room was a cell and could barely make out the faces of the people standing around him.

Mathias knelt beside him. "I told her."

Kaiden grinned. His best friend was there with him. It wasn't a good thing, but then again, it wasn't a bad thing either. "Mat," he rasped. "You're alive."

"Rest for a bit. You took quite the beating," Mathias said.

"What about the others?" Kaiden asked.

"We're here, Captain." Zade walked up, along with George and Isaac. They all appeared to be bruised up, but not nearly as bad as Kaiden.

"Raijinn?" Kaiden asked.

Mathias shook his head and glanced down at his clasped hands. "He didn't make it."

Kaiden didn't know how to tell his best friend that he'd let Audrey die. He glanced down at his calloused hands and searched for the words.

"I know," Mathias said, "about Audrey. George told me."

A lump formed in Kaiden's throat. "I'm sorry."

"Shit," Mathias whispered, glancing down at the floor as a look of sorrow crept onto his face. A few seconds passed before he continued. "It's not your fault. She knew the risks when she joined the unit." Mathias placed a hand on his shoulder. "I'll cherish her memory. Let's make sure her death isn't in vain."

Kaiden nodded and sat up straighter, noticing a handful of people spread throughout the small cell. "I saw Blaise. She's worse off than me." His heart skipped a beat as he said her name and remembered her crimson-covered body. They didn't have any time to waste. Rowena was on the verge of releasing her army.

"You should take off your chest plate. You'll breathe

better," Mathias suggested, and then he helped Kaiden slip it over his head and tossed it aside.

Zade knelt in front of the captain and asked, "What's that?"

Kaiden glanced down at the purple crystal hanging low around his neck. "It was my mother's. My sister gave it to me before I left Elatora."

"Huh, so that's why," Zade said as he placed a finger to his chin.

"Why what?" Kaiden furrowed his brow.

"I can't see into your mind. I never could, and I wondered why. Now it makes sense. I'm surprised Rowena overlooked it." Zade paused. "That crystal you're wearing is a shield." He examined it more closely. "When the color fades from it completely, you'll no longer be shielded."

Kaiden nodded and understood why the sirens' song hadn't affected him as they'd crossed Thessalynne Lake. "We need to find a way out of here."

"Zade tried to use his satori on the door, but he failed. There's no way out. It would take a miracle to escape this dungeon," Mathias said.

"I'm sorry, I'm still a bit weakened by the events on the lake . . . Wait." A look of concentration overcame Zade's face as he muttered, "We may have one coming our way." He rushed to the thick cell door and banged on it. "Blaise! Blaise, we're in here!"

Mathias helped Kaiden to his feet.

How had she even escaped? "That's impossible," Kaiden whispered. "I just saw her chained to a wall."

"Stand back." Zade leaped away from the door, and as he moved, blue streaks of electricity enveloped the wood, causing it to crackle and pop. Within a few seconds, a flash occurred, and the door flew against the cell wall and crashed to the ground.

When the smoke cleared, a figure limped in and collapsed onto the stone floor. Kaiden's eyes widened as realization washed over him. *How did she get out of her cell?* He rushed to her side, falling to his knees. "Blaise. Blaise, I'm here." His own pain became nonexistent at the sight of her battered, tortured body. He examined her wounds closer. They were so deep that he wondered how she was still alive. The one on her side was especially bad, the skin and meat there mangled.

Warmth ignited within his stomach as the urge to spill blood overwhelmed him. And not just anyone's blood. He wanted to inflict the same torture Blaise had suffered on Rowena and watch as her blood soaked into the ground.

He brushed Blaise's hair away from her unconscious face, chest tightening more and more with each of her shallow breaths. He wanted to breathe *for* her. "Don't you dare think about leaving me," he whispered, cradling her in his arms.

Nira knelt next to Kaiden and said, "This isn't good."

"Can you help her?" He shot Nira a pleading look, holding Blaise close to his chest.

"Lay her on her stomach and step away, Captain." Nira rubbed her palms together.

He obeyed and gave her space to work. Mathias placed a hand on his best friend's shoulder, flashing him a comforting grin.

Nira placed her fingers on Blaise's largest wound. She massaged it, and new skin materialized before Kaiden's eyes. He'd never seen how gitros worked. It amazed and disgusted him at the same time. Nira continued the motion on the other wounds, healing them one at a time.

A few minutes passed before Nira told Kaiden to help flip Blaise onto her back. He did, and the healer hovered her hand over Blaise's chest. He witnessed black smoke emit from the palm of Nira's hand. The smoke worked its way into Blaise's mouth and nostrils.

Blaise's chest rose. Her eyes flickered open and met Kaiden's worried gaze. He looked at Nira with a grateful expression.

"I couldn't heal her completely, but she should be able to walk now," Nira stated, rising slowly to her feet.

Mathias helped her, slipping his arm around her waist. "Are you okay?"

Nira nodded. "Just a little weakened, but I can carry on."

Isaac kept watch at the door. "We should get a move on before we're discovered," he said.

"It's only a matter of time before Rowena senses our escape." Zade paused. "Come, we must hurry. There are tunnels that lead into the foothills just outside Balam."

Nira frowned. "We can't just leave the other refugees."

"I'll make sure everyone gets out." Blaise sat up with help from Kaiden.

"I can help," Zade added.

Kaiden gazed into Blaise's eyes for a moment, fully aware of the inappropriate timing. Heat radiated through his chest, and a tingling sensation coursed through his hands. Maybe they could survive this after all. "Let's go then." He helped her stand. Everyone followed Zade down the narrow hallway.

They passed many cells as they rushed through the dungeon. Blaise used her katai to free the prisoners inside. Zade was able to help using his satori. The group became larger with each cell they opened. They found the imprisoned akrani alchime as well. George unchained Andreas's ankles and told him to follow them.

"How do you know about these tunnels?" Kaiden asked as they ran down the corridor, having no idea where he was going.

Zade didn't look at Kaiden. "Raijinn escaped through them when he was little. He told me where they were in the event he didn't make it this far." A glint of sadness could be seen on his face.

"I'm sorry." Kaiden knew it didn't make matters better, but it felt like the right thing to say. He assumed Raijinn and Zade were close like he and Mathias were. His heart sank at the thought. What if Mathias hadn't made it? He pushed it away.

Zade glanced at Kaiden and nodded, and then they came to a dead end.

"Great. Now what?" George banged his fist against the stone.

"This is where Blaise comes in," Zade replied.

Blaise's eyebrows came together. "What?"

"You must use blue flames in order to open the passage," Zade said.

Kaiden looked behind the group of refugees, and a gigantic revenant appeared from around the corner of the long narrow corridor. "We have company."

"Goddess of chaos, that thing is inhumanly large," George remarked.

"We don't have our weapons," Isaac stated.

"All we have to do is keep it distracted." Kaiden turned to Blaise and said, "You can do this."

She shook her head. "I don't think I have much akrani left."

He grabbed her by the shoulders and gazed into her chestnut eyes. "I believe in you. Always have. Always will."

She swallowed and gave him a nod.

He turned, running toward the monster. The thing had a battle-axe fused into its arm and wore a black helmet that appeared melded to its head.

Kaiden fell to his knees and slid between the revenant's legs, avoiding a strike from the axe and ending up behind the creature. From the distance, he saw George, Isaac, and Mathias running to aid him. The space they were fighting in was difficult to maneuver.

Isaac leaped, running up and across the wall before landing on the revenant's shoulders. He used his elbow and slammed it against the creature's temple. It appeared dazed from the impact. Isaac jumped down. But the monster was relentless, and it swung its other arm, knocking Mathias against the wall. It swung the other way. Grabbing George by the throat, latching onto him. Kaiden jumped onto the revenants back and wrapped his arm around its throat. He used the weight of his body to lean back, causing the creature to loosen its grip enough for George to escape.

A blue light flashed from down the hall. *She did it.* Kaiden grinned. "She got it open. You guys go." He still had the thing in a choke hold.

At that moment, Blaise ran down the hall, lightning in the palms of both hands, her eyes glowing azure. That was Kaiden's cue to let go. He did not want to get hit by her katai a second time. He ran backward as he witnessed her power immolate the revenant. The monster radiated with blue fire. It just stood there trembling for a few seconds before it exploded into a thousand pieces. Small remnants of the creature showered Kaiden as the acrid stench of burnt flesh filled his nostrils. He wondered where she'd found that sudden surge of power—not that he was complaining. He stood there staring at her while Mathias, Isaac, and George wasted no time running toward the open passageway.

"What're you doing? Let's go," she said with a hand gesture.

Kaiden knew she had it in her to overcome whatever obstacle was thrown her way. Tension released from his muscles at the thought. Mathias was right. She didn't need to be protected. She'd had the strength inside her all along.

27

ROWENA

She'd left Blaise in the deepest part of the dungeon to fester in the physical and mental brokenness she'd inflicted upon her. Rowena reveled in it. She peered into the pool of water once more, staring at her reflection. Maybe if she kept Blaise alive, the premonition she'd heard earlier wouldn't come to fruition.

The sun would rise eventually. Rowena climbed the many steps to the top of the tower. Her armies appeared miniscule from where she stood. The night breeze flowed through her hair as rows of her precious creations awaited orders. With the flick of her wrist, a large battalion of revenants marched away toward the Onyx Mountains in the direction of Elatora. She flicked her wrist another time, sending another legion in the direction of Haven.

With a smile on her face, she watched as her armies disappeared over the horizon. One of her Wayward servants interrupted, clearing his throat.

"What is it?" she asked, venom in her voice.

"The warden is no more, and the refugees have escaped," said the servant in his raspy terrified voice.

Her nostrils flared, and her fingers flexed, causing her knuckles to crack. She closed her eyes and inhaled. After releasing her breath, she summoned a group of her strongest revenants to search for the refugees and bring them back.

"There's more," said the servant, shrinking backward.

"What?" Her teeth clenched as she shot him a warning glare.

"The girl and the akrani alchime have escaped as well." Fear dripped from his voice.

"Fool!" she spat at the man. "Find her and bring her to me. And kill everyone else, including Andreas."

Her servant bowed. "Yes, my queen." Then he left her to her solitude once more.

As the sun rises in the east, she will rise. As it sets in the west, you will fall. The voice came from the depths of gehheina.

Rowena held her head, shaking the thoughts away. She clutched the onyx crown sitting atop her raven hair. "Leave me alone. You had your chance to make things right." She calmed herself and concentrated on Blaise. Where had the little bitch gone? She should have killed her when she had her chained in the dungeon, but a part of her didn't want to see her die. It was a waste of power and potential, even though it was what she had been ordered to do.

He'd told her she could be free from the life of servitude, had told her she could do whatever she wanted with Crenitha. *He'd* even told her she could *have* Crenitha. Freedom had never felt so close, so tangible. All she had to do was end Blaise's life.

Rowena paced the flat stone tower, peering past the battlements. Blaise looked so much like Maxima—the same chestnut eyes, the same raven hair. The only thing that wasn't the same was her confidence, and Rowena had taken full advantage of that, fed off it.

She focused her mind, letting loose invisible threads of akrani. She searched the stairways of the dungeon, the hallways, and then the dungeon and its cells. Where could she have gone?

The tunnels. Rowena pushed through the walls of the dungeon and found Blaise. She reached out to her with satori, spoke to her, warned her what would happen should she continue to attempt escape.

Blaise stopped in her tracks and turned back.

Good. The dry night air caressed Rowena's pale cheeks. She unsheathed the sword at her hip, readying for the fight ahead. It would be quite fitting she kill Blaise with the same blade she'd murdered Maxima with. A sadistic grin crept onto her face as she continued to watch her army begin their invasion upon Crenitha.

28

BLAISE

Blaise didn't have time to process everything. She was half god? Kaiden was half ellorian? And Rowena had been sent to Alymeth to kill her?

One question led to another. If one of the gods had broken a rule and fallen for a realm dweller, did that mean Blaise was a mistake? Had Helena or Jocelyn known? Blaise held Kaiden's hand, following him down the long drafty passageway. They had made it out of the dungeon. A quarter of the way down, Blaise stopped in her tracks at the sound of Rowena's voice in her head.

Where are you running to? Wherever you go, I'll find you, pet. I'll make you watch your loved ones die, and then I'll kill you. Blaise held her head. She attempted to push Rowena out, but she was still there. She would *always* be there.

Kaiden came to a halt as well. "What is it?"

She shook her head slowly and whispered, more to herself, "This is never going to end."

"What?" Kaiden studied her as Zade caught up to them.

Blaise grabbed Zade's arm before he could pass them, stopping him in his tracks. "Where's Rowena?"

He had a befuddled look about him as his gaze bounced from Blaise to Kaiden, then back to Blaise again. Zade closed his eyes, and a few seconds passed before he replied, "She's in the north tower bedchamber." He paused. "You're going to face her, aren't you?"

Blaise nodded. "Rowena will always know where I am. She won't stop unless . . ." She trailed off in thought.

"Unless what?" Kaiden asked with a knowing expression on his handsome face.

She inhaled a deep breath. "Unless *I* stop her."

"No, not in your weakened state," Kaiden said as the last group of refugees passed them.

Zade intervened. "She has to do this, Captain."

Kaiden shot him a warning look. "Regroup with the others."

Zade sighed, but he conceded, leaving Blaise and Kaiden in the tunnel.

"What choice do I have?" She swallowed. If she ran, it would put him and the people in jeopardy, and she wouldn't do that again. "You know the consequences if I continue with you."

"Then I'm going with you." He started back toward the dungeon.

She held up a hand, stopping him once more. "No. This is my fight, and my people are going to need your help getting out of here alive." It was the first time she'd claimed the refugees as her people. Something about those two words sent an empowering chill up her spine. "I really need you to trust me."

He spent a few seconds staring. "Here, take this." He took off his necklace and placed it around her neck. "It'll protect you."

Blaise glanced at the fading purple crystal and gave a faint grin. "Take care of them. Please." She walked up and kissed him on the cheek, but he obviously didn't think it was enough because he gripped her waist, drew her against his body, and pressed his lips to hers. She gasped into his mouth, hands braced against his hard chest. Their tongues danced against each other as one of his hands slid to the small of her back and the other cupped her nape. The memory of the intimate moments with him in the cave flooded her mind. It was completely inappropriate and caused her to forget about Rowena, about her lineage, about her akrani. She became completely and utterly lost in the taste of his lips, in his sandalwood scent, in the warmth of his embrace.

Reality came crashing down at Mathias's abrupt voice in the distance. "Kaiden, Blaise, we need to move! The revenants are closing in!"

She pulled away from Kaiden and stared into his eyes. It looked as if Kaiden wanted to say something more, but she didn't give him the chance. She turned and ran back toward the dungeon, hoping to finally put a stop to Rowena.

Blaise didn't have a choice; she had to find the courage and strength to confront Rowena and end this once and for all. Even though she'd been able to survive the torture and abuse, a part of her was still afraid. But she couldn't let that hold her back. *Not anymore.*

She walked up the steps out of the dungeon, where a few of the Wayward seized her, binding her wrists in iron cuffs. They led her down an open corridor. Light from the full moon illuminated the grand arched windows and shone down from several staircases. The walls on the inside of the fortress were covered in shriveled black vines. They climbed the last long staircase, and she finally got a full view of the kingdom and what it had become. Her heart ached. The obsidian soil appeared to be rich in nutrients, but everything for miles around was lifeless. A few trees still stood, shriveled up, thirsty for water. And in the distance, the trees of Daagan Forest and the foothills of Balam would be next.

They walked down another long corridor, and one of the Wayward gestured to a double-doored room after uncuffing her. Hesitantly, she stepped toward one of the doors and pushed it open. The bedchamber looked familiar. She'd seen this place before. The memory crystal had brought her here. It didn't take long for her to realize that it used to be her mother's chamber. Blood from her face rushed to her heart as it quickened.

The lighting was dim, like in the rest of the fortress. Dark curtains shrouded the large windows of the room, prohibiting any light from entering. The bed appeared to be worn and dusty as Blaise approached it. There was a sword on the royal-purple velvet covers. It had an exquisite black galydrian grip with an etched silver pommel. The fuller was gilded, and the rest of the blade was highly polished silver.

"That was your mother's," said a voice from behind her.

Quickly, Blaise gripped the weapon and pointed it at Rowena, meeting her sword. "You're a sick woman," Blaise sneered.

The false queen glanced at the crystal around her neck. "Ah, I see you came prepared. Nevertheless, it'll do you no good." She struck with a series of combinations, and Blaise parried them all. "I expected you to be well trained, which is why I also came prepared," Rowena crooned with a delighted smile on her pale features.

In that moment, the double doors of the bedchamber flew open, and there stood a revenant. This wasn't just any revenant. It had Queen Maxima's facial features, but they were deformed and void of any emotion. Blaise shrank backward a few steps as she muttered, "Mother?" It wasn't her. Maxima had died in that sword fight all those years ago. *This isn't her,* she reminded herself.

"Come, meet your mother," Rowena said in such a taunting way that it made Blaise's blood boil.

The undead queen stepped toward Blaise. Its legs were no longer connected to the body; instead, there were six metallic limbs resembling those of an arachnid. Its chest had been plated as well, and it wore a crown of steel thorns on her head.

"You're fucking sick," Blaise spat once more as her chest

tightened. Her breathing was shallow as she asked, "Why would you do this to your own sister?"

"She's not my sister!" Rowena's outburst echoed against the high ceiling of the room. Then she whispered something into the revenant's ear, and it advanced toward Blaise.

The revenant swiped its bladed fingers at Blaise. She dodged and rolled to the other side of Rowena. Rowena sliced down at Blaise, but she blocked and sliced upward simultaneously blocking the revenant's attack.

"You won't be able to fight both of us together," Rowena said with a sadistic grin.

Blaise's stamina was dwindling, but she continued to fight. The fact that she couldn't engage Rowena and the revenant for much longer had begun to sink in. Her legs ached. Her arms were sore from swinging the blade. With each blow, with each parry, her physical strength lessened. She needed to defeat them soon.

She ran out of the chamber, slashing at the revenants who were standing outside. She managed to immobilize both of the guards. She had no idea where she was going. The fortress had many rooms and corridors. All she knew was that she had to take the defensive.

The revenant queen trailed behind. Its spiderlike legs were quicker than Blaise's human ones. The monster swung one of its sharp legs horizontally. Blaise dodged it, falling to her knees and sliding into the sanctum. She recovered to her feet, but the revenant swiped a bladed leg once more. Blaise wasn't quick enough that time. She fell to her knees from the impact of the creature's claws, reopening some of the wounds on her back. The agony of her wounds was reflected in the dark waters of the pool as a piercing scream escaped her lips.

Blaise's heartbeat thrummed in her ears as she swung her sword upward. The revenant queen parried and dodged every blow she delivered. As she lunged, the revenant swiped at her neck. Blaise reacted with lightning reflexes. The blade whispered against her throat, and the crystal was cut loose from her neck. From the corner of her eye, she watched it fall into the dark pool of water.

Blaise had to gain distance from the monster. She rushed out to the balcony adjacent to the room, and the revenant followed closely. Rowena came out of nowhere and slashed at Blaise with her weapon. The revenant attacked next. Blaise slid between its sharp legs and ended up on the other side of it, closer to the railing of the balcony. Her heart thrummed against her insides as she realized how far of a drop it was.

The revenant lunged toward Blaise, knocking her over the railing of the balcony. Her sword was knocked free when she had to grab the railing, and she watched the creature fall thousands of feet. Rowena peered down at Blaise, and she entered her mind once more.

Let go. She heard the false queen in her mind, and her grip slipped as she attempted to regain a semblance of control over her own body. She had to do something, or this would be the end for her.

I think it's high time you discover that power. It's high time you discover yourself. Helena's voice popped into her consciousness.

Kaiden sees something in you, Blaise. Although I couldn't see it at first, I can see it now. She remembered that moment with Mathias. He'd appeared so sincere when he'd said it.

Then she heard Kaiden's voice. *I saw something in you, Blaise.*

Lastly, she heard Daniel's words before she'd left Elatora. *I believe in you.*

Sparks rose in the pit of her stomach, and warmth enveloped her body. Rowena's eyes widened in both terror and surprise. Blaise had been able to occupy her thoughts with her loved ones, leaving Rowena powerless over her mind.

A gust of wind pushed Blaise up and over Rowena. She landed hard on the floor and retrieved her sword from the balcony's edge. Gathering akrani in her hands, she expelled bursts of lightning, hitting Rowena. It stunned her momentarily.

"You little bitch! You're nothing but the bastard child of a dead queen!"

Moving backward, Blaise parried each quick blow Rowena delivered. Finding her footing, Blaise sliced down. Rowena blocked. Blaise swung horizontally. Rowena dodged that attack as well. Blaise didn't let her frustration get the best of her. She rushed the false queen, spun, and struck again. With a kick, Blaise was able to knock the weapon from Rowena's hand.

A cold glare crept onto the false queen's crazed face. She fell to her knees and just continued to stare.

"You were never the queen of Balam," Blaise spat. She drove her sword into Rowena's chest, straight through her heart, and then she gave her weapon a brief twist.

Rowena lurched, then met Blaise's eyes. "*He* won't stop until you're dead," she whispered, and then her body deteriorated before Blaise's eyes, her youthful appearance turning haggard.

Blaise pulled her sword from Rowena's chest and sliced off her head, ensuring that she stayed dead. Rowena continued to deteriorate into nothing but ash, and a howling gale scattered her remains across the three kingdoms.

The sword made a loud clang as Blaise collapsed onto her knees. A wave of exhaustion hit her, and the violent rapping of pain washed over her insides. Where was Nira when she needed her? She glanced down at herself and realized that at some point in the fight she'd been stabbed in the chest. Fresh crimson liquid stained her tunic once more as her vision blurred before she fell to the ground. While the darkness enveloped her sight, the sun rose on the horizon.

29

KAIDEN

Half ellorian. But who in gehheina was the full-blooded ellorian amongst his parents? His mom or dad? And did that mean Elizabeth was also a half blood? Did he harbor satori like the ellorians? He really didn't have time to think about that. The revenants were everywhere. He tried to extinguish as many as possible, tried to save and protect as many refugees as he could, but he was simply outnumbered. Kaiden and the rest of the team formed a protective circle around the group of people, including the akrani alchime. Mathias, Zade, and Isaac fought against steel and bone revenants alike.

Kaiden, his unit, and the refugees were cornered in the foothills of Balam with nowhere to go. He accepted the possibility that he would die in battle against these cursed creatures. Then, as he sliced one's head off, the rest of the surrounding monsters disintegrated, turning into ash and blowing into the crisp breeze of the dawn. An expression of peace crept onto their faces as they faded out of existence.

"What's happenin'?" George exclaimed, still fighting off a few of the creatures, but they soon turned to dust.

"She did it," the akrani alchime, Andreas, said. He stopped fighting and just observed as the revenants turned to nothingness. "Blaise defeated Rowena!"

That dizziness drifted over Kaiden again. He sensed Blaise's familiar akrani somehow. He glanced behind where the tunnel stood in one of the foothills. It led back to the dungeon. He sprinted through the ashes of revenants without another word. Kaiden was glad they'd been set free from a life of servitude and suffering. Their souls could finally rest.

Vibrations rolled through Kaiden, new and strange, leading him through the fortress dungeon, up the countless stairs, and past corridor after corridor. A mixture of blood and ash coated the dark stone floors. He hoped none of the crimson liquid was Blaise's. His heart thrummed in his ears as he came to a room with a rectangular pool of dark water. Remnants of revenants still lingered in the air.

When he came to the balcony, his breath hitched. His heart seemed to stop. She lay there on her back, wounded and still. Too still. He swallowed, forcing his legs to move, and when he finally reached her, he fell to his knees. He cradled her limp body in his arms. "Blaise," he rasped as he brought his face to hers. "Open your eyes." It had come out as an order. Her soft, slow breaths caressed his cheek, which was covered in a mixture of dried blood and dirt. "It's done. You did it." His eyes clenched shut, hands shaking. He buried his face in the crook of her neck and drew her against his body. Her breaths became even more shallow as he held her. A sense of helplessness overwhelmed him. He would give anything to see those chestnut eyes staring at him, looking at him as though he were an idiot for worrying so much. He should've gone with her, fought beside her. For *her*, even. He should've been more honest with her about . . . everything.

She was a half god. Didn't that mean anything? Or was that simply the extent of it? God in title and akrani only? Did being half of anything ensure an immortal existence? And he'd never heard of a god falling for a realm dweller. Blaise *had* to be the first of her kind. But did that mean he was also the first of *his* kind?

Kaiden didn't look away from Blaise as Mathias, George, Zade, and Isaac rushed onto the balcony. Then Nira and a few other Balam refugees entered with solemn expressions on their faces.

Nira knelt and checked Blaise's pulse in her neck. "We must work quickly. Follow me."

Kaiden carried Blaise's body to one of the many bedchambers of the fortress and laid her on the velvet covers of the bed. He stared at the wound in her chest and realized how much blood she'd lost. He glanced at her blood on his hands.

Nira placed her hands over Blaise's wound and began to work her gitros.

"Is she going to be okay?" Kaiden asked, holding Blaise's cold hand. "Tell me she'll be okay." He tried to keep it together. A million thoughts rushed into his mind, most of them memories of Blaise. The kisses they'd shared, the banter, how she'd risked her life for him and the members of their unit multiple times. She didn't deserve this.

"It's hard to tell, Captain. I need you to wait outside," Nira stated, working her fingers into the wound, blood spurting from it. "Shit."

He shook his head. "I'm not leaving her."

"Please, Captain, trust me. I will do everything in my power to save her." Nira's determined cobalt eyes locked onto his as she cauterized the wound with her gitros.

Kaiden let Blaise's hand slip from his grasp. Each step he took away from her caused his heart to physically hurt. He finally made it out of the room, closing the doors behind him. The uncertainty of his choices haunted him as he paced the corridor. The vibration in his chest had ceased and he hoped that was a good sign.

What would the realm be like without her? The horrible thought invaded his mind, causing the pain in his chest to intensify. He didn't know what he would do if she died. Never mind the fact that he'd trained his whole life for this mission. Never mind the disappointment he'd receive from his father, from the king. Never mind the fact that Balam would be without a ruler. If she died, part of him would die with her.

A DAY PASSED, and Nira was still in the bedchamber with Blaise. She hadn't walked out for anything, not even to update Kaiden on Blaise's status. He hoped it could only mean Nira had been working hard to heal her.

Kaiden sat against the wall next to the chamber doors. His eyelids were heavy from lack of sleep. His whole body throbbed. He didn't take into account his own injuries. There were cuts and bruises in the exposed places of his body. His clothes were dirty and worn, but he didn't care. *She's going to make it. She has to make it.* If he'd had a chance to switch places with her, he'd have taken it.

Mathias walked up to his best friend. He'd cleaned up and the dark circles under his eyes had lightened. "You need to rest."

"I'm fine," Kaiden replied stubbornly, arms crossed over his chest.

"Captain, please. You're no good to anyone in your weakened state." Mathias copied his movements and smirked.

Kaiden shot him a half grin. "Fuck you," he scoffed, then gave a conceding sigh. "Fine." He grunted, moving his stiff muscles and struggling to his feet.

Mathias leaned against the wall next to one of the doors of the bedchamber. "I'm sure she'll be just fine."

Kaiden said nothing.

"How're you holding up?" Mathias asked, a look of genuine concern on his face.

"I'm fine." Kaiden's shoulders tensed.

Mathias cut him a sidelong glare. "Really? You don't seem fine."

Kaiden walked away and let out a breath.

"We've been through a lot." Mathias fell into step with him. "It's okay to feel a certain way. After everything."

Kaiden halted and faced his best friend. "Okay. Why don't you tell me what *you're* feeling first?"

Mathias's eyes narrowed. "Fine." He loosed a breath.

"I'm sad about the deaths in our unit." He swallowed. "Especially Audrey."

"I'm sorry." Kaiden looked at the ground. "I know you two grew close."

Mathias swallowed, and his eyes turned glossy as he pulled his shoulders back. "Your turn."

A lump formed in Kaiden's throat. He couldn't say what he was feeling, or he'd lose it. "Honestly?" He met Mathias's blue eyes with his hazel ones. "I'm numb." He started walking again.

Mathias followed. "You do know I can tell when you're lying, right?"

"What do you want me to say?" Kaiden blurted. "I'm scared, okay?" His voice wavered. "Blaise is the first woman who's made me feel more than my title, more than my social status, and just . . . *more*. Like I could have a life outside of taking orders. She doesn't have the same expectations everyone else has of me."

Mathias's eyebrows rose. "Wow," he murmured.

"Yeah." It was finally all out in the open, but would he be courageous enough to act on everything he'd just told his best friend?

"A few of the refugees scrounged around for some vegetables. They were able to make a nice broth out of them. You should go to the kitchen and grab some." Mathias fell back as Kaiden proceeded down the corridor.

"Thanks," Kaiden said before he was out of earshot.

He made it to the large kitchen, where a handful of Balam's people had gathered to have their evening meal. The room went quiet as he passed the threshold. A young man walked up to Kaiden and asked, "Is she okay?"

Kaiden grabbed a bowl and spoon from a wooden cabinet and studied the green-eyed boy before he replied, "I don't know. Lady Nira is still in there with her." The words were difficult for him to get out.

The boy nodded and said nothing more about it.

Kaiden quickly slurped down his bowl of soup, then made his way down the corridor, finding an empty bedchamber with a washroom. It had been quite some time since he'd had a nice hot bath. He washed himself in the stagnant lukewarm water in the built-in stone tub.

Blaise never left his thoughts. The wound in her chest had looked irreparable. Even though his surroundings incited relaxation, his heart still pounded in his chest at the thought of losing her. He stared down at his empty hands, the same hands that had cradled her limp body, hands that were stained red with her blood. He was unaware of what the future might hold, and despite the warmth of the bath, his body grew cold.

He had to figure out so much. Rowena had disclosed so many shocking details about both him *and* Blaise, things he'd never thought possible. He needed to go back to Elatora and confront his father about . . . everything.

When he'd left Elatora, he'd been so sure about who he was and what his path in life would be. But after discovering the truth about his bloodline, he'd never felt so lost, so insecure, so afraid. Who was Kaiden Atherton?

After his bath, he retreated to the large bed and plopped down on it, wondering how he would ever get sleep with his mind wandering. His body betrayed him, and he fell asleep within minutes of lying on the soft bed.

30

BLAISE

Her body pulsed with pain as she attempted to move her arms and legs. A stifled grunt escaped her throat. Familiar voices echoed throughout the room as Blaise opened her eyes. Her blurred vision focused on the lovely countenance of Nira, who sat at her bedside. Next to her stood Zade with a smirk on his handsome face.

Nira placed a hand on Blaise's. "It's best if you don't move, Your Majesty."

Blaise rasped, "What happened? Where is everyone?" She knew what had happened and had meant to ask who'd survived. "Kaiden. Is he okay?"

Zade nodded. "He's fine. Everyone on the team made it except . . ." He trailed off, and a look of sadness washed over his face. "Raijinn and Audrey."

It couldn't be true. Not Raijinn and Audrey. Tears welled up in her eyes. "How?" Part of her didn't want to know how they'd died.

"When Calun caved in, Raijinn was still in there. The sirens pulled Audrey into the depths of Thessalynne Lake while we were crossing," Zade replied.

"Ollie and Piers, are they okay?" Blaise's voice had become less raspy.

"They're fine. Piers took a beating from one of the bone revenants, but he'll live," Nira said as Zade walked out of the room. He'd probably gone to tell everyone that she'd woken up.

It still saddened her. Raijinn had died. He'd played a significant part in her new life. He'd even pledged to stay loyal to her. Her heart ached at the thought.

There was a knock on the door. Nira answered. George, Isaac, and Zade walked into the room and gathered around her bed.

"Look who finally decided to wake up," George said with a grin.

"We've been worried sick about you, Blaise—I mean, Your Majesty," Isaac corrected with a bow. "It would've been a shame to have to find a replacement queen for Balam."

Zade's brow furrowed as he smacked Isaac on the arm.

Blaise let out a light chuckle and for once didn't mind being called by her new title. "There for a moment, I didn't think I'd come out of this alive."

They all conversed and enjoyed one another's company, relishing the fact that they had survived the impossible and honoring those who hadn't. Where was Kaiden? Even though the others said he was fine, she wanted to see him for herself.

They spent a few more moments in playful banter before Andreas, the akrani alchime, walked in and requested a private moment with Blaise. With much hesitance, they all walked out of the room, leaving the door cracked.

"How are you feeling, Your Majesty?" Andreas asked, taking a step toward her bedside.

"Feeling better by the second," was her reply. "And you don't have to call me that."

He smirked. "But I do. It is you who'll be queen now. My name is Andreas Calvulti."

"It's a pleasure to finally meet you, Sir Andreas." She paused. "It must have been horrible being held captive by Rowena," Blaise said, pushing herself up on her elbows and leaning against the wooden headboard of the bed. *Does he know about my godly blood?*

Andreas nodded and appeared downcast. "All that is behind us. Now we can start anew. We can make Balam great again."

Blaise studied him for a moment. She'd just met this man a few seconds ago, and he was already speaking about reform in the kingdom. He appeared more enthusiastic about her becoming ruler than she had ever been. Perhaps he really cared about Balam. Perhaps it would do her well to trust this man.

"You won't have to worry about anything. I knew your mother, Queen Maxima, and how she ran things before Rowena destroyed everything." Andreas placed his hand on hers. It was cold and clammy.

With a wry grin, she replied, "I appreciate that, Sir Andreas, but right now, I would like to get some more rest."

He bowed his head. "Of course, Your Majesty. While you rest, I will begin the preparations for the coronation ceremony." In saying that, he walked out of the room.

She closed her eyes, hearing ringing in her ears. Everything seemed to be happening faster than she'd anticipated. Killing Rowena meant *someone* would have to ascend the throne. Enough time hadn't passed for her to process everything. Part of her didn't want to go through with the coronation ceremony, but she couldn't leave her mother's kingdom without a ruler. She couldn't leave the *people* without a ruler. How would she ever figure out how to turn things around in Balam? Learn politics? Bring life into the land once again?

More thoughts surfaced as she lay in the plush bed in the chamber. Which one of the gods had fallen for her mother? And where in gehheina was her father? Had he just agreed to having his own daughter killed? Or perhaps he hadn't had a choice in the matter.

She stared out beyond the stone balcony of the room and knew her days as a sentinel had ended. Only a few weeks had passed since she'd been on the Teaos wall, guarding it. It seemed so long ago, and she'd never fathomed she would end up in this fortress, in the place she would soon call home.

Helena and Daniel took precedence over her thoughts. She was still bitter at her adopted grandmother for lying to her about her lineage, but Blaise understood why, and her heart ached to see them despite the lies. And not being blood related, they were still her family, and she still cared for them. Whether she wanted to believe it or not, she'd forgiven Grams the second Philippa had told her that her whole life had been a lie. In a way, Blaise admired Grams for fulfilling her duty to her mother, Maxima. For that reason, Blaise wanted to carry out her duty as queen of Balam.

COLORS OF ORANGE and gold illuminated the balcony as the sun set on the horizon. Blaise still hadn't seen Kaiden. Even Mathias had had the courtesy to pay her a visit the day before. Did Kaiden know that she'd regained consciousness? Someone must have told him, right?

One of the bedchamber doors swung open. In walked Nira with a tray of hot soup. She carefully placed it on Blaise's lap and said, "The broth is made from vegetables we found in the courtyard. Apparently, Rowena was smart enough to have her own personal garden."

"It smells delicious," Blaise stated, taking a whiff of the liquid. "Thank you, Nira." She paused, gazing down at the metal spoon in her hand.

"What's wrong? Aren't you hungry?" Nira sat on her bedside.

"I don't know if I can do this. The whole queen thing." Blaise kept her gaze downcast. "I'm not my mother. I've been told I look like her, but I'm not her."

With a sigh, Nira said, "I know we hardly know each other, but I can see you have a lot of your mother's determination in you." She placed her hand on Blaise's arm and gave it a light squeeze. "You *can* do this."

Blaise met her sincere gaze. "Maybe you're right."

"I know I'm right. You're not alone in this."

"Well, I have a request for you." Blaise then took a cautious sip of the soup.

Nira's eyebrows came together. "What is it?"

"I would like you to take back your position as a handmaiden here. My handmaiden." Blaise offered her a gentle smile. "And possibly a friend?" Nira didn't express her emotions outright, Blaise had noticed, so when a smile crept onto her face, Blaise gleamed in surprise.

Nira gave a calm response. "Yes, of course I will."

A gentle crisp breeze drifted into the bedchamber as a ripple of ease flowed through Blaise. She was glad to have met Nira, not only because she had healed Blaise twice now, but because she had become such a light in her new life. Maybe Blaise's role as queen wouldn't be as complicated as she anticipated.

Her thoughts were interrupted by a knock at the door. Nira straightened and walked over to answer it, but Kaiden had already let himself in.

Nira stopped him. "She's eating her evening meal," she stated, arms crossed. "You should come back later."

"It's okay. Let him pass," Blaise called from her bed, setting the tray and empty bowl aside. Nira glared at Kaiden and said nothing else as she took the tray from the bed and walked out, closing the door behind her.

Blaise's heart rate increased as she stared at him, taking in his appearance. He had a few small cuts on his face that had already begun to heal. His armor had a few scrapes on the pieces that were made of lightweight steel. Some of the leather had torn, and there were a few slashes in his undergarments. Despite that, he still looked handsome, still looked like the insufferable man she'd met on the Teaos wall. But was he?

Kaiden finally said, "I'm sorry it's taken me this long to visit you."

"Why *didn't* you visit sooner? Was there another pressing matter you had to attend to?" Sarcasm dripped from her voice as she crossed her arms over her chest. "Didn't you care about the state I was in?"

His brow furrowed. "Of course I care. I just thought it'd be best to leave you to recover for a few days."

"Yeah. Right," she scoffed.

He walked around the bed and faced the balcony. The sun had set, and stars twinkled brightly in the night sky. "I can't stay here, Blaise. I need to go back to Elatora."

Those words, such simple ones, made her heart sink. They twisted her organs in a way that made her nauseous. She masked her emotions with a blank expression, swallowing the lump in her throat. "Of course you do." Tears were on the verge of spilling over, but she blinked them back.

He took a seat at her bedside. "I need to figure things out, talk to my father about what Rowena said in the dungeon."

She wanted to understand. Gods knew she had to figure out her own issues. But she was hoping they could solve them together.

"I'm sorry"—he placed his hand over hers—"for not being completely honest with you in the beginning."

"I think we have bigger things to worry about." She shot him a faint smile.

He shook his head, gazing at her lips before looking to her eyes. "Do you forgive me?"

She studied the specks of gold around his irises and tilted her head, loosing a breath. "How could I not,

Kaiden?" Those gods damned tears were surfacing again. She tore away from him. "I wish you a safe journey." Her stomach warmed. She wanted to ask him to stay.

He gave her hand a squeeze. "I'll stay for your coronation ceremony."

Not wanting to make this more painful than it had to be, she said, "I don't want you to feel obligated to stay. You have a long journey ahead of you, after all." She buried her emotions deep down where they belonged.

He pulled his hand away, raising his eyebrows. "Is that how you truly feel about it?"

She stared into those hazel eyes she'd grown to admire, then moved to his lips. Why did she still want to kiss them? The promise she'd proclaimed to Mathias came to mind. She wouldn't be the one to keep Kaiden from his obligations as a sentinel. As much as it pained her to say, she kept her eyes on him and replied, "Yes."

His face became cold and void of any emotion. "Very well, *Your Majesty*." He straightened. "I'll take my leave first thing in the morning."

"Very well, Captain," she replied with just as much resolve in her tone.

He walked out of the room without saying another word to her. Blaise swallowed and breathed deeply. She wouldn't cry for him, even though that was all she wanted to do at that moment. This was for the best. There would be no way they could work out. *Just let him go.* She stared out into the night sky and watched as the waning moon rose.

31

KAIDEN

He'd done the right thing. Things would never work out between him and the soon-to-be queen of Balam. If he'd done the right thing, why did it feel like his heart had been torn from his chest? Why did a torturous emptiness plague him? He hated himself for not having more control over these emotions, hated himself for having developed feelings for her in the first place. He walked into the chamber he'd been sleeping in and immediately prepared his satchel for the long trip home in the morning. Without much thought, he picked up the empty vase from his bedside table and threw it across the room into the wall. It shattered into a million pieces.

A familiar voice said, "Whoa, careful with the decor."

Kaiden had been so focused on his emotions that he hadn't seen Mathias walk in. He stole a glance at his best friend and continued to pack without a word in response.

Mathias took a few steps toward him. "Where do you think you're going?"

"Where do you think? Back to Elatora." Kaiden couldn't keep the bitterness out of his voice.

"You're not attending the coronation ceremony?"

"What do you want me to say, Mat?" Kaiden confronted his best friend with a slightly furrowed brow. "She doesn't want me to stay."

Mathias laughed, quietly at first, and then it became louder, heftier. "You do not know women as well as you may think, my friend."

"What?"

With a shake of his head, Mathias muttered, "Never mind. I know for a fact that you won't listen to a *thing* I have to say about it."

"Will you do me a favor?" Kaiden changed the subject.

"Is it a favor or an order?" Mathias cut him a sidelong stare.

Kaiden rolled his eyes and stopped what he was doing. A look of annoyance spread across his face. His best friend could be insufferable sometimes.

Mathias grinned. "You want me to stay and look after Blaise."

"Just until after the ceremony." Kaiden continued stuffing his satchel.

"I promise to keep a close eye on her." Mathias placed his hand on Kaiden's shoulder and winked.

Kaiden's eyes narrowed, and a muscle in his jaw ticked. "Not *too* close."

"Do you plan on ever coming back?" Mathias asked.

Did Kaiden want to come back? Yes, he did. Could he give up his life in Elatora and leave everything behind though? He replied, "I don't know. Someday, I suppose."

Mathias groused, "That's awfully vague." He didn't prod the issue any further and changed the subject for a second time. "Did you hear about Zade?"

Kaiden shook his head.

"Blaise offered Zade a position as a member of her royal court, and Andreas is going to be her advisor," Mathias said, leaning against the tall wooden bedpost as Kaiden continued to toss items into the bag.

"Good for them." He paused to glance at Mathias, then let out a breath. There'd been a weight on his shoulders ever since he'd walked out of Blaise's room, and he couldn't rid himself of it. Another long sigh escaped him as he sealed up his satchel.

"Stay for the coronation ceremony. You owe her that at least," Mathias said, a severe look in his blue eyes.

Kaiden stayed quiet for a few minutes before he said, "I don't want her to know I stayed."

"Don't worry, she'll be busy preparing for it, I'm sure," Mathias replied.

THE DAY OF the ceremony arrived, and Mathias had been correct in assuming Blaise would be too busy to notice that

Kaiden had stayed. Nira, however, had run into the captain one time on his way to the kitchen. She'd told him it would be best to keep his distance. He had no qualms about her suggestion.

Many people came to witness the coronation of the lost princess. Captain Wilhelm arrived and took his place in the large crowd as well. Kaiden was impressed. Andreas had put together an event to remember. He'd even recruited a few people to clean and make parts of the fortress somewhat respectable.

A raised wooden platform had been set up in front of the dark pool. Kaiden assumed that was where Blaise would be crowned. There were people walking about on the open balcony across from the still water, soaking in the afternoon sun. Kaiden made sure to remain unnoticed in the back of the room. Mathias stood a few rows ahead of him, along with the rest of the unit.

The ceremony began, cued by the string quartet playing a lovely melody as Blaise walked into the sanctum from the side doors, escorted by Zade.

Kaiden took in a sharp breath, jaw falling open at the sight of her beauty. It should've been him escorting her to the stage. She wore a violet three-quarter-sleeve gown. The heart-shaped bodice accentuated her bust in a modest way and showed off her slim waistline. She'd worn light makeup, which highlighted her beautiful chestnut eyes, and violet color for her plump lips. His heart fractured at the realization that he could never have her. He couldn't do this.

"Thank you, one and all, for attending this momentous event in the history of the kingdom of Balam," Andreas announced as the crowd became so quiet a needle could've been heard hitting the stone floor. He went on to say how he and Maxima had a long history as queen and advisor and how he'd be honored to carry on the tradition with Blaise.

Blaise appeared to be searching for someone in the crowd. She couldn't have been searching for him. He'd already told her he wouldn't be there. Her countenance went from hopeful to what looked like melancholy within a few minutes of Andreas's long-winded speech.

Kaiden couldn't stand to be there any longer, couldn't take the heaviness in his heart, so he eased his way through the crowd, nudging George and Isaac, signaling them that it was time to go, and strode out the door of the sanctum. It didn't take long for them to catch up to him.

After a few long moments of them walking in silence, Isaac asked, "Now what?"

Kaiden gazed at the sparkling Thessalynne Lake ahead and shrugged. "For once, Isaac, I don't know." He planned to take the pass through the Onyx Mountains to get home. He signaled the men to follow, and as the breeze caressed Kaiden's face, he inhaled the fresh air. He made it a point to stop and stare at the glistening Thessalynne Lake.

"We should probably start walking if we're going to be home in three days," George stated, walking up beside him.

"Wait." Kaiden stopped them. "Let's just take our time for once."

The three men just stood there, enjoying the sounds of nature and the calm water.

Kaiden had completed a mission he'd been training for his whole life. At first, he'd resented his father for deceiving him. But if it weren't for him and King Vaughn, he probably never would've met Blaise, and she was quite possibly the best thing that had ever happened to him, despite how they'd parted ways. She would always have a place in his heart. *Always.*

In no hurry at all, Kaiden took his time traveling home. He wasn't ready for the responsibilities that awaited him back in Elatora. And maybe once he arrived, he wouldn't regret the choice he'd made: leaving her.

Dammit, I didn't mean to fall in love with her.

32

BLAISE

A plethora of thoughts bombarded her mind. Did Blaise really want this? Had she made the right choice in accepting her mother's crown? Could she rule Balam competently? And the most important question—who or what would try to end her life next? She stood on the solid platform in front of people she didn't know, about to accept the biggest responsibility of her life. Her eyes swept through the crowd of onlookers. She met Mathias's gaze, then saw Captain Wilhelm and a few other people she didn't know. Where was Nira?

Andreas's voice snapped her out of her thoughts. "Blaise Everleigh of Balam, do you promise to uphold the laws and traditions of the land?" He held a beautiful crown fashioned out of lustrous galydrian.

"Yes," she announced loudly.

Andreas's deep voice boomed through the sanctum once more. "Do you swear to keep the people of Balam in mind in every decision you make?"

Blaise let out a sharp breath as her stomach clenched at a sudden pain in her stomach. She looked down at herself, eyes wide. An arrow had burrowed into her stomach. It appeared to be from a sentinel's crossbow. *Who did this?* Her blurring eyes wandered through the screaming crowd. Blaise's eyes met Mathias's. His face was stoic amongst the panicked expressions. Her vision became even more hazy as crimson liquid leaked out of the wound. She caught sight of a crossbow in Mathias's hands. *Why?* Andreas reached a hand out to Blaise, but it was too late. Blaise plunged into the onyx pool of water, falling into a familiar darkness, falling into oblivion.

Thank you for taking the time to read book one of The Akrani Gods!

If you enjoyed this book (even if you didn't) please leave a review.

ACKNOWLEDGMENTS

This was originally supposed to be a standalone book, but my critique partner/Slytherin friend, Brittany Riley, saw the potential for it to be more. So I owe this trilogy to her. I want to thank my critique partner, Kasey Le Alma, for always giving me ideas on how to make my story really come to life. And to Lana Staux for coaching more eloquent words out of me during our line-editing sessions. All these kind (sometimes terrifying) women have really helped bring this story together in a way I could've never imagined. They are my critique partners, my story coaches, and most importantly, my friends.

I want to thank my editor, Natalia Leigh, for just getting my writing style and putting up with my many comma splices. To my proofreader, Lisa G., for implementing the finishing touches and making sure the book is polished and prim. To my awesome formatter, Greg Rupel, for creating an interior that is so aesthetically pleasing. And of course, my super talented cover designer, Thea (I think the cover speaks for itself. I'm in love). All these wonderful, talented people work at Enchanted Ink Publishing. They really know how to make a book look gorgeous, inside and out.

To my beta readers: Thank you for taking the time to give me so much valuable feedback. You helped me put the finishing touches on Blaise and Kaiden's story. Rebecca Brynne, Lexie, and Amy Mirashi. You're awesome!

Honestly, this book was more challenging than my last one in many ways, but I'm proud of how it turned out. I've lost sleep coming up with ideas, fixing plot holes, and making sure everything in the story stayed consistent. I'm so grateful to my husband, Bobby, who continues to support me through my author journey. I'd like to thank my close friends and family for their continued support. Lastly, I'd like to thank *you*, the reader. I appreciate *you* more than you know!

ALYSSA GREEN

When Alyssa isn't writing, she can be found editing for clients and traveling the U.S. (safely, of course) with her husband and pup (Fiona), living full-time in their camper. She loves hiking, exploring new places, and just living life!

WWW.AUTHORALYSSAGREEN.COM

Instagram: @author_alyssa_green

Facebook: @authoralyssagreen

TikTok: @authoralyssagreen

Printed in the USA
CPSIA information can be obtained
at www.ICGtesting.com
JSHW011653130823
46473JS00002B/67